Wolf

State Changers

Book 1

CHRIS FENWICK

HELLBENDER BOOKS

Hellbender Books

Mechanicsburg, Pennsylvania

HELLBENDER BOOKS
an imprint of Sunbury Press, Inc.
Mechanicsburg, PA USA

For information about special discounts for bulk purchases, please contact Sunbury Press Orders Dept. at (855) 338-8359 or orders@sunburypress.com.

To request one of our authors for speaking engagements or book signings, please contact Sunbury Press Publicity Dept. at publicity@sunburypress.com.

ISBN: 978-1-62006-217-3 (Trade paperback)

Library of Congress Control Number: 2019949251

HELLBENDER BOOKS EDITION: October 2019

Product of the United States of America
0 1 1 2 3 5 8 13 21 34 55

Set in Bookman Old Style
Designed by Chris Fenwick
Cover by Chris Fenwick
Edited by Erika Hodges

Continue the Enlightenment!

More from Chris Fenwick:

State Changers:

Wolf

Fae

Human

Hero

the 100th human – 15-year anniversary edition

Character and Pronunciation Guide

(Note: Pronunciations can vary greatly depending on what part of Ireland you are from.)

Casidhe Keneally: *KAS-ih-dee (Cassidy)*
Cian Keneally: *KEE-an*
Colleen Keller: Casidhe's aunt
Amanda: Casidhe's high-school friend and co-worker
Cal: Amanda's older brother
Judy: Colleen's friend and co-worker
Jessica Palmer: caseworker
Finn and Nola Kenneally: Casidhe's parents

<u>Keneally Pack in Butte, Montana:</u>
Inner circle:
Kelly Moore: Keneally pack Alpha
Lesslyn Moore: Keneally pack Alpha-She
Dana Moore: Kelly and Lesslyn's daughter
Ronan: Keneally pack Beta wolf and physical trainer
Brody: Works for Kelly and Lesslyn
Blaire: Works for Kelly and Lesslyn
Aedan and Claire: mated
Brian and Cara: mated
Bronagh: *Bro-nah* - a Police officer in Butte, married to a human, Sam.
Cormac: oldest, storyteller, mated to Neala
Siobhan: *Sha-Vawn* – mated to Elf named Thebieas, four children

2nd String:
Liam: not mated
Derry: not mated
Neala: doctor, mated to Cormac
Sean: *SHAWN* – registered nurse
Brendan: mated to Cathleen
Cathleen: mated to Brendan

Newest members:
Kevin: mated to Sinead
Sinead: *shi-NAYD* – mated to Kevin
Seamus: *SHAY-mus* – not mated

Darcy: not mated
Fiona: not mated

Other names and places:
Saoirse: *SEER-sha* - the White Wolf
Senan: *SHAWN-in* - brother of the White Wolf
Aoife: *EE-fa* – Casidhe's great, great . . . grandmother
Mac Tire: *mok cheer-a* – wolf in Irish, name of original State Changer twin, and pub in Butte.
Mac Dearg: *mok dearg* - red in Irish, name of original State Changer twin
Tír na nÓg: *tēr nə nōg* – Name of the land of the Fairies/Fae, underground.
Sidhe: *Shee* – another name for Tír na nÓg.
Dagda – The good god, Father of the State Changers
Tuatha Dé Danann: *too-uh dey dah-nuhn* - a race of gods or demigods who defeated the Fomorians and ruled Ireland during a golden age, original Fae.
Fúath: *foo-a* – means hate, a general classification for Fae who hate humans.

A Grá: *Ah ghraw* - love, dear.
Sláinte: *slawn-che* – health, cheers.

Tuatha Dé Danann's four magical treasures:

- Claíomh Solais – the Sword of Light
- Lia Fail – Stone of Destiny
- Sleá Bua - the Spear of Lugh
- Coire Dagdae - Cauldron of Dagda

♪~ W o l f theme song: "Secrets" arranged and played by Jennifer Thomas, on the Illumination album. It especially fits the final chapter. Look for the note symbol. ♪

CHAPTER ONE

C asidhe Keneally always enjoyed the comfort she found in the small patch of woods out past the back yard. Now, it sent a tremor of fear through her body. Now, she steered clear of large stands of trees, butcher shops, and mirrors whenever possible. Casidhe was sure she was losing her mind, destined to frighten small children. And to be alone. Casidhe sighed, knowing her latest symptoms, which started just under a week ago, guaranteed her solitude.

She could smell Aunt Colleen in the kitchen making dinner before she got out of her car and headed for the front door. Dropping her bookbag in the foyer, she went into the kitchen, where her aunt ladled vegetable soup into two thermoses. Aunt Colleen naturally seemed to side-step Casidhe's sensitivity to meat. She had not thought twice about it before, but she wondered. Was Aunt Colleen a vegetarian for herself or Casidhe? She shook her head.

Casidhe thought her aunt looked older. Colleen had always been hard working and active. Perhaps it was a little plumpness around the middle of her average frame or a few greying streaks through her mousy blonde hair. Casidhe felt it was something more but couldn't quite put her finger on it.

"Be sure to set your alarm clock this evening, dear. I won't be home early enough to wake you for school. I am covering for Judy in the morning. One of her kids has a dentist appointment, and the hospital is short nursing staff as it is."

"I will. I'm working until 10:00, and then I have a paper to write," she groaned. "I can't wait to graduate."

"You only have a few months left." She handed her the thermos. "I don't like mornings either; that's why I work nights. The coffee pot is set to go off automatically." She kissed Casidhe on the cheek, grabbing her lunch bag to go.

"Thanks." Casidhe ran upstairs to change. It was Amanda's turn to drive, and she'd be here any minute. She and Amanda cleaned an office building in Greenville on weeknights. Amanda was her best friend, though really, they were just two girls who preferred working in quiet office spaces rather than food service or some other job that would put them too close to people. It's not that she hated people; she simply didn't feel like she related to most. Now, she was afraid someone would find her strange or scary. Amanda was usually too wrapped up in her own problems to notice. Casidhe zipped up her sweatshirt as she heard the car honk out front. Picking up her wallet and phone, she locked the door on her way out.

Aunt Colleen was right, only a few months, and she would graduate from South Central High School. After that, she'd continue to work her two jobs and take some classes at Pitt Community College. She couldn't imagine being a nurse like Aunt Colleen; the smells of the hospital would overwhelm her. Perhaps she was more suited to engineering or computers, something solitary.

Amanda immediately started complaining about her parents. Since Casidhe's parents were dead, she didn't relate to Amanda's stories of their fighting. Today the rant continued the whole 35-minute ride. Sometimes, Amanda apologized for her constant complaining, but today there was no end in sight. Casidhe couldn't imagine living in such chaos and was relieved for the distraction; happy Amanda didn't notice anything amiss.

The changes Casidhe experienced lately confused her. As they passed neighborhoods, she could smell dinner being cooked in houses. Meat, she could always smell meat. When they made it to the highway, she picked up the scent of gas and oil, exhaust, and dirt. At school, one girl used a particularly strong shampoo, making Casidhe sneeze. Casidhe always used unscented products for her own long bright red hair, tying it back in a ponytail. Last week, someone came in after drinking too much and threw up in the cafeteria. Casidhe smelled it down the long hall as she exited her classroom and ran straight for the bathroom, losing her own breakfast. She often tucked her face down into her blouse or jacket, covering her nose to avoid smells that entered with her classmates. Body odor and cheap perfume were usual, but Casidhe could now smell what they had for breakfast and what type of soap they preferred. Amanda used soap with lavender, or was it her deodorant? Maybe both.

At first, the chemicals in the cleaners they used overwhelmed her as she worked to dust and vacuum offices and cleaned bathrooms. But after a while, it all blended, and she went on methodically until each floor was clean for the night. Tomorrow they would do the same task on the next level. She never knew what would happen at school, but here at work, things were predictable, and right now, that was comforting. They worked independently, each going off in different directions. They met at 7:30 for a half-hour dinner break, then Amanda dropped her at home around 10:30, and she let herself into the dark house. She was tired, but nighttime was always better for Casidhe. There was less stimulus, and her brain just functioned better at night. After a snack, she sat down with her computer and began writing her paper. It was midnight before she switched off the light.

Casidhe smashed her alarm at 6:30 to make the noise stop. *Was it louder this morning?* She nearly fell back to sleep, but the smell of coffee brewing wafted into her consciousness. Its robust and rich aroma flooded into the room, waking her taste buds and enticing the rest of her body up and into the kitchen. She took her cup to the bathroom to shower, wondering what time Aunt Colleen would make it home. She'd be tired after working the night shift and now the morning, as well.

Casidhe exited the house forty minutes later, heading for her little, black VW Jetta hatchback. It was an older model but had always been reliable. A chill touched the autumn morning, coloring the leaves which were littering the ground and sidewalk. As she walked to her car, the sound of her short, black boots hitting the pavement gave a loud tippy-tap. She set her travel mug on the top of the vehicle and rubbed her head with the back of her hand before inserting the keys into the lock. The door to the car swung open with a loud creak. *Is something wrong with my car door? Perhaps, it needs oil or something?* She settled in, closed the door as quietly as she could, and started the engine. As the gas and air mixed and combusted in the machine, allowing the motor to rumble alive, Casidhe rubbed her head again. During the ride, horns and screeching breaks made her cringe and grit her teeth. As soon as she entered school, she went to the office to request ibuprofen from the nurse, unsure she'd make it through the day.

She sat in the rear of her AP English class, fishing around in her bag for her headphones. She plugged them into her phone and put on music. *No good. Too chaotic. Too many levels of sounds.* She put on some white noise she sometimes used to help her sleep, and that helped some. *One mundane sound–ahhh.* But the bell rang, and over the white noise, her ears exploded. She bent her head and covered her ears with her palms until it stopped. *That was bad, really bad. What the hell is happening to me now?* As class started, she removed her hands from her ears and turned down the white noise. Fortunately, everyone else shut up while the teacher lectured. She could still hear a hundred other sounds from around the school and down the hallway, but it was tolerable. If her sense of smell was acute, her sense of hearing now seemed superhuman. As the medicine kicked in, she relaxed a little. *This is my most bizarre experience yet.*

Hearing everything classmates talk about might be cool in the beginning, but eventually, it's unnerving. About her, they'd say things like, 'she's a loner.' 'She doesn't have parents, poor thing.' 'She's odd, doesn't have many friends, 'cept that Mandy girl. She's strange too.' 'She's pretty; I'd do her.' 'You'd do any girl, Andy, but she is pretty.' And it wasn't only conversations about her that Casidhe would overhear. She could hear every argument, each hallway flirtation, and every sloppy kiss exchanged. Walls helped some, but when she went outside, she could hear squirrels scamper and leaves skip across the pavement from 100-yards away. She kept in her earplugs to listen to the fan-humming, white noise, which was her first choice, but water-running worked well too. She tried hard not to flinch or cringe at loud noises, so she didn't look too weird. But nothing could help hide her reaction to high-pitched sounds. She turned up her headphones just before the bells went off each period. When the trash truck came by, she ran to the upper library on the opposite side of the building, turned her headphones way up, and covered them with her hands, having nowhere else to hide.

Since her last class was a study hall, she skipped out early. Braving the traffic sounds, she pulled up in front of their little cottage in Winterville, near the small patch of woods at the end of the road. *That's weird; Aunt Colleen's car isn't in the driveway. She usually would be home by 6:00 AM, after a 12-hour shift. But since she filled in for her friend, I expected her home by 10:00. She should be getting some much-needed sleep.* As Casidhe entered the foyer and dropped her bag softly, she heard Aunt Colleen's car drive up. She glanced at the clock on the wall: 2:00. *Hmmm.*

Aunt Colleen entered, looking haggard and exhausted.

"Did you work all day?"

"No, I mean, ah . . . yes. Judy's son was sick, so I ended up pulling a double."

Casidhe raised her eyebrows but didn't question further.

"You look tired too. Did you stay up working last night?"

"No, I just have a headache, and I wanted to lie down a little before work."

" I think there is a little more soup leftover, would you like some before you lay down?"

"No, I'm not hungry. You go ahead, and then you better get some sleep too before you fall down"

"I know, I will, dear. I'll be fine."

Aunt Colleen's master suite was on the main floor. Casidhe had the whole upstairs to herself. She took some Tylenol and dropped into the bed. She should talk to Aunt Colleen; she is a nurse, after all. *Maybe I have some illness that is causing these issues. Maybe, I have a brain tumor that is accentuating my sense of smell and hearing? Maybe, I'm going crazy?* Casidhe shook her head. *No. Aunt Colleen is way too tired to worry her about this now. Maybe after she's rested.* Casidhe's last thought before she drifted off was why Aunt Colleen had first said no about working all day and then changed her mind.

Casidhe woke up an hour later and noticed her headache was gone. It was her night to drive, but she still had time before picking up Amanda. She went downstairs to get some food and noticed Aunt Colleen's door still closed. She marveled at how she could hear Aunt Colleen's quiet breathing behind the door.

Casidhe ate some soup while standing at the back door, looking out at the small forest behind the house. Perhaps tomorrow, she would take a walk in the woods to relax. She always felt at home among the trees and nature. Before she left the house, she stood outside of Aunt Colleen's door, listening to her breathing. She noticed a faint smell that Casidhe couldn't identify–something not quite right. Deciding to let it go for now, she turned away, gathered her things, and left.

Later that evening, she entered the house as quietly as possible. She heard no sounds, and only a single light glowed in the kitchen, telling her Colleen was still asleep. *Sweet dreams, Aunt Colleen.* The strange smell was still coming from her aunt's room, but she was too tired to investigate it further.

Casidhe drifted off to sleep, thinking about her over-sensitive hearing and smell, wondering if she had a brain tumor or a disease, and if Aunt Colleen would insist she visit the doctor.

Late the next morning, she ambled downstairs in her PJs. On Saturday, she did not have to rush off to school or work. Her second job, night-stocking the local drug store, would start later that evening, 8:00 to midnight. She chose this job again because she could do it without interacting with many people. She had the day to do what she wanted. By the smell of things, Aunt Colleen was making breakfast–oatmeal and toast.

"Good morning, dear. How are you feeling today?"

"I feel fine. How about you? Are you rested up?"

"Yes, I slept like a baby until early this morning." But even as Aunt Colleen said this, Casidhe noticed she still looked tired. She had dark circles under her blurry eyes. And the smell was definitely present, though Casidhe still couldn't place the cause.

"Do you have much to do today? Maybe you should take it easy?" Casidhe suggested.

"Oh, I am not going anywhere this morning. I'll do some laundry, and I should go to the grocery store this afternoon. But other than that, it's an easy day."

"Good. After breakfast, I think I'll go for a walk in the woods. I haven't been out there in weeks."

"Sounds nice, dear. Would you like some milk with your oatmeal?"

They ate in silence. Aunt Colleen seemed preoccupied, while Casidhe tried to decide if she was ill or just tired. And the odd smell was beginning to bother her. "Aunt Colleen is there something in the fridge or pantry that has gone bad?" she asked as she got up and began poking around.

"I'm not sure. What do you smell?" Aunt Colleen eyed Casidhe curiously.

"That's it. I don't really know. Something pungent."

Aunt Colleen watched Casidhe search and smell items in the pantry. "Well, if you find something rotten, throw it out. Maybe it's the trash?"

"Could be. I'll take it out, just in case."

After taking out the trash, Casidhe went upstairs to dress for her walk in the woods. She put on her hiking boots and a warm jacket and grabbed her journal. Walking in the woods gave her solace almost every weekend since she was a child. The trees, the grass, and the sense of nature had always been a source of comfort to her. She felt at home in nature. But as she neared the woods today, odors intensified. She could smell the earth and the decaying leaves littering the ground. She made out the woody scent of the trees and their bark and could hear the creak of the branches as they swayed slightly in the breeze. The sights and sounds made her twitchy. Her skin piqued. Her hair, though pulled back, as usual, felt like it stood on end, making her whole body alert as she listened hard for the sound or smell of a rabbit or a squirrel. She wanted one, to chase, to find, to . . . what exactly? She wasn't sure. The desire overtook her, and she could feel her eyes shifting back and forth with all her senses sharpened. She wondered who, or more accurately, what she was becoming. She wanted to hunt, to catch, to eat her prey. This urge became so powerful; she nearly kicked off her shoes to run in the dirt. But as she bent down to undo her laces, she noticed her feet–the feet of a young woman in hiking boots. She was not an animal. She fell to the ground. "No, NO! What is this?" She pulled her knees to her chest tight, closing her eyes and covering her ears with her hands. *Something is seriously wrong with me!*

After a moment of unsuccessfully trying to block her senses, she jumped up, ran back into the house, and up to her bathroom, where she showered and scrubbed herself like she could remove her ailments with soap and cloth. Finally, she got out, dried off, and laid in her bed, exhausted. She was sad her precious woods could not bring her the calm she needed. What kind of ailment would make you want to hunt small animals? She had never heard of an illness like that. *Since when were small fluffy animals prey?* She decided she should tell her aunt. If Casidhe had to brave the doctor, then she must. She went downstairs to find her aunt, but Aunt Colleen wasn't home. *Maybe she left when I was in the woods or the shower? I was so upset; I wouldn't have noticed.*

Casidhe thought of calling her aunt on her cell but decided to wait. *I don't need to frighten her. Didn't she say she had to go to the grocery store?* Casidhe went back up to her room to do some research online, trying to diagnose herself. She didn't find anything specific to her symptoms, and what she did find caused her to worry more.

She heard the front door, followed by Aunt Colleen coming in with groceries. Casidhe could tell most of the items her aunt purchased by the smells that drifted up the stairs. And that other smell had returned. She now associated it with Aunt Colleen. *Maybe it was a new soap that doesn't agree with me.* She ran down the steps to help her aunt and found her sitting in a kitchen chair, winded and pale.

"Aunt Colleen, what's wrong? I thought you weren't going to the grocery store until this afternoon. You don't look so good."

" I just got tired suddenly. Can you get me a glass of water?"

Casidhe brought her the water and waited beside her as she drank it. "I'll put these away. Why don't you go sit down in the living room for a little?"

"I think I will." As she got up, her aunt staggered a little. Casidhe caught her arm and helped her to the couch, insisting she lie down and rest. Her aunt only put up a little fuss before complying and putting her head down on the small pillow. Casidhe covered her with the throw blanket on the back of the couch. Her aunt looked so frail. This was new. Aunt Colleen was the quintessential nurse–kind and caring to everyone. Casidhe returned to the kitchen and put the groceries away in record time without noticing what they were. In just a few minutes, she came back to the living room and knelt beside her aunt. The smell was overwhelming at that moment, and

Casidhe turned her head a little, brushing her nose with the back of her hand to lessen the effect.

"Is there something wrong, dear?"

"No, no. I am just worried about you. You aren't looking too well." She wanted to add, 'and you don't smell right,' but that would give away too much, and she didn't know how to open that conversation with Aunt Colleen looking so unwell. She put aside her issues for now.

"I think I overdid it in the last couple of days at work. I have a few days off now. I will be fine."

"Good. You should rest. Do you want to lie in your bed, or can I get you anything?

"Could you bring me my phone? I think I'll take a nap here for a while."

Casidhe found her phone in her purse, put it on the table beside her aunt, and then left her to rest. She decided to go to the library for the afternoon. The local library was another one of Casidhe's favorite places. She could be quiet and alone, and besides, she loved books! She checked on her aunt once more before she left, relieved that her aunt was asleep.

As Casidhe left the house as quietly as possible, she worried more about her aunt than her own strange symptoms. Aunt Colleen had always been a rock. She could not remember the last time she had been sick. Casidhe knew something was wrong–something serious. She should convince her to see a doctor. *This is great; both of us displaying odd symptoms at the same time. What are the chances?* Casidhe used the time in the library to work on her term paper due the following week and tried to keep her mind off illness and disease. She did text her aunt once, checking in to make sure she was okay. Aunt Colleen told her not to worry.

Casidhe got home in time to help with dinner and clean up. Aunt Colleen had regained some of her coloring. She sat in her chair, watching her favorite show when Casidhe came down, ready for work.

"If you need anything, call me."

"I will be fine. I don't plan to move much off this chair."

"Good!" She leaned over and kissed her aunt on the top of her head and left.

Work went without incident, other than the now always present acute sense of smell and hearing. Casidhe was grateful there were no new shipments of soap or shampoo to stock that evening. The boxes were filled with cans and well-packaged food items that didn't overwhelm her. She got home a little after midnight and could hear Aunt Colleen sleeping in bed. Casidhe ignored the smell and went off to bed. It could wait until tomorrow.

She dreamt that night that she was walking through the woods alone without fear or distress. Up ahead on the path, she saw a light and could smell a fire. She heard people talking as she approached slowly, staying in the shadows. She came upon a young woman sitting on a log across from a young man. Both of their faces were lit up by the flame of the campfire in front of them. They were deep in conversation but to Casidhe's surprise, she could not make out what they were saying. She walked closer, drawn to the woman and her undeniable beauty, with dark, shiny hair and clear skin that seemed to glow. Casidhe became less interested in the conversation, wanting only to look into this woman's eyes. She approached them carefully until she stood right beside her.

The woman did not look up. Casidhe could feel the man looking at her but would not shift her gaze to him. She waited, looking down at the dark crown of the woman's head. Finally, after many moments, the woman turned and lifted her chin, her eyes leading the way to Casidhe's face. The moment their eyes met, Casidhe stood transfixed, her need for oxygen a bygone luxury. She never wanted to look away from those ocean blue eyes. Finally, slowly, ever so slowly, she drew in a breath, and as she did, the scene clouded and faded from view until it disappeared into a mist and was gone.

Casidhe woke up astounded. She'd never had a dream like that before. Her heart pounded, and tears streamed down her cheeks, but a smile creased her lips. She breathed long, ragged breaths for a few minutes until her heartbeat slowed.

Casidhe always suspected she was gay since she had never been attracted to guys. When she watched movies, she was more fascinated with women than men. She never acted on any feelings of attraction. And lately, with all the changes happening in her body, she stayed as away from everyone. But here in her dreams, she knew she could love someone. Especially if that someone was the beautiful woman in her dream. Her smiled turned upside down as she remembered her strange symptoms.

Before sleep reclaimed her, she decided to allow the idea of finding this woman to remain in her dreams. Having lost her parents when she was an infant, it had always been just her and Aunt Colleen. That's the way it always was.

CHAPTER TWO

S unday morning Casidhe woke up thinking about the black-haired, blue-eyed woman and smiled. Something new stirred within her. But suddenly, she heard a crash in the kitchen. She jumped out of bed and ran down the stairs.

"So sorry to wake you. I was putting away the dishes when I lost my balance. I couldn't hang on to them and catch myself at the same time."

"I was awake. Are you okay? You're not hurt or cut, are you? Don't move. I'll clean this up." Casidhe rushed into the laundry room adjacent to the kitchen and grabbed the broom and the dustpan. As soon as it was safe to do so, her aunt sat down in the chair and waited. Casidhe poured them each a cup of coffee and sat down across from her aunt.

"What's wrong, Aunt Colleen. I know you are not well. You must tell me."

"I am so sorry, Casidhe. I wanted to tell you."

"Tell me what?" She peered into her aunt's eyes, imploring her but also frightened of what she might hear. Aunt Colleen let out a long sigh and then gripped her hands together on the table.

"I have cancer. On Friday, I wasn't covering for Judy. I was at the hospital in Greenville, getting treatment. I'm afraid it is already too advanced to do much about."

"Cancer?" She said slowly, not believing it could be real. Aunt Colleen had always taken care of everyone else–of her. She was a nurse. How could she get cancer?

"But they can give you medicine, right? Chemotherapy? Or radiation? Can they operate?"

"Yes and No. No operation. I started chemo and radiation, but it's unlikely to help. If my numbers don't change in the next couple of weeks, it would be better to stop the treatments as they will take too much out of me. It's too advanced." Tears began to stream down her aunt's face as she reached for a tissue. Casidhe jumped up and got the box for her.

"But can't they do *something*?" She whined.

"They will do everything that can be done, but it is unlikely I will recover." Casidhe's face turned pale. She took a sharp intake of breath and held it. In almost a whisper, she asked: "How long?"

Aunt Colleen was sobbing now. "Six months at the most. I am so sorry, Casidhe; I do not want to leave you."

Casidhe sat there, speechless. She wanted to run, but to where? She wanted to cry, but the tears seemed to be stuck. She wanted to scream, but her voice faltered. She froze, opening her mouth a couple of times to speak but closing it again. Nothing came out.

Casidhe had always been a loner, but she never doubted that her aunt was there when she returned home. Aunt Colleen was her home, the only one she ever had. Now what? Her brain couldn't produce an answer.

After a few minutes, Aunt Colleen blew her nose and gained some control.

"We have lots of plans to make. You will finish high school, no matter what. I will need help as my illness progresses."

"I can take care of you." Casidhe finally found her voice.

"No. I won't allow it. You must finish school and continue your jobs. We need to discuss the house and such, and I have been keeping some things for you from your parents. I was going to give them to you when you graduated, but I think we can do that sooner. But not today. Today, we need to let this settle in."

"But who will take care of you?

"We will get hospice help when I need it. Until then, I will take it easy, and you can help me here and there. Okay?"

"Do you have to continue to work?" Casidhe didn't know if they needed Aunt Colleen to continue to work to pay the bills. Casidhe worked to have her own money and not be a burden, but she wondered if she would need to support herself soon.

"No, dear. I went on long-term disability last week, and I have insurance to cover the medical costs. I have been with the hospital for a long time, so I think we will be fine. And, after I am gone, you will have plenty."

It wasn't sinking in. That smell . . . That was it. It was cancer. Casidhe vaguely remembered Aunt Colleen telling her once that dying people had a particular smell. She had not paid it much attention since she had no reference for such information. Now, with her increased sense of smell, she knew what it meant. Neither one spoke until Casidhe got up from her chair and knelt beside her aunt, hugging her tight. The tears finally came as the situation began to sank in.

"You can't leave me alone."

"I am so so sorry, Casidhe. You have always been so mature, far beyond your years. But I fear this will force you to be an adult before you need to be."

Casidhe sobbed until there were no tears left in her, then stood, blew her nose, and wiped her face. No matter what Aunt Colleen said, she would take care of her.

"From now on, I put away the dishes." Casidhe teased her aunt as she blew her nose again. "Otherwise, we will have to get new dishes."

Her aunt smiled faintly through her tears. "Agreed."

"Shall I make some eggs and toast for breakfast?"

"That would be nice, but I think I will lay on the couch for a few minutes until it's ready. The medicine makes me tired."

Casidhe helped her aunt to the couch and went into the kitchen to make breakfast. It took longer than usual to fix such a simple meal.

She decided she would try to keep things as normal as possible for them. She'd quit her office cleaning job to be with her aunt more. She would do more of the housework and cooking and make sure Aunt Colleen rested. She only has a few months before she graduated.

Casidhe forgot about her strange symptoms and the beautiful dream she enjoyed that morning. She ended up eating breakfast alone, lost in her thoughts. Her aunt had fallen asleep on the couch, and she didn't want to wake her.

She did some laundry and cleaned up the house as quietly as possible. When her aunt awakened, she remade her breakfast.

"Casidhe, there is a lot about the past I have not shared with you. Now, it is important you know more about where we came from, as it will affect your future." Just then, Casidhe's phone rang. It was Amanda. She ignored it, thinking Amanda would leave a message, and she could get back to her later.

Her aunt pushed around the food on her plate. "There are some important things you need to know. I am sure you have questions."

Casidhe raised her eyebrow. What could her aunt be talking about? She couldn't know about her strange symptoms. Casidhe was sure she had hidden them well enough. Then her phone rang once more. It was Amanda again.

"That's strange; Amanda never calls me twice. I wonder if something is wrong?"

"Go ahead, answer it, make sure she is okay." Her aunt offered almost too quickly.

"Hello. Oh. Are you okay? Um, I guess, yes, of course." She glanced at her aunt, apologizing for the interruption and the fact that they both knew Casidhe needed to rescue her friend. Aunt Colleen nodded her head to Casidhe, letting her know it was okay.

"I will be there in ten minutes. Just get out of the house. I'll pick you up at the gas station down the road. No, it's okay. Don't worry. I'll be right there."

Casidhe hung up the phone and told her aunt Amanda's parents were fighting, threatening each other, breaking dishes, and yelling.

"She doesn't sound good. I need to go pick her up; she is in no condition to drive. Worst possible timing."

"It's fine, dear; we'll talk later. That sounds awful for Amanda!"

"Yeah, her parents fight a lot, but this sounds like the worst. I am gonna take her to her older brother's apartment. She'll crash with him for a couple of days."

"Good. I'm glad she has someplace to go. If she needs to, she can stay here."

Casidhe nodded but didn't want that to happen. She felt terrible about it, but with her aunt being sick and Casidhe's symptoms, she didn't think she could handle Amanda too.

"I'll be back as soon as I can." Casidhe grabbed her keys.

"I've got some paperwork to keep me busy while you're gone." Pausing a moment to get her balance, Aunt Colleen stood. When she looked up, she could see the worry in Casidhe's face. "I just need more time to catch my balance. It's the meds. I'll be fine." She found her book and glasses and headed for her bedroom.

Once Casidhe settled her aunt at her desk, she ran out the door to pick up Amanda. *She won't be fine, and we both know it.* As she drove the few minutes to Amanda's house, thoughts and emotions ran through her mind, keeping her from staying on any one topic. *Focus on driving, Casidhe, before you have an accident and make life even worse.* The day was chilly, with the smell of winter in the air. Had she ever thought about the scent of winter before? She arrived to find Amanda standing outside the gas station with a soda in her hand. She had been crying, her long brown hair hanging in her face. She got in the car and harrumphed down into the seat.

"Where does your brother live?"

"He lives on the east side of Greenville. He drives a truck and isn't back yet from this week's haul. I talked to him on the phone, and he said he would be home later this evening. He'll be off the next couple of days and promised to talk to our parents and find out what the hell is going on. Thanks for picking me up."

"No problem. Are you hungry? Do you want to get something to eat?" Casidhe felt anxious to get back to her aunt, but she wanted to be sure her friend was okay, too. And if she were honest, Amanda's problems were more comfortable to think about right now.

"Sure. I don't think I can eat much, but we could talk for a little while."

"What time do you think your brother will be home?"

"Cal said by dinner time. You don't have to wait with me till then, though. I'll need to get my car. Let's go over to Plaza Pizza." Casidhe hid her relief. They sat in the booth at the rear and ordered iced tea while Amanda did most of the talking. After an hour, Casidhe texted her aunt to let her know she would be a little longer before returning home.

Three hours later, Casidhe pulled up in front of her house again after dropped Amanda off to get her car. It was time to fix dinner, and Casidhe was planning what to prepare.

Aunt Colleen was not in the living room, so she went to the kitchen, hoping to find her there. She saw an empty teacup but not her aunt. Continuing the search to her aunt's bedroom, she began to worry when she found no sign of her. She checked the bathroom and all the rest of the house. Her car was in the driveway. Where could she have gone? She ran back down the stairs and through the house to the kitchen and out the back door. There she found her aunt crumpled on the ground below the laundry line; a sheet still clutched in her hand.

Casidhe let out a gasp and ran to her side. "Aunt Colleen, Aunt Colleen?" But there was no answer. Casidhe's senses told her what she did not, could not accept. "Please, Aunt Colleen, wake up!" Tears flowed down Casidhe's face as she collapsed beside her aunt, cradling her head at the same time, reaching into her jacket pocket for her phone. She managed to dial 911.

The ambulance came and worked to resuscitate her aunt and then whisked her off to the hospital in a wale of sirens. A police cruiser came and took Casidhe to the hospital too. She sat blank-faced in the emergency room waiting area until the doctor came out.

"Hello. I'm Doctor Jackard. Is Ms. Keller your mother?"

"Yes," a small lie that didn't matter to anyone else. "How is she?"

"I'm afraid she did not make it. She had a massive stroke. Her cancer was pretty far advanced, and it isn't uncommon. I am so sorry."

Casidhe just stared at him.

"Is there someone who can be with you? Can we call some-one for you?"

"No. No one." Those words rang inside Casidhe's head, sounding empty and hollow. Her heart clenched in her chest. She involuntarily reached up with her hand to cover it, finding it hard to breathe.

The doctor didn't seem to notice her pain. "The police would like to ask you a couple of questions. Is that okay?"

Casidhe nodded her head but didn't speak. She thought it was the same officer who drove her to the hospital, but she honestly wasn't sure. He asked what had happened and took notes as Casidhe numbly relayed the events of the last hour. He asked if there was anyone he could call for her. She could-n't face saying 'no one' again, so she shook her head. He offered to take her home, and they rode in silence. He left his card with her when he left her alone.

She walked into the dark house. She had not eaten since the slice of pizza she'd convinced Amanda to share with her, but she wasn't hungry. Without switching on a light, she slid down onto the floor in front of the couch, sobbing, not sure how much time passed before climbing up onto the sofa. How would she face the next day, or the day after that, or the rest of her life? She wished she had not gone off to help Amanda. Maybe if she had been there, she could have saved her aunt. And what about what Aunt Colleen needed to tell her? She would never hear it now. She would never hear Aunt Colleen's voice again. How can you not know when you wake up in the morning that something so tragic is about to happen? How can there be no warning? She knew her aunt was sick, but she couldn't have imagined she'd die - so soon.

At some point in the night, she got up from the couch and went into Aunt Colleen's room. Casidhe could smell her aunt in here. The odd smell was now gone, leaving only her aunt's soft and sweet fragrance. *Can you sum up a person by their smell? Maybe not until they're gone.* Casidhe curled up in a ball in her aunt's bed and fell asleep, clutching her pillow, willing the pain to subside.

The next day was Monday and school, but Casidhe didn't care. She woke up mid-morning and called the school, telling the receptionist about her aunt's death and that she would be out for a while. She didn't care about school, only Aunt Colleen had cared, and she was gone. She went to the kitchen and made coffee and toast. Her stomach hurt, or was it her heart? She wasn't sure; just generalized pain throughout her whole body. After chewing on a piece of dry toast, she left it and took her coffee cup back to her aunt's room.

As much as she wanted to sleep for days, she knew she had to figure out where and how to bury her aunt. She went over to the big window on the opposite wall and sat down at her aunt's desk. There were some bills in a pile. In another collection, she found a letter with her name written on the envelope in her aunt's curly script. She was about to open it when she saw a piece of paper under it, listing names and numbers.

- Judy
- Pfeiffer's Funeral Home
- Jack Poletti, Attorney
- Jessica Palmer, Case Worker
- Hospital Administration

Of course, Judy. She forgot about her aunt's co-worker and friend. Maybe she would be able to help Casidhe figure out what to do. At the very least, Casidhe knew she should let her know. She dialed the number.

"Hello?"

"Hello, Judy? This is Casidhe, Colleen Keller's niece. Do you remember me?"

"Yes, of course; how are you, dear? Is there anything wrong?"

"Yes, Aunt Colleen died yesterday." Casidhe could hear the gasp of breath on the other end of the phone and wondered if there was a better way to say that, but right now, she couldn't think straight. "She had a massive stroke, and they couldn't revive her."

"Oh, my. I knew she was sick, but I thought she would have more time. Oh, no." Casidhe didn't know what else to say. She wasn't sure if she was supposed to comfort Judy or not. She listened as her aunt's friend cried.

After a few minutes, Judy seemed to gather herself. "Casidhe, I am at work, but I can get off early. The kids are still in school, and I will have Ted pick them up later. I can be over there in about an hour, and we can figure things out together. Okay?"

"Thank you."

"Of course. I will see you soon."

Casidhe hung up and crossed Judy off the list, then stared out the window for long moments. She wondered if she should wait for Judy or if she should call the rest of the numbers her aunt left her. *Does it matter?*

There were other papers, a copy of her aunt's will, and a copy of the deed to the house. There were also legal papers on juvenile emancipation with the same number written at the top as on the list, next to the caseworker's name. Reading through it, Casidhe remembered she was not yet considered an adult. Now that her aunt was no longer her legal guardian, what would become of her? To her amazement, her aunt had thought of this and contacted someone to have her considered an adult before her 18th birthday. Casidhe dialed the caseworker's number.

"Hello, Jessica Palmer."

"Hello, my name is Casidhe Kenneally. I believe you spoke to my aunt, Colleen Keller?

"Yes, and since you're calling me, that means tragedy has struck and your aunt's worst fears realized?"

"Yes, she died yesterday, and I guess I have to do something?"

"Yes. Your aunt already began the process, just in case she didn't make it to your 18th birthday. I will need to come by and interview you. Will you be at the house this afternoon?"

"Yes, I think so. My aunt's friend Judy is coming here soon to help me with the funeral arrangements. But I would like to begin the process as soon as possible. I do not want to leave my house. I have my work and all of this to figure out."

"I am so sorry for your loss, Casidhe. I can be there around 2:00. Will that work?"

"Yes, thank you."

As Casidhe hung up the phone, she felt cold and shivered. She heard Judy's minivan drive up and accepted a hug more stiffly than she wanted to but couldn't seem to relax. Judy wasn't as old as Aunt Colleen, maybe early-forties, and she wasn't a tall woman, but she made up for it in attitude. She gave an air of confidence that Casidhe thought would work well for her as a nurse. Her blonde hair was cropped short, and her brown eyes shone brightly behind fancy tiger-colored glasses. Her smile was warm and made Casidhe feel glad she called her. Casidhe told her about the caseworker and the appointment that afternoon. Then she showed Judy the list.

"Yes, of course. You are not 18 yet." Tears welled up in her eyes as she said the words. Casidhe could hear the 'so young' part of that sentence, even though Judy didn't say it aloud. Judy brushed away a tear and asked Casidhe if they could make some tea. Casidhe escorted Judy into the kitchen and realized her aunt's teacup was still sitting on the table. Judy noticed the cup too and how Casidhe stared hard at it. She rushed over to pick it up and put it in the sink, then went about making tea for them both. Casidhe didn't need tea but allowed Judy to fix it anyway. It appeared she needed something to do.

"Let's have a look at that list then," she said as she sipped her tea. "I think we should give the funeral home a call next, as the hospital will need to know who is taking care of arrangements. Is that okay with you? Then we'll call your aunt's attorney."

"Sure."

Judy pulled her phone out of her purse and dialed the number. It wasn't a long call, as Colleen had already made her own arrangements, and they knew just what to do. All had been paid for in advance, Judy informed Casidhe after the call. Judy must have seen the confusion in her eyes.

"Don't worry, dear. The funeral home will handle it. They will let us know if there is anything else needed. Otherwise, they'll call back with some days and times for the funeral, and you can decide."

"Will they let me decide?"

"I think you take the reins as much as you want to. If you want me to talk to them, I will do that. But since Colleen made most of the preparations, there isn't much to do or decide. Colleen had the utmost confidence in you, which is obvious since she already began the emancipation process for you, just in case. She must have known how sick she was."

"Yeah, I wish I had known how sick she was. Maybe I should have known." She whispered the last part.

"Nonsense, you couldn't know. Now, let's call the attorney, shall we?"

Judy dialed the number and told the receptionist she was calling on behalf of Colleen Keller, who had passed away and that Colleen's niece was here. The woman put her on hold, and Judy pushed the speaker button. They listened to elevator music for a couple of minutes. Then a man came on the line:

"This is Jack Poletti; I am Colleen Keller's attorney. Can I help you?"

Judy repeated what she had told the receptionist. Casidhe heard the words spoken again; it was hard to make her mind accept her aunt's death.

"I am so sorry for your loss."

"Thank you. Colleen had you listed here to call if this happened." Casidhe said.

"Yes. I can review her will and get the paperwork moving along. She has left everything to you, Casidhe. However, you need to be 18 or given emancipation to receive your aunt's estate. Otherwise, it will go into a trust. I don't believe the process will take long. When do you turn 18?"

"March 1st, but I am speaking to the caseworker this afternoon."

"I think this will just be a formality, and then you can receive your aunt's estate. The state of North Carolina will not want you as a ward this close to 18, so I think things will move quickly. Can you give me the number of your caseworker, and I will touch base with them? After the funeral and I have a death certificate, I can do a reading of the will. I'll have my secretary call you and schedule that for next week. If there is anything else in the meantime, please do not hesitate to call me."

They gave him the case worker's name and number and thanked him. When they hung up the phone, Casidhe felt like they had accomplished something, though she wasn't sure why. After all, Aunt Colleen had done most of the work.

"I will let the hospital administration know of Colleen's passing. Don't worry about that one. I will talk to our boss tomorrow. Let's get some lunch before the caseworker arrives. It looks like you have not eaten much today." She was referring to the uneaten piece of toast still on the counter.

"I am not hungry."

"I know, but you must eat. Besides, Colleen would be furious with me if I didn't get some food in you. Let's go down to the Workaday Diner. It'll be good to get out of the house for a little while."

Casidhe did not look forward to the many smells of the diner, but Judy was trying to help, so she agreed to go and did her best to keep her nose to herself. Casidhe did end up eating half of a BLT sandwich and chips. Judy recommended a shower before the interview. Still disheveled from the previous day's events, Casidhe looked in the mirror and agreed.

The hot shower calmed Casidhe's nerves, but if she weren't about to be interviewed by a caseworker, she would have collapsed into bed again. Instead, she gathered her strength, put on fresh clothes and a blank face, and went downstairs just as the doorbell rang.

Jessica Palmer was younger than Casidhe expected, but she seemed competent and was already versed in Casidhe's case. Her keen eyes and small hands wrote down notes in Casidhe's file. Jessica agreed with the lawyer. Since Casidhe was about to turn 18 in a few months, the State would be

happy not to have another ward and quickly grant emancipation. She asked Casidhe to confirm what was written in the
file. Casidhe was not so committed to finishing school right
now, but she told Jessica she was. They also discussed
Casidhe's jobs and her plans for the future. Casidhe answered
as if her world had not recently been turned upside down, and
her one and only family member hadn't died. She tried to act
mature and together, even though she felt neither. Jessica
took notes while commenting that all looked good and was in
order. She would talk to the attorney and give her report. They
might get lucky and get before a judge as early as next week,
although that was wishful thinking. Still, it might not take too
long, and the state would be motivated. She left with a 'sorry
for your loss' statement, most people said automatically, but
few understood.

Judy stayed in the kitchen throughout the interview. Later,
Casidhe noted that Judy had busied herself by doing up the
few dishes, wiping the table, and throwing the sheets left in
the back yard into the washer.

After Jessica left, Judy came back in to check on Casidhe.
"All okay?"

"She said we might get in front of a judge as early as next
week. In the meantime, she'll put in her report and recom-
mendation that I remain in my own house. That's good, right?"

"Very good. Unless you don't want to stay here, you could
always come to my house and stay as long as you want."

"Thanks. I appreciate it, but I would rather stay here. I'll be
okay. I have some things to do, and I think I will turn in early.
Maybe watch a movie to take my mind off it all."

"That's a great idea. I'll call you later to check on you. If you
need anything at all, please let me know. I left the other half
of your sandwich in the fridge in case you want it later."

"Thanks," Casidhe tried to put some heart in her words,
but to her own ears, she sounded flat.

Judy hugged her, and this time Casidhe tried to return the
hug. She wouldn't have known how to get through this day
without Judy. She listened as the minivan pulled away, then
called her office cleaning job, letting them know she wouldn't

be in for the rest of the week. They could get someone else to fill in. Amanda had called her and left a message, wondering if she was okay, but she couldn't talk about it right now. Changing into sweats, she parked in front of the TV. Watching someone else's story, real or not, might make her forget her own. She fell asleep on the couch the second night. At around three o'clock in the morning, she woke up stiff. The sofa did not provide her room to stretch out. She went into Aunt Colleen's bedroom and curled up in her bed again, sleeping until late morning.

CHAPTER THREE

he midmorning sun streamed in through the windows caressing Casidhe's face as she awoke. The clock reflected the time as nearly 10:00. For a moment, she didn't remember the events of the last couple of days. When she realized she was in her aunt's bed, it all came back to her, and she slid down into the bed, not wanting to face it. How would she live with such emptiness? When the silence nearly suffocated her, she threw back the covers and got out of bed.

While the coffee brewed, she went over to her aunt's desk and picked up the Last Will and Testament. She was surprised to learn, not only would she inherit Aunt Colleen's estate, but her parents had left her something as well.

Why didn't Aunt Colleen tell her about this? She didn't know much about her parents, only that they were killed in an accident when she was an infant, and Aunt Colleen had taken her in and cared for her ever since. Occasionally, her aunt would comment about Casidhe's eyes reminding her of her mother, Colleen's sister. And when she was younger and more obstinate, Colleen would say she was more like her father. This always made Casidhe wonder who they were. She never mourned for them, not knowing how she could miss someone she did not know. Still, she wondered if her solitary style related to them in some way or the absence of them, perhaps. Casidhe put down the Will and stacked the papers into a pile. Just then, the envelope fell out with her name on it. When she turned it over, she saw an old-time wax seal stamped into it. It looked like a Celtic knot but inverted and elongated to resemble a wolf head. She stared at it for a long moment, frowning, then she pulled it open, breaking the seal to read the letter:

Dear Casidhe,

   If you are reading this letter, then I have passed on, and my attempts to transform and heal were unsuccessful. It is a longshot to try with my disease being so advanced. I am so sorry to leave you, my dear! There is so much I hoped to have the opportunity to tell you, but I am writing this letter in case I don't get that chance.

   First, I want you to know it has been my greatest joy to have you all these years, and I am very proud of the woman you have become. You are more beautiful, intelligent, and talented than you know. But that is not surprising considering the family you come from. Which brings me to the big thing I must tell you—you are NOT alone. Your parents were not from North Carolina, as I allowed you to believe all these years. When you were born, we all lived in Butte, Montana, and there are people there who still care for you. Again, I am sorry you are reading about this instead of telling you in person. I always thought I had more time, and some of these things are delicate and difficult to understand.

   My guess is you are exhibiting some peculiar physical symptoms of late. Yes, I could see the signs, and besides, I knew they were coming. At first, I figured I would let them happen (and eventually pass), and that would be best for you. But in the last couple of days, I have been second-guessing my decision, so I was going to tell you, (there is no easy way to write this) -you are a wolf.

   I know, now you think my illness has messed with my brain, and I have lost my mind. But think about it. If I remember correctly, you are showing signs of an increased sense of smell and hearing. Right? Maybe, you have wondered if you are going crazy or have some strange illness, and for that, I am sorry. You are not going crazy; you are a shapeshifter—specifically, a wolf shapeshifter called a State Changer. Your whole family were State Changers going back thousands of years to the early days of Ireland—which is where your ancestry is from. I know you won't have a hard time believing you are Irish, with your red hair and green eyes. You look like your great, great, great grandmother, Aoife. But I'll stick to the issue at hand for now. There is time to learn about your family tree later. Just know I am not crazy (and neither are you), and I am telling you the truth. You are a shape-shifting-wolf-fairy from the old world of Ireland.

Now, my guess is you are wondering why I never mentioned anything remotely like this before. The truth is, I was afraid to. You see, your parents didn't die in an accident, they were killed, and you are also at risk. That is why I took you away from your hometown, raised you as human, and never told you about your heritage and specialness. Facing my own death, I realize it was a mistake not to tell you, but I only wanted to keep you safe. Now that you are alone, I know you will need the pack. Yes, our family of wolves has a pack. And yes, I too, am a State Changer. I haven't shifted in 17 years to keep you safe. I couldn't risk it.

Now that I am gone, you must decide if you want to be a wolf and part of the pack. If you don't go through the final transformation before your 18th birthday, you will live the rest of your days as a human with no unusual symptoms or abilities. This choice was given to us by the Dagda, our ancestral godfather, many centuries ago. He was a Fairy King (they prefer Fae since Walt Disney has redefined fairies). Fae are mighty beings that you will learn more about if you go to the pack in Butte, which I recommend you do, even if you decide not to go through the transformation. They can protect you and tell you more about who and what you are.

In the same envelope as this letter, you will find a safety deposit box key. Take it to my bank, tell them who you are and that you have the key. I have already given you official permission to access the box. You will find things from your parents, information on who you are, and where you come from.

I know this is all very confusing, and you don't have to go, of course. You can choose to keep the house, graduate from high school, and go to college. After you turn 18, if you have not gone through the initiation and transformation, the symptoms will pass, and you can live out your days as a human and forever safe from the forces that killed your parents and put you and your brother at risk. You read that correctly. You have a twin brother. Your parents decided for both of your safety to separate you and raise you independent of the other. He knows not of you either, at least I don't think so. I have not had contact with the pack in a long time. More information is in the safety deposit box.

I am so sorry, Casidhe. I should have told you and given you the choice we all had. I should have shifted long ago myself, and I would not have gotten ill. I know this is a lot to take in. My only excuse is my love for you and my fear for your safety. Please forgive me and remember whatever you decide to do; I will always love you and be proud of you. Stay safe and find happiness and love, my darling daughter/niece.

Colleen

Casidhe let the letter fall open on the desk, looking up and staring out the window. *I don't care what she says; she IS crazy. Wolf-fairies? State Changers? Pack? Irish? Twin brother? Okay, the last bit could be real, but the other was too fantastic, too ridiculous, too far out there to be true. And why didn't she tell me sooner? I have so many questions. Am I in danger now? What kind of danger? Why were my parents killed and killed how exactly? I have a twin brother?*

All the questions swirled around in Casidhe's head until it hurt. She decided to dismiss the entire idea as fantasy. Aunt Colleen had obviously lost her mind before she died because it would be too cruel to play a joke like that at a time like this. Her brow knit together, and her eyes narrowed as she stomped off to the kitchen, leaving the letter, key, and all the other papers on the desk, hoping it would all be gone when she returned. She had to call Judy and finalize the arrangements for the funeral. This is the real world, and she had real problems. She jumped as her phone's ring intruded upon her thoughts.

"What is going on?" Amanda demanded.

"What do you mean?" Casidhe hedged.

"I mean, you called off sick from work, and you aren't coming to school this week. Are you okay? Is your aunt okay?"

"Oh, yeah, I mean no." She took a deep breath and went into the story about her aunt's death, leaving out the part that Casidhe was with Amanda when it happened. She didn't need to make her feel bad. Of course, she spoke nothing of the wolf-fairy thing. No one would believe her anyway, not even Amanda, and she didn't want anyone else to know how crazy her aunt had become.

"Oh. Oh no. I am so sorry, Casidhe. What can I do? Do you want me to come over and stay with you?"

"No, it's okay. I have a lot of arrangements to make, and Aunt Colleen's friend is helping me. I'll be fine. I just have a lot on my mind."

"Well, at least let me come over later to see you. I have to work and the new girl . . . But what about after work, for a little while."

"Okay, just for a little."

"I'll see you around 10:30. Text me if I can bring you anything."

"Thanks, Amanda."

Casidhe wondered if she was too curt with Amanda. Absently pouring cereal into her bowl, she thought, *what is a fairy-wolf anyway? I have never heard of it. I am obviously a human. Does that mean I am a werewolf—part human and part wolf?* That idea spooked her. Was she going to turn into a monster the next full moon and start eating babies? The thought made her nauseous. She knew for sure she didn't want any part of being a werewolf. *But that's not what Aunt Colleen said. She said I had to go through an initiation to transform. Wait, am I actually thinking about this? No! Aunt Colleen must have been out of her mind with illness to tell me such a story.*

Casidhe ate the cereal without tasting it. After a couple of bites, she dropped the bowl into the sink with a loud crash. *Why didn't Aunt Colleen tell me!* She left the kitchen wondering if she could allow her questions to go unanswered. Should she go to Montana to find out the truth, or was it all as fictional as the wolf story? How could she know for sure if she didn't go there to find out? Wouldn't it be worth the trip if only to discover that she, in fact, could have a twin brother? If it were true, Casidhe would not be alone; she would still have a family. Could she take that seriously, given all the other crazy ideas her aunt had written about?

Casidhe's mind tumbled over itself. Always coming back to 'Why?' She'd go to the safe deposit box and find out if there was anything in there about her parents and a brother. She would focus on that; the rest was too outlandish to believe.

She took a second cup of coffee with her to the bathroom to shower. When ready to go, she glanced at the clock. 11:30. The phone rang.

"Miss Kenneally? "

"Yes?"

"This is Pfeiffer's Funeral Home; we would love it if you could come by this afternoon to make the final arrangements for your aunt's funeral. Would that be possible?"

"Yes, but can we make it later in the afternoon, I would like for my aunt's friend Judy to come too, and I don't think she gets off work until 4. Would 4:30 work?

"Yes, that's fine. Ask for Stella when you arrive, and we'll have everything ready."

"Thank you."

Casidhe hung up after calling Judy to confirm the timing. Her phone rang again. This time, the caseworker informed her they had gotten lucky and would go to court next Tuesday. They made a date to get together on Monday to review the paperwork and prepare for the court appearance. Jessica assured her it would be an easy case to make and had full confidence all would go well.

Casidhe looked at her watch. She still had plenty of time to go to the bank and retrieve the safety deposit box contents before meeting Judy at the funeral home. Stepping out the door and turning to lock it, her super-sensitive nose kicked on. She went around the side of the house and peered out past the yard to the trees beyond. The musky scent of a rabbit filled her mind. She remembered her experience in the woods just days before, even though it felt like much longer ago. Her mind tried to reject the whole wolf thing, but Casidhe's body was not allowing her to dismiss it so quickly. Terrified, she spun around on her heels and ran to the car. Her tires squealed as she tore off, taking several breaths until the rabbit scent no longer tormented her. She tried to relax, focusing on what she might find at the bank.

After standing in line for a few minutes, she presented her key to the woman behind the counter, asking to see box 47.

"I'll need your ID, please."

Casidhe presented it, and after checking the computer, the woman led her to a back room where a hundred small locked doors lined the wall. The woman entered her key and Casidhe's key and opened the door to slide out a long metal box from its home. Then she escorted Casidhe with the box to a private room, telling her to call out when finished.

After the woman left, Casidhe just stood there and stared at the box. Eventually, she decided it was worse not to know. Inhaling deeply, she raised the lid.

Inside, she found a large, full-sized envelope with a metal clasp at the top. The front was bare except for her name written in a script she didn't recognize. She lifted it, surprised to feel how heavy it was. It obviously contained more than paper. When she turned it over to look at the back, she saw the same red wax Celtic knot wolf head–like the one Aunt Colleen had used on her letter. Realizing someone else had written her name on the front and used the same seal on the back made her heart skip a beat. Besides the large, bulky envelope, the box was empty.

She tucked the envelope under her arm with the seal facing inward, so no one could see it and returned the box to the woman, thanking her. For the second time that day, her tires squealed as she took off toward home. She had planned to stop at the grocery store, but now she didn't want to stop. The idea of leaving the package in the car while she did something as mundane as shop for groceries was no longer reasonable. She drove directly back home, and after entering, locked the door behind her. *Why am I so cautious? Am I afraid someone is watching me? Perhaps, I just don't want anyone to know how crazy my family is.* That made her sad again. And then angry. *Why didn't she tell me!? I could have asked her all the questions in my head, and I would know if she was telling me the truth or not.* Casidhe realized she was revisiting questioning the wolf story again.

She sat at her aunt's desk and, turning on the lamp, put the heavy envelope down with the red wax wolf head looking back at her. The symbol gave her an uneasy feeling like it was angry with her or something. *It's only a story, a fantastic tale.* She flipped the envelope over and stared at the writing on the front. *Casidhe Kenneally* was written in a sweeping, black script. Nothing about it was familiar to her. She was sure her aunt had not written it. She flipped the envelope over again and broke the seal, ignoring the wolf and dumping the contents onto the desk.

First to fall out was a small, smooth, milky stone with flecks of gold running throughout. It rolled around on the desk for a second and then landed at the base of the lamp. It was beautiful. She started to pick it up but noticed a small black velvet ring box tumble out after the stone and picked it up instead. She sucked in her breath when she opened it and saw a uniquely stunning black pearl and diamond ring staring back at her. Was it her mother's? She wanted to put it on her finger, but it felt wrong somehow. Was it hers to wear? She quickly snapped the lid shut.

Once she decided the ring couldn't be hers, she noticed a small wooden box with the name *Kenneally* engraved on the top. Inside were the contents needed to create a wax seal, including wax sticks, ladle, and a silver ring, obviously used to create the same wolf-head symbol. Casidhe tentatively allowed her fingers to touch the wolf head. Was this part of her family heritage? The stirring in her heart surprised her as she caressed it. *Could any of this be true?*

She read the papers before her. The first, a contents list:

- Nola Kenneally's ring
- State Changers wax seal kit
- State Changer Moonstone
- Personal letter for Casidhe and Cian Kenneally
- Kenneally Pack Alpha lineage

She paused. Something was shifting inside her, and it frightened her more than being alone–more than anything had ever scared her before. *How could this be true?* It was clear from the envelope's contents that her aunt wasn't the only one who believed the story to be real.

She stared wide-eyed at the list as her hand absently reached out to pick up the milky stone on the desktop, which according to the list, was a moonstone. When her fingers lightly grazed its smooth surface, a bolt of power struck her, traveling up her fingers to her arm and into her heart. She convulsed back so violently; she fell out of the chair and onto the floor. Stunned, cradling her hand and arm, still feeling the buzz left from the zap of energy that came out of the stone, she gapped. *What was that?*

Her cell phone rang from the other room. She had been in a different world since she walked into the house with the envelope. She stumbled to get to the noise in time, but not recognizing the number, she didn't answer it. Instead, she went into the kitchen to get a drink, welcoming a break from the trance the contents of the envelope had put on her. *What was that stone that shocked me, and how can a stone shock anyone?* She poured some iced tea and grabbed a pack of crackers, eating them absently from the package while walking around the kitchen. She stared out the backdoor for a moment, but so many emotions flooded her, she turned away. No matter what else was happening, she missed Aunt Colleen. *Why didn't she tell me?* This time when she asked the question, she felt anguish and regret. *Death is so damn final.* Tears streamed down her cheeks.

Brother? Maybe I do have a brother. She put the empty cup in the sink and returned to her aunt's desk, where she found another smaller envelope with the same wolf-head seal on the back. On the front, in the same script as the front of the larger envelope, was written: *Casidhe and Cian.* She opened it.

Dearest Casidhe and Cian,

We are writing this to you both so you will know of each other and our love for you both. Though I am writing this, your mother is right here beside me. Things have gotten out of hand with a couple of members of the pack and a fraction of the Fae who would do us harm. We, your mother and I, are unique within the pack, which makes us a target, and you both are at risk. I won't write too much about that, as we do not want this communication to cause you fear. We only wish to inform you that we did not leave you by choice and hope you are both happy and well cared for. It breaks our hearts to think that you may not know us or each other. But if you are reading this, then that is undoubtedly the case.

Casidhe, you are the oldest, though only by 6 minutes. You will live with your mother's sister, Colleen. She has offered to take you away and raise you separate and safe in case something happens to us. She will not live as a State Changer, which is a great sacrifice, but one she is graciously willing to do since we believe having you raised together will be too much of a threat to the forces that move against us.

Cian, you will go to live with my cousin, Colm, in Canada. He is strong within his pack, and we believe anyone who would consider you a threat would think twice about challenging him. He and his mate will raise you with their other children. With Casidhe gone, you should not draw anyone's interest.

Once you both become State Changers, you will be given these letters. We hope you seek out each other and find the common heart of the Kenneally family. We hope by the time that happens, the dangers will have passed, and you no longer have to stay in the shadows and can become healthy members of your pack. During your initiation, questions might arise that need answering. Seek out Saoirse, the white Wolf; she can help each of you. Cian, you can trust your uncle Colm. Casidhe, you will have Colleen. But if needed, seek out the Butte Montana Alphas, Kelly, and Lesslyn Moore—assuming they are still well. They have a small pub in Butte. Look for the State Changers symbol to find them. They will guide you in the ways of the pack there.

We have passed along family heirlooms to each of you. The Kenneally and Keller families date back to the ancient times of the State Changers. We regret not being able to guide you ourselves as you become a State Changer and as you enter into the magical and mystical realm of the Fae. But please know we love you both with all our hearts and have done everything we can think of to keep you safe.

Eternally loving you both,

Your parents,

Finn and Nola Kenneally

Casidhe sat there until the sun went behind the trees casting shadows on the small side yard. Thoughts swirled around and around, just out of reach. She heard a few birds chirp outside. She heard a truck rumble past. She heard a siren off in the distance. Still, she sat in a daze until her phone rang again.

"Hello"

"Hello, Casidhe, dear. I am running a little late, but I am on my way. I will meet you at the funeral home if that's okay?"

"Oh, hi, Judy. Yes, that's fine." Casidhe said in a far-away voice.

"Are you okay, dear?"

"Yes, fine. I was just a little distracted. I'll see you there."

Casidhe hung up, looked at her watch, and realized she would be late too if she didn't get going. She shoved the papers and boxes together and then carefully, using a pencil, rolled the stone back into the envelope without touching it, tucking it all in a drawer. She ran for her bag and coat and out the door before she could consider any other questions that might leap into her mind. She had to push all aside for now. The real world could not entertain such queries or offer any answers.

CHAPTER FOUR

T he funeral was a small event that Saturday. They laid her aunt to rest in a plain casket with a few flowers adorning the surrounding grounds. The only mark distinguishing the casket was the wolf head symbol, which she now knew represented the State Changers, burned into the top. Casidhe wondered if this request from her aunt had caused any raised eyebrows. The service was outside, as patches of sun and clouds peppered the sky on a breezy November day. The priest, someone with which Aunt Colleen had made arrangements, said pleasant things about her. Casidhe did not think he knew her aunt well. They had never gone to church, but it didn't matter. Her aunt was gone, leaving Casidhe alone with a world of questions.

Judy and her family were there, and some others her aunt worked with. Amanda and her brother came. Other people were there that Casidhe knew she had met before but could not remember their names or when she had met them. Each came by to hug her and tell her how sorry they were for her loss. Casidhe tried hard to keep her mind on the events of the day, and her aunt, the only family she had known. But her mind often strayed to the contents of the envelope and the letters.

They didn't host a luncheon afterward; Casidhe insisted they didn't need it. After the benediction, she tossed a small shovel of dirt over the casket as if that were a suitable good- bye, and then everyone dispersed. Judy wanted to drive Casidhe to and from the ceremony, and Casidhe didn't see the harm in allowing it. She was playing a part, as any dutiful daughter would.

Judy offered to come in and stay with her for the afternoon, but Casidhe refused, citing her desire for a nap before work that evening. She knew Judy worried about her and insisted Casidhe call her later.

After Judy drove away, Casidhe slumped down on the couch. *Now what? What am I supposed to do? Continue with my life alone? Go to work, finish school. Get used to being alone?* That idea crushed her.

"No!" she screamed, though there was no one around to hear her. She didn't care. "Why didn't you tell me?" She threw the pillow she had been squeezing against her chest across the room. "WHY?!" She pulled another pillow off the couch and screamed into it as tears soaked the fabric. "UGH!" She shouted again and again until her throat hurt, and her nose ran. The only response was the oppressive silence of the house. Finally, exhausted, she curled into a ball and fell asleep on the couch. Later, she woke long enough to call in sick to work, then slept the rest of the night fitfully in her aunt's room, no longer able to sleep in her own bed.

By morning, she knew she would follow the clues that had been given her, no matter how fantastic and absurd they were. It was the only option. Everything else was a black hole that threatened to consume her. If she did have a brother, perhaps she could live near him and get to know their cousins. If there are people who knew her parents, she will find them, even if the stories surrounding them were unbelievable.

Casidhe spent the rest of the afternoon coming up with a rudimentary plan to get through the next couple of weeks. After reviewing her high school transcripts online, she discovered she had enough credits to graduate at the end of this semester. She needed to finish the current classes, but that wouldn't be hard, and she was almost positive; she could cite her aunt's death to convince the school to let her finish early. She would meet with them as soon as the judge granted her freedom. She didn't want to risk that decision.

She also would get back to work, not knowing when she would receive her inheritance. She had money saved up but decided every little bit would help. Working would also help her look like she was a responsible adult to the judge. After her court date on Tuesday and finishing the semester, she would be off to Montana to find Kelly and Lesslyn Moore—whoever (or whatever) they were. Maybe she could be there by Christmas. It's not like anything or anybody was keeping her here for the holidays.

One night she had a similar dream to the one she had before Aunt Colleen died. The last thing she remembered before sunlight hit her face through the window was the beautiful woman with the dark, silky hair and ocean blue eyes smiling back at her. For a moment, Casidhe forgot everything else she was dealing with and felt what it must be like to have someone. A warm feeling washed over her, and she smiled for a second, wondering if the woman could be real. *Don't be ridiculous.* Casidhe ran her hands through her hair, got up and dressed in warm sweats, and went down to the kitchen to make coffee.

It had been one week since her aunt's death. Perhaps it was too soon to move on. Others would think so. All she knew was, the only thing that didn't consume her with dread was the idea of finding her brother and the people who knew her parents. So today, she'd bring in the boxes she had brought home from work and begin packing. She would go through her aunt's things, keeping a few items and donating the rest. She found no sense in keeping it all. While she was at it, she'd get rid of a bunch of her own things as well. She needed to clean the house and begin anew. She had to move forward or lose herself, and that meant finding the Moores in Montana.

That thought always made Casidhe feel hope and dread at the same time. *What if I find my brother, but he doesn't care about me? What if he doesn't want to know me as much as I want to know him? Wouldn't he at least be curious? I wonder what kind of person he is and if he looks like me.* She needed to find some answers, no matter what they might bring.

After a bite to eat and cup in hand, Casidhe went into her aunt's bedroom. Going through her aunt's closet, she packed up all the scrubs her aunt had worn to work. She pulled out a sweater she knew her aunt loved and brought it close to her face, breathing in the scent that was so familiar. Tears welled and spilled down her cheeks while her heart clenched. *Oh, Aunt Colleen, why did you leave me?* She decided to keep the sweater and put it aside, pressing on, determined to get through it all. Most of her aunt's personal belongings were either bagged to go or packed to save by lunchtime. A few things she would keep. As she got up to go to the kitchen for lunch, her phone rang.

Amanda wanted to come over and visit. Casidhe felt bad that she didn't have more of a connection to Amanda. She hurried to put the boxes back in the bedroom and the bags to go into her car trunk. No one else needed to know her plans yet. Casidhe wasn't sure why she felt the need to keep everything so secretive. Could she ever learn to trust?

Casidhe heard Amanda's car come down the street long before she could see it. Having stayed all day indoors, no wild smells or sounds from the woods had enticed and confused her. Amanda chatted for a while about work and school and nothing important. Casidhe tried her best to be more open, but it took effort. They decided to go out and get pizza and see a movie. Several new films were coming out this time of year that looked good. After a pleasant evening, Amanda dropped her off at 11:30, saying she'd see her at school in the morning. Casidhe got ready for bed, thinking she'd had a nice time despite everything, but the quiet house quickly reminded her how alone she truly was.

Casidhe went to school and pushed herself to get through the classes. The talk about her behind her back or from across the room was thankfully at a minimum since the football game win on Friday night occupied everyone's mind. She had a study hall at the end of the day, so she left early to meet with Jessica and discuss their court appearance preparations.

They wrapped up by dinner time, and Jessica assured her she thought all would go well. After Jessica left, Amanda came by to pick her up for work. She got home at 10:30 and climbed into her aunt's bed. With her anxiety about the court appearance the next morning, she had a hard time sleeping.

The judge read over her paperwork and asked her about school and her intentions to graduate. He inquired about her jobs and complimented her on her work ethic.

"Looks like you have no other family?" He stated aloud as he read over the papers before him and then glanced up and over the rim of his glasses as if asking if that were true. Casidhe cringed inwardly. *Does a twin brother I've never met count?* She stumbled a moment and then looked down to cover her pause.

"No, your honor. Aunt Colleen was the only family I have ever known," she said honestly, looking up at him a little teary. Fortunately, the judge misread her stumble, assuming she was broken up over her aunt dying.

"I am sorry for your loss, Ms. Kenneally. As you only have about three months until your 18th birthday, and you are doing well in school, at your jobs, and in your own house, I see no reason to put you in a foster care situation. You are granted emancipation from any adult supervision and have the rights and responsibilities afforded any other adult on this day, November 19th. Best of luck, miss."

"Thank you, your honor."

When the judge lowered his gavel and struck the base, Casidhe felt it in her chest. It was done. She was officially a solitary adult, in need of no one. Casidhe thanked Jessica, got into her car, and drove home. When she entered the house, the judge's words replayed in her mind. She gritted her teeth, refusing to cry again. She would keep moving forward. She had to. She got a glass of water in the kitchen, but she dropped it when she went to put it in the sink. It shattered all over the kitchen floor, reminding her of when her aunt had broken dishes not that long ago. All her resolve melted, and she slumped into the chair and sobbed. Once again, she had to pull herself together enough to keep going.

Fortunately, she'd already made the appointment later in the week to meet with her school advisor. She called the attorney's office and asked if she could bring by a copy of the court order and get the ball rolling on the transfer of her inheritance. By the time she left the lawyer's office the next day, she felt a little chipper. It invigorated her to be making her own decisions without having to ask anyone else. But after a moment of elation, it was gone. She would give up her independence if she could have Aunt Colleen back. *How can you live with someone your whole life, see them every single day, and then, in a moment, they are gone?*

By the time the semester ended mid-December, Casidhe had all the credits needed to graduate high school. She didn't have the diploma yet; she'd get it when May came around, and all the other students got theirs. The whole house was boxed up, and she had her banking arranged so that any other deposits would be automatic. She had given notice and left both jobs. She emptied the fridge and freezers and cleaned everything, throwing sheets over the furniture to keep the dust down to a minimum. She packed her bags and her car for the long trip, hoping the weather would cooperate, especially when she reached the northern states. She felt nervous to see new places; she had never been so far from home.

Casidhe's body changes were coming and going in waves, sometimes manageable but occasionally out of control. One afternoon, she had gone to the grocery store to pick up a few things after school. When she entered the store, she went through the aisles, dropping some fresh produce and fruit into her basket. On her way to the dairy section, she went past the meat case. Most of the time, this didn't faze her. She had never eaten meat; her whole life, they had been vegetarians. She never craved meat because she never had it. But on this day, the smell of the raw beef filled her nose and entered her brain until there was nothing else. She stood there at the counter as the butcher came over and asked her what she would like. She heard her voice whisper, 'no, thank you,' but couldn't move away. He stared at her for a few seconds and then asked if there was something else he could help her with. Still, she did not move; her eyes remained fixed on the large steak in front of her. She heard drumming in her ears, and her nostrils flared. Suddenly, a small child nearby let out a shrill cry demanding a candy bar. She jumped and spun around to see who had broken the spell. Then turning back to the man behind the counter, she gave him a quick smile, said 'sorry,' and hurried to the dairy aisle, grabbing the creamer and heading to the front check-out. She had not gone near raw meat since.

Casidhe could learn to live with an extreme sense of smell and hearing and even the occasional nightmares where she found herself tearing into a live rabbit with her bare teeth. But in the last couple of weeks, she noticed more strangeness. One morning getting ready for school, she peered at her reflection in the bathroom mirror. Her emerald eyes had turned a golden color. She blinked several times, and it went away. At first, she thought she was seeing things. But since then, it had happened several more times. She bought a pair of sunglasses and started wearing them to school. They added to her "freak" status but far less than if others saw those golden eyes. She felt so relieved on her last day of classes, knowing she didn't have to worry about anyone there noticing her strange symptoms.

The body changes created an air of deep curiosity around the "fairy-wolf" idea instead of the previous skepticism. No matter how absurd it was, she couldn't deny things were happening to her body. The wolf story made more sense than she could have guessed. Why else would these bizarre things be happening? She repeatedly searched online for references regarding fairies and wolves, but nothing gave her the answers she needed and often frightened her, especially when stumbling across werewolf information. She decided to wait and find out when she got there.

She had filled in Amanda of her plans to visit distant relatives for the holidays, not having a return date as yet. She was as ready as she would ever be. Amanda took her out on her last night and made Casidhe promise to keep in touch. Casidhe asked her to check in on the house occasionally, and of course, she could call her cell anytime. Casidhe decided she would miss Amanda and her life some, but she knew she couldn't stay after Aunt Colleen's death. It was just too empty.

She was anxious for what she might discover in Montana. She had focused on everything that needed attention before she could leave. Now that she would drive off the next day, a wave of fear wash over her. Amanda noticed.

"You okay?"

"Yeah, it's just . . . a lot, you know?"

"Yeah, I know. But you are going to be fine. I am sure those cousins up there in Montana are gonna love you, and you need people, girl. You gotta find your people!"

"Thanks. Are you going to be okay? How are things with your parents?"

"Better, actually. Since I moved in with Cal, I guess they realized they needed to get help. They have been going to marriage counseling and doing better. I am not sure they will make it, but they are trying. I go back and forth between them and Cal's apartment. This gives us all some space since Cal travels all the time. I think Christmas will be interesting, though. We'll see."

"Well, I'm glad things are better! You take care of yourself and keep in touch, okay?"

"Of course, we will keep in touch!"

They embraced for a long hug. Amanda teared up a little and promised to talk to her tomorrow on the trip. Casidhe waved as she drove off, wondering if she would ever see Amanda again.

That night, Casidhe didn't sleep well; visions of running through the woods as a wolf filled her dreams until she woke early with a start. She got up and showered to wash away the thoughts and emotions that always coursed through her when she had those dreams. It was hard to come to terms with such violence and such freedom at the same time. She put the ideas away for later and concentrated on turning everything off, locking up the house, and getting on the road. Then she focused on the directions, doing whatever possible to keep her mind clear. *One step at a time.*

She decided to head west to Colorado before turning north. This decision would put a couple of hours on the trip, but it seemed prudent after consulting the weather apps. She had picked out several stopping points along the way. If she traveled eight hours a day, she would arrive on the 5th day–Christmas Eve. She wondered if that might cause a problem or was in some way presumptuous. Should she try to call ahead? Who would she call? Lesslyn Moore? She had already checked, and there was no listing for that name. There were multiple Kelly Moores. How would she know which one? And what would she say? She decided it best just to go. If she found the Moores and they didn't want to talk to her, maybe they'd at least point her to where her brother lived.

When she pulled the house door shut and locked it for the last time, melancholy swept through her. She was leaving everything that was familiar, everything she had shared with Aunt Colleen. But what else could she do? She stood there for a few long moments in the cool morning air, staring at the door, hand still on the handle. Slowly, reluctantly, she released it, turned, and walked to her car without looking back. She got in, turned on the engine, and drove away, maybe forever.

The first day of driving passed uneventfully. Since she got such an early start, she decided to travel to Lexington, Kentucky. It took about nine hours with stops, but she checked into her hotel on the east side of town before dark. She turned on the TV and found a movie, and ordered room service. It was a splurge, but she deserved it. She needed to keep her spirits up. She had seen the movie before, but it was a favorite. She fell asleep before it was over and slept without disturbing dreams for the rest of the night.

The next morning, she hit the breakfast bar, filling her plate, when two young guys entered the dining area. Her senses piqued, and she felt the hair on the back of her neck go up. Turning in the opposite direction, she was nearly out the doorway when another of their group entered. He looked old enough to be their dad. Immediately, her bad feeling got worse. He stopped in front of her and smiled sweetly, too sweetly.

"You need any help, missy?"

"No, I'm fine." She tried to move around him, but he stepped back in front of her. She could feel the other two come up behind her.; her senses now on high alert.

"Now, why you gotta be rude? We were just trying to help a young lady in need."

"I am not in need. Please get out of my way."

"Oh, I see. You are one of those independent women. My guess, you've never been taught to respect a man." The two behind her began to snicker.

Casidhe didn't feel the growl from deep in her chest bubble up until it escaped between her lips. It wasn't loud, but it was low, long, and menacing. Her lips curled back, and her eyes turned golden. At that moment, she shifted from the prey to the predator. The man in front of her stumbled back in surprise, his eyes going wide. The two behind didn't see the changes to Casidhe's face, but they heard the growl and saw the fear on their father's face.

"What the . . . ? What are you?"

Casidhe paused for only a moment before she was able to snarl out, "Just an independent woman!" as she side-stepped and turned toward the elevator. She decided against it and ran up the stairs. Her hands fumbled with the key card, but she entered her room alone. She breathed heavily. Turning, she caught a glimpse of her face in the mirror, shocking herself. Her eyes were still golden, and her eye-teeth were elongated. She stumbled back, panicked. She looked away from the mirror and collected her things. No longer hungry, she pitched the food in the trash. With her overnight bag, she carefully exited the hotel, watching to avoid any other encounters.

It was nearly lunchtime as she crossed over the Illinois state line and began feeling like herself again. She decided she rather liked not feeling a victim to guys like that but also didn't know what she was capable of, which alarmed her. Gritting her teeth, she looked into the sky and asked, "Why didn't you tell me!" But just like every other time she had asked that question, no answer came.

After filling up the gas tank and getting a sandwich, Casidhe turned on the radio and tried to clear her mind of all things wolf. She sang along and, at the end of another day of driving, found herself not too far from Kansas City. She'd go the distance and put in another long day in an effort to get to Montana as soon as possible. She found a hotel, stayed inside, and ordered room service again. Afterward, she took a long bath and snuggled under the covers. They smelled sterile but tolerable.

She began to feel the wear of driving but was happy with how far she had traveled in only two days. She didn't stop to see many sights and had very little interaction with others. Her nature was to stand off from others, but she was even more cautious after what had happened in Lexington. She talked on the phone with Amanda a couple of times, which helped. But the isolation was beginning to close in on her.

Just before the alarm went off the next morning, she dreamed of the black-haired, blue-eyed woman again. She couldn't remember the details, but she felt lighter when she opened her eyes. *Maybe someday I'll find a woman like that. But for now, I'm off to Colorado.* She quickly went in and out of the breakfast bar, only noticing an older couple who barely looked up from their newspaper. Dismissing them, she was back on the road, thinking of the dark mystery woman in her dreams.

Driving across Kansas was the worst. It offered nothing to distract her mind, which often strayed to fearful thoughts or unanswered questions. She tried the radio but couldn't find much she liked. She tried her playlist on her phone but grew tired of it. She needed a distraction. Truck stops became her respite, offering a bathroom, food, and gas. While perusing the isles with her sunglasses on, just in case her golden eyes made an appearance, she saw some books on CD. She picked out the first two Harry Potter books, figuring they were an excellent way to pass the time and get through Kansas.

Back on the road, the world of *Harry Potter* and the adventures and woes of the young wizard filled the small VW and her mind. She was about halfway through the first book as she approached the Colorado state line.

As she traveled west, the scenery changed. Off in the distance, she could see mountains, grey against the brilliant blue sky. At first, they were slight and in the distance, but by the time she stopped at a little Best Western on the east side of Denver, the front range of the Rocky Mountains stretched as far south to as far north as she could see. They were still some distance away but stood tall and permanent against the skyline as the sun sank behind them.

As Casidhe pulled in for the night, the sun was no longer visible, but darkness had not claimed the evening yet. Across the street, she spotted a family diner and entered just after the dinner rush. No one noticed the girl in the side booth, even with her sunglasses on. She ate quickly and was paying the bill when she saw someone watching her from across the room. She glanced over the glasses as casually as she could to see a young woman dining with what looked like her brother. She didn't sense danger; it was something else–something new to Casidhe. The woman was looking at her with curiosity but not idle, more attraction. This idea made Casidhe's heart race and her face blush. Casidhe didn't think of herself as unattractive, knowing she didn't have the beauty of the black-haired, blue-eyed woman of her dreams. Still, the idea of this woman looking at her like that made her feel funny. She picked up the pace as she walked across the parking lot towards the hotel. She went in the front entrance, even though the side entrance was closer to her room. Would she always need to be so careful?

Casidhe fell asleep that night with a TV show playing in the background and thinking about the woman. She had never had a relationship but hoped one day she might. Though tired, she tossed and turned. The idea of reaching Butte soon began to loom in her mind. While on the road, she was in a sort of no-man's land. It had its dangers and its curiosities, but it belonged to no one, including her. Once she arrived, things would change. Or would they? The truth is, she had no idea what to expect, and that troubled her. By tomorrow evening, she would be in Montana, and by early the day after that, she would be in Butte. Would she be able to find the Moores? What do State Changers look like? Will they welcome me? She just didn't know.

The next morning, Casidhe headed out early. She drove west for a few more miles before hopping on the I76 loop around Denver to reach highway 25 north. As soon as she cleared the morning traffic, she turned on the second half of the Harry Potter audiobook and entered imaginary Hogwarts again. It felt safer there than her own thoughts right now. More than once, she wondered at her sanity for taking off from her home and life to go to Butte, Montana, to meet a bunch of werewolves. She knew that term didn't sit well, but when her thoughts turned especially dark, she went there.

No. It was far better to deal with "he-who-must-not-be-named" than her own dreadful ideas about what was or who was ahead.

Wyoming presented an interesting drive. Much like Colorado, the mountains loomed large to her left, and the flat snow-dusted plains stretched out to her right. Witnessing such a drastic difference in terrain was fascinating. Casidhe had never seen anything like it before. After a while, she realized highway 25 had veered west, and now the mountains were to the south, though still to her left. When she reached Casper, Wyoming, she stopped to fill up her tank and grab a bite to eat. When she stepped out of the car, the wind whipped through her jacket, and her teeth began to chatter. Reaching behind her seat, she grabbed the new parka she bought before leaving home. She quickly finished her business and climbed back into the warm car. The highway turned north again, and as she got closer to the Montana state line, she merged into highway 90.

The west looked very different than her home back east. Gone were the green trees and lush undergrowth that covered North Carolina. Gone was the humid air the Atlantic Ocean breezes delivered. There were far fewer populated areas—far fewer people in general. Montana appeared wide open, with fewer trees and less of everything else. The air was dryer, the wind colder, and the clouds billowed white and light grey against a pale blue sky as far as she could see. It was so different; she felt like she had entered another world.

She reached Billings by late afternoon, but since the highway went around and south of the city, there weren't many places to stop. Eventually, she saw an Econolodge and decided that would do. She pulled in, donned her coat, and zipped it up before getting out. She realized there were several places to stay after she got off the highway but settled into the motel. She walked across the street to the Casino that had a restaurant inside. The noise from the machines and the people overwhelmed her, so she stayed to the edges and out of the lights. There were all types of people milling about, sitting at the slots and card tables. She asked for a booth in the rear of the restaurant and ordered. Eating quickly, she hoped to get away without incident. While paying her bill at the front register, an old native woman looked at her sharply. Casidhe tried to ignore her, but the woman left her slot machine and came right up to her.

"You belong in Butte, don't you?"

"Who me? I am going to Butte. Why do you say that?"

"Oh, you got the look, dearie. Irish miners, the lot of you. I married one, but he ran out on me. He was after the fairy gold. Crazy Irish! And they think we natives are strange." Her eyes drifted off as if lost in a memory, and Casidhe took that opportunity to exit as quickly as she could. She could hear the woman calling after her, "Stay away from them mines; they'll make you mad as a hatter!" She smiled an eerie smile that showed off how few teeth she had left.

Casidhe tried to feign a smile as she scooted out the door and back to her room. She pulled out the key and was putting it into the lock when a large truck pulled into the parking lot, brakes squealing to a stop. This made her jump and her heart race. Once inside, she double-locked the door and leaned against it. She was on edge, but she didn't know why. Why was she so damn jumpy? And what did that woman mean by fairy gold? "Crazy old woman!"

Casidhe took a hot shower to wash away the road and to ease her muscles and her mind. She had the heat up high and was about to crawl under the covers when she heard a key turning in the lock. She froze for a second, just before fear could shift to rage, knowing a growl was forming in her chest. Then she heard a woman outside the door.

"That's the wrong number, Jack. You are trying to get into someone else's room. Down there. Number 108!" she yelled to Jack, presumably her husband.

"Oh yeah, thanks, Alana." Jack half laughed and moved along down the corridor. Casidhe exhaled, but it took some time before she felt her body return to normal. *Whatever Butte had to offer, I hope I find some way to deal with this . . . thing, this wolf inside me, or whatever it is.* She was beginning to worry about what could happen.

In the morning, Casidhe dressed and packed her overnight bag quickly. It was only a three-and-a-half-hour drive to Butte. She didn't know what she would find there but was tired of the unknowns of the open road. She would deal with one thing at a time, and for now, that meant getting to Butte.

The terrain changed again soon after she left Billings and headed west. Hills, rocks, and trees entered the scene, bringing a warmer feeling versus the desperation she felt on the prairies and planes, even as a light dusting of snow covered all. When she stopped to get a late breakfast, the wind had died down, and the air felt crisp with a distinct flavor of pine. Her spirits lifted some as she drove the final leg of her long journey. This was the fifth day of being nowhere and everywhere. Tonight was Christmas Eve, and though she didn't have high hopes for a jolly welcome, Casidhe was ready to find someplace to settle, even for a little while.

CHAPTER FIVE

hen she arrived in Butte, she found a hotel along the highway that seemed welcoming with a Christmas tree out front and a wreath hung on the door. She decided it would be her home base for a few days as she got the lay of the town and looked for Kelly and Lesslyn Moore. After checking into a lovely king-size room, she unpacked a few items and went down to the hotel restaurant for some lunch. The people were nice but not overly friendly, which helped her relax. After hauling in a few more bags from the car, she ventured out into the town.

What had made this her family's home? Casidhe had researched the Butte area. It boasted the highest density of Irish per capita in the United States, due to the silver and copper mining, at the beginning of the twentieth century. The Irish immigrated here in droves with the hopes of finding riches, or at least steady work. At one time, a full twenty-five percent of the population was Irish. You could still see their influence in establishing the town by the names of the restaurants and pubs. O'Malley's, Kelly's, Sullivan's–they'd all come from the old country.

After the mining eased off in the late '70s and early '80s, the area was deemed an environmental disaster, and the big-rollers had to clean up the mess. The most extensive cleanup in the history of industrial pollution had happened here in Butte. Aside from bringing in the Irish, which it seemed were her people, she didn't see any connection to wolves. Was it something more that brought and kept the Irish-wolf-people here? Perhaps it was the surrounding area. *Or maybe they aren't even real.* She poured over the maps she had collected from the hotel lobby and saw the vast wilderness surrounding the city. Perhaps the proximity to all that open wilderness kept them here.

As she drove into the town center, she saw the old brick buildings and obvious traces of a once-thriving mining town now turning and stretching into a new age. She wondered what it was like in this western town a hundred years ago. It must have been a rowdy place. She saw modern stores in renovated spaces, allowing the town's folk to hang on to the history but still stay in business. She drove down street after street, seeing signs of new, old, and ancient. It fascinated her how they all coexisted, like ghosts from the past dancing with spirits of the future.

Casidhe noticed there were young people as well as old who walked the streets on their way to the coffee shop or the local pub. All were bundled in coats, hats, and gloves with rosy cheeks and bright eyes. They seemed happy if a bit hurried. *Funny how you see things when you are new to a place.* Casidhe wondered if her perspective was because she felt so completely a drifter, with no place or person to attach herself to.

Christmas was in the air and appeared to put most people in a good mood. She noticed a Scrooge or two, but they were few and far between the merry passers-by.

After driving around for over an hour, she didn't see anything that said, 'werewolves enter here,' not that she had expected it to be so easy. She found nothing with the name of Moore or any sign of the wolf symbol. She wondered where they were hiding in this northern town and how she would find them.

Getting hungry on the way back to the hotel, she saw a little pizzeria that looked promising and was happy to find it open. Adjusting her sunglasses, she ordered a slice and a drink and sat in the back to eat. She wanted to head back to the hotel but knew she should try to stay out. She wasn't going to find her people in the hotel. But though the pizza tasted good, the lack of clientele brought no insights. She thought she might go to the mall if it were still open and buy herself something. She could use a few more warm clothes, and afterall, it was Christmas. She asked the man behind the counter the best place to buy warm clothing on Christmas

Eve. He did a once-over of Casidhe and agreed she would need extra clothing to manage the cold Butte winter.

"There's a Supercenter about a mile down the road." He gave her directions and went back to the kitchen. When she went out of the door, snow had begun to fall. The surrounding mountains were already snow-capped, and the grassy lawns were dusted, but the roads had been dry and clean. That would soon change.

The atmosphere in the Supercenter was familiar and comforted her. She did a little shopping, purchasing some long underwear and a fleece sweatshirt. She also picked up a wool hat, scarf, and gloves set. As she checked out, she asked the woman at the register if a lot of snow was predicted.

"It's amazing we haven't had much snow yet, quite a dry winter so far. But yeah, honey, we'll be getting a lot of snow; you can count on that."

As Casidhe drove back to the hotel, she was extra careful as a thin coating of snow had already covered the streets. When she entered the lobby, the sweet smell of cinnamon filled her head. It reminded her of past Christmases with Aunt Colleen and the hot spiced cider she made every year. Her eyes filled with tears, and once inside her room, she sat down on the bed and cried.

"What am I doing here? At least in North Carolina, there are people I know, and I would not be alone for Christmas." She curled up in her bed, crying for all she had lost. Hopes of finding her brother fell away, and only loneliness filled her. It poured out of her and surrounded her like a thick, dark cloud. On Christmas Eve, she was far away from everything she had ever known. She slept fitfully and dreamed of running through the woods, desperately pursuing someone but never quite reaching them.

She woke very early, drenched in sweat, and decided to take a shower. It was still dark outside, so she turned on the desk lamp. When she went past the full-length mirror on her way to the bathroom, bright golden eyes stared back at her, causing her to stumble away from the mirror. As she stared back at the strangeness that had too often become her reflection, she knew again she must find answers, no matter what else came of her time here in Butte.

On Christmas Day, it snowed–a lot. Casidhe stayed in her room, only venturing down to the breakfast bar late in the morning and filled up on waffles and bacon. The older woman who worked at the front desk and the breakfast station didn't seem to notice her much. Casidhe guessed she would rather have been anywhere else.

She spent the day alternating between watching Christmas movies and studying maps and websites about Butte. It snowed about a foot, and not much moved outdoors that she could see. Everyone was snuggled in their homes with family, and Christmas dinner, and gifts, and warm fires. Of course, she knew not everyone was that fortunate, but that was all she could imagine. She worked hard to keep her spirits up, but by evening, when darkness fell, it also fell in her own heart.

That night she pulled out the envelope her parents had left her, reading it for about the twentieth time. *Why didn't they tell me exactly where to find Kelly and Lesslyn? Why didn't they give me an address or place to look? A pub with the wolf symbol? Do I have to go down every street? AND, why didn't Aunt Colleen tell me?* She had asked this question so many times; she tired of the silence that followed. *Safety is not a good enough answer. It was an excuse.* This line of thinking always made Casidhe angry and then sad. *Why, Aunt Colleen? Why?*

The day after Christmas didn't bring her any more answers. The snow continued, and still, no one moved outside. She tried to keep her mind occupied, walking outside in the snow for about an hour during the middle of the day to get some fresh air. In the afternoon, she pulled out a novel from one of her bags but found it hard to concentrate. By evening, the snow had finally stopped, and she fell asleep watching a classic movie.

The next morning, the snowplows were out clearing the streets, and Casidhe couldn't wait to venture out and look for any sign of the Moores and the wolf symbol or anything that might lead to her brother. She carefully drove around the outskirts of town, but nothing looked right. She went back downtown to the older areas that made you believe the Irish were still around. The history was downtown, and she hoped she would find the Moores there too.

She reached the end of the commercial district on one street and was about to turn around, avoiding a residential area, when she spotted something familiar out of the corner of her eye. There, tucked between two larger shops, was a tiny, narrow pub that looked like it was in desperate need of an upgrade. The single, window-less door had been painted bright yellow many years before. Now it was dingy and had dark marks scaring the bottom-half as if it had been kicked far too many times. But what surprised her was the inverted Celtic knot on the window. It was the same wolf-head symbol that was in the wax seal kit her parents had left her. Above the emblem, in fading letters, it read: Mac Tire Pub. Casidhe didn't understand what tires for a Mac truck had to do with a wolf, but she wanted to find out. She parked her car and got out, zipping her coat up to the top and pulling her hat down tight to stay warm against the frigid day.

She walked up to the yellow door and turned the knob, but it was locked. She wasn't old enough to enter a bar, but she figured it was worth a try. She turned to look through the window and saw the hours in small letters. They didn't open for another hour. Casidhe turned to go when the yellow door swung outward, and a large man came out. He turned and gazed down at her. Casidhe's eyes widened like she had been caught where she didn't belong. His eyes were brown and beady. Dark, greying hair and beard covered most of his head, save for his narrow nose and sneering thin lips.

"What do you need, lass? You can't come in here; ye're not old enough to be drinkin', even if it is Christmas. Go home to your folks."

It took Casidhe a few breaths to answer, "Ah . . . sorry. I was just looking for someone."

"Found someone you have, then." His sneer grew broader.

"Um, no, I mean, I was searching for someone specific. Lesslyn . . . Lesslyn Moore?" she stammered out the woman's name in the face of such a giant man.

"Lesslyn? What would you be needin' Lesslyn for?"

"You know her?"

"'Course, I know her. She's me wife."

"Oh, right. Um . . . I um, wanted to know if she, if you . . . knew my parents." Casidhe had not rehearsed what she would say if she found Kelly and Lesslyn Moore. Everything coming out of her mouth sounded scattered and bizarre, even to her own ears.

"Why would ya wanna ask her that? What're ya up ta, lass?"

"Oh, sorry. I was just trying to find someone."

"You've said that." His eyes narrowed more, which she wouldn't have believed possible.

"Ah, never mind. I am sure she . . . or um, you aren't who I'm looking for." Casidhe, feeling dumb and frightened, turned to leave, but he put a large hand on her shoulder, stopping her. She could feel the heat rising inside, partly from embarrassment and partly from fear of this large, hairy man. She was about to run when she heard a woman's voice behind her. She spun around to see the woman standing in the doorway.

"What's going on, Kelly?"

"This lass wanted to talk to Lesslyn Moore. Don't know what she's up ta."

"Kelly, why are you such a brut? She's just a young lass. I'm Lesslyn, but it's too cold out here to be talkin'. Come inside, and I'll fix you a cuppa tea."

Casidhe was unsure at that moment. Lesslyn looked a little younger than her husband; perhaps it was the long dark hair that whipped around her face. Casidhe thought she might have been lovely in her youth, with dark blue eyes and long eyelashes. You could tell she had lived through some hard times. It wasn't exactly her face that told the story, but her demeanor. She was confident, comfortable but also a bit sad.

Kelly had removed his hand from her shoulder but still stood menacingly nearby. The place was dark inside, and for a moment, Casidhe wondered if she went in, she'd ever come back out again. She shivered from the cold wind, and that convinced her. Lesslyn had turned and held the door while Kelly went in first, and she, smiling back at Casidhe, offered the warmness of the pub. Casidhe knew it was an impossible coincidence to find them like this. But the symbol on the window stared back at her from behind the woman named Lesslyn, and she figured she should at least talk to them. What else was she here for? There was no way it wouldn't be awkward no matter where she had found them, so she shouldn't be surprised. All this musing in her head took about half a second before she turned toward the doorway and stepped inside. The woman turned and locked the door behind her. Casidhe noticed, hoping she could unlock it if she needed to escape.

"Set yourself down at da bar, aren't any room for tables."

Casidhe agreed there was no room for tables; the place was narrow with a long wooden bar down the right side of the room, taking up more than half the available space. Kelly had gone to the back, and they didn't see him again for a couple of minutes. Casidhe was glad. She thought for sure, of the two, the woman was her safest and most agreeable source of information. Lesslyn busied herself behind the bar getting cups and tea ready. Before long, Kelly returned, putting a pot of hot water on a wooden platter on the bar as if to protect it from the boiling kettle. Which was interesting to Casidhe because the bar looked like it had been beaten up and marked on by everything possible and for a lot of years. No one spoke until the tea was poured and a couple of Christmas cookies placed on a plate before her, which gave Casidhe a chance to think about the Moores' way of talking. It was much more Irish than she had expected. The words were the same, but the accents were very different.

"A dear friend gave us these biscuits for the holidays." Lesslyn smiled at her and shooed Kelly to the back room.

"Now, what can I do for ya, luv?" Lesslyn's eyes were piercing but kind.

"Thank you for the tea and cookies. It's very kind of you. As I was telling your husband, I was looking for Lesslyn Moore to see if you knew my parents."

"What's your name, lass?"

"Oh, I'm sorry. I was a bit flustered. My name is Casidhe Keneally." As the words left her lips, the woman's expression froze, and the teacup fell with a clash on the floor as she took a step back from the counter. Her mouth opened a bit, and words Casidhe didn't understand escaped.

"*Go bhfoire Dia orainn!*"

Lesslyn stood there, frozen in place as if someone had come back from the dead, and stood alive and well in her dingy, old bar. Casidhe was afraid to break the spell, but Kelly came running forward to see what had caused the noise. He saw his wife standing stunned in front of the girl, the broken cup at her feet.

"Everything okay?"

Lesslyn whispered, "Casidhe Kenneally."

CHAPTER SIX

Kelly walked toward Casidhe, staring at her wide-eyed. His great height and bulk grew nearer, and soon, she was looking up into his hairy face frightened, and sure she had made a big mistake in coming here. She wanted to shrink away, but his eyes held her in place. Just when Casidhe knew she was done for, Kelly's bushy lips curled back into a huge smile as if he'd decided she was who she said she was. It took a moment for Casidhe to register the relief in his face and relax. Before she was ready for it, Kelly scooped her up into a huge bear hug.

"'Course ya are! Jesus!"

When he released her, Casidhe saw Lesslyn had come around the bar and reached to embrace her too, with large tears rolling down her cheek.

"I can't believe it. I can't believe it! Oh, Casidhe, we've hoped to see ya for all deese long years but, we'd all but given up. Where's Colleen?"

With the mention of her aunt's name, Casidhe looked down, her shock at their welcome giving way to the pain of losing her aunt.

"She died of cancer about a month ago."

This news seemed to rock them both. Kelly's dark eyes grew bright as tears welled and spilled onto his bristly cheeks. Lesslyn gasped, bringing her hands up to her mouth to stifle a sob. She sat on a barstool and openly cried. Casidhe didn't know what to say. The moment had turned from surprise and glee to deep sadness in a blink. Who was her aunt to them? They had obviously been close. Casidhe was filled with questions but decided to wait as they needed to sit with the news of Colleen's death. Finally, Casidhe could wait no longer.

"How did you know my aunt?" It seemed Casidhe was destined to shock these people again and again. Neither spoke at first as they stared at her with their mouths open.

"Um, she was a member of our pack, *a gra*." Kelly said at last, a bit confused by the question, but there was something else too. Something in the way he answered that was yet unspoken.

"And she was me best friend growing up." Lesslyn chimed in. Then as if she had made an important decision, she changed the conversation entirely.

"Where are you staying, Casidhe?"

Confused by the sudden shift, it took her a moment to answer. "The Best Western out by the highway."

"Kelly, is it safe?"

"Aye, I know da manager, but I doubt any red flags been sent up yet. We didn't see the resemblance, even after she walked into our own pub."

"Aye, quite. They won't be looking for her, though if anyone opened their eyes, they could see both Finn and Nola in this young lass, now wouldn't they." Casidhe felt uncomfortable that she would look like the parents she had never known. She wasn't used to looking like anyone other than herself. Then the 'safe' question registered in her mind.

"Safe from what?"

Her lack of understanding appeared to create certainty in Lesslyn.

"It's good'n safe here at the Mac Tire, but this is not the place to have that conversation. Kelly, can you have Brody fill in for me here at the bar tonight? I want to take her out to the Ranch, if that's okay with you, darlin'?" she said, turning toward Casidhe, who was trying hard to keep up. The Moores' speech rhythm made Casidhe need to pay close attention so as not to miss anything. She noticed how Lesslyn pronounced what she assumed was the name of the pub. She tried to repeat it.

"What does *Mc'Teeda* mean?"

"Wolf . . . Kelly, I'll call you later to check-in. It's probably best not to mention anything about Casidhe here to anyone else in the pack just yet. Give us some time to catch up first?" She winked at her husband, who smiled and nodded his agreement.

"Where are you parked, darlin'?"

"Out front."

"Good, I'll be in the big, black truck; just follow me."

"Okay." She hesitated a bit. "How far is it?"

"About ten miles down the road. Not too far, but far enough." This time Lesslyn winked at her, but she wasn't sure why or what she meant by 'far enough.' She followed Lesslyn out of the pub and got into her car. As she pulled out to follow the dark, oversized truck Lesslyn was driving, she thought about what had just happened.

She had found the Moores, as her parents' letter instructed her to, and they seemed genuinely happy to see her. But Casidhe still had all her questions bottled up inside and wondered if Lesslyn could or would answer them all. It was apparent there were hints to an implied connection to wolves. *I mean, Kelly practically was wolf-like with all that hair.* But that didn't mean anything; he certainly wasn't the only hairy man Casidhe had ever met. Aside from the noticeable Irish connection, Casidhe was still not sure what any of it meant.

As they drove out of town, the landscape changed. They first steered southeast, then turned northeast, then directly east into the foothills. Snow white fields filled in with trees around them, and snow-capped mountains loomed ahead. In no time, it felt like the hills came down to meet them, surrounding them. They turned off onto a dirt road that took them deep into the forest and up to an arched stone gateway, which joined two ends of split rail fencing, which took off in either direction as far as she could see into the trees. At the very top of the arch was the same Celtic wolf-head symbol that Casidhe was now associating with her parents and what they described as State Changers.

The moment they crossed under the archway and onto the Ranch, Casidhe felt something stir inside her. At the same time, she had a ringing in her ears, and her nose picked up the scent of something? *What is that smell? It's familiar, but I can't remember where I have smelled it before or what it could be.* She also saw sparkles twinkling in the air around her as if she had just entered a child's storybook world. She was trying to decide what was happening. *Snow? No, the skies are clear and crystal blue. Crystal? That's it. The air sparkles crystal-like. This can't be real.*

As they drove closer, Casidhe could see several buildings. Off to the left of the driveway stood a large barn, towering against the tree line, which came down behind it. There were other smaller out-buildings, but Casidhe was not sure what they were. They pulled around the wide circle of a driveway in front of a mammoth log . . . cabin? No, more like a log mansion. It had wings that branched off in different directions and windows everywhere, reflecting the blue sky above. The porch spanned the entire front of the house and wrapped it on both sides, giving the impression it continued around the entire structure. Large tree posts stood on either side of the main stairway supporting the roof over the expansive porch and leading up to the doors beyond. *Wow. These people must come from money. There is no way that little pub makes enough to pay for all of this.* Lesslyn had parked and walked up the broad wooden stairs that led to the porch and the heavy double doors with full brass hinges that loomed ahead. Casidhe had turned off her little car behind the truck. She tried not to gawk as she ascended the stairs and attempted to keep up with Lesslyn.

Lesslyn appeared different in this place. The years fell away from her face. The lines faded, and her cheeks were rosier. Her hair shook free, full, and lush, and when their eyes met, they too sparkled. *This is very strange? Maybe it was something I ate?* Casidhe did feel light-headed.

Lesslyn noticed the confusion dance across Casidhe's face.

"It's not your imagination *a gra*. This land's been touched by the Fae. Only a true State Changer would notice it. I had to be sure of you." She smiled as she went up to the doorway.

The knotted wolf symbol was burned into a wooden plaque above the door. As she entered, she noticed smaller doors inset into the more massive doors at the bottom. Dog doors on the front? Casidhe had never seen anything like that before. Otherwise, there were no handles or locks on the doors that Casidhe could see.

Lesslyn had already entered the enormous house, and the doors had begun to swing shut. But when Casidhe approached the doorway, they swung open again automatically. When she was through the opening, she looked around for who might be operating them, but there didn't seem to be anyone.

"Only Fae and State Changers can walk through those doors; otherwise, you'd be forbidden entry. Many things around here are charmed." Lesslyn smiled at Casidhe.

"Lesslyn, I hear what you are telling me. But I don't really understand." Casidhe also noticed that Lesslyn's accent seemed far less pronounced here on the Ranch. Did Fae magic have something to do with that too?

She smiled and led Casidhe into what she called the great room, and for good reason. Dark gigantic wooden beams spiraled out from a central spot in the ceiling like a wagon wheel supporting the roof that loomed to the second story overhead. Glass windows were plentiful and strategically placed to allow for the best views and the most sunlight. A massive stone fireplace and exposed chimney took up one whole wall with a hearth so wide and deep it could seat ten people at least. There was a fire roaring in the fireplace with plenty of firewood stacked nearby. Around the room were many cavernous brown leather couches and chairs with bright pillows and throw blankets littering the scene. A huge fur rug covered the stone floor in the center. Despite the room's vastness, small lamps scattered about on luxurious oak tables gave it a warm and comfortable feeling. The very tall, magnificent sparkling Christmas tree still standing against one wall helped. Casidhe remembered it was Christmas time and was admiring the beauty of the space when Lesslyn invited her to sit by the fire and asked if she would like anything to eat or drink.

"Some water would be nice. Thank you."

"Certainly." As soon as Casidhe had made her request, a young woman entered the room carrying a tray with two water glasses and some more Christmas cookies.

"This is Blaire. She works with us. Blaire, this is Casidhe."

"Nice to meet you," Casidhe said automatically. Blaire, who looked to be in her mid-twenties, had a full head of brown hair that she tried to pull back from her face but was not altogether successful. She had fine features and dark brown eyes that made her look like she knew more than she was telling you. Casidhe wondered if she, too, was a State Changer. *But wouldn't she have to be if she were able to enter the house, as Lesslyn said?*

"Casidhe Kenneally. Nice to meet you too." She said genuinely, looking into Casidhe's eyes, and then looked up at Lesslyn before she left the room.

"Casidhe, darlin', let's start with what happened to Colleen and how you found us," Lesslyn began.

"Right. Well, there isn't much to tell, really." Casidhe said as she launched into the story of her life in North Carolina with her aunt and her sudden death. She told Lesslyn about Colleen's letter and how shocked she was at such a revelation.

"I can't say I believe it all. I mean, I know there are coincidences I can't explain, but wolves and State Changers? This is all very strange to me. If it weren't for the symptoms I've been dealing with, I probably would have dismissed all of it."

Lesslyn's interest was piqued. "Yes, tell me about your symptoms and when they started."

Casidhe told her about her acute sense of hearing and smell and how disconcerting that was. But it was nothing compared to the feelings she had in the woods of hunting down prey, the scene in the grocery store, and the nightmares of hunting, catching, and eating her prey. Her voice had become high with anxiety, signaling her discomfort over the idea. Casidhe was surprised she didn't mind revealing all this so soon to Lesslyn.

"So, you had no hint of who or what you are before Colleen's death and the letter?"

Casidhe shook her head. "No. I still am not sure what this all means."

"Well, my dear, it seems you have much to learn in a short amount of time."

"But why didn't Aunt Colleen tell me? How could she have kept something like this from me? I keep asking myself this question, and of course, she can't answer me now." Casidhe was nearly in tears. Perhaps it was all the stress of the trip and now all the strangeness happening around her. Or maybe it was the first time she was asking these questions of someone who might be able to answer them. Casidhe knew she sounded desperate and a bit pathetic, but she couldn't help it.

"It's okay, darlin'. We'll figure it out together. I can tell you more of the story about why you came to live with Colleen and why she was desperate to keep you safe. But before we get to that, what did the letter from your parents say?"

"It said I should come here and find you and that I have a twin brother named Cian. Is he here too?"

"No, Cian does not live here. He is still in Canada with his cousin, I presume. I have only seen him once since the two of you left, and he was a young lad then."

There was no question about whether Cian existed or if he was, in fact, her twin. But there was something about the way Lesslyn spoke of her brother that made Casidhe wonder if she didn't like Cian. But why would that be? She seemed so friendly and open to Casidhe.

Lesslyn interrupted her thoughts. "You are a State Changer by blood as both of your parents, Finn and Nola Keneally, were State Changers from a long line dating back to the ancients. There are forces at play you cannot understand as you are still human and have been taught nothing of our ways. Each of us has the opportunity and choice to embrace that part of ourselves and go through the initiation to become a full State Changer. If we do not do this by our 18th birthday, we continue to live like other humans. The strange symptoms you have been exhibiting will disappear, and you may go out into the world to live a human life. You are dangerously close to the point of no return. If I remember correctly, your birthday is March 1st. But there is time in the next two months for you to learn our ways and complete the initiation if you so choose."

Casidhe was surprised that Lesslyn knew her birthday but remembered that she had lived here at birth. "What do I need to learn?"

"State Changers have the ability to change shape from a human form into a wolf in an instant (well, it takes a few moments, but not long). Like wolves, State Changers live in packs. Our pack is led by my mate, who you met–Kelly. He is our Alpha. As I am his mate, I am the Alpha-She. There are specific dynamics to pack life you are not familiar with. Some of it is comforting, and some of it will be difficult for a loner such as yourself, I think." She looked knowingly at Casidhe.

In any other setting, Casidhe would have asked if she were kidding. But somehow, Lesslyn made it all sound completely feasible. Perhaps it was the house or the grounds or Lesslyn herself. Whatever it was, Casidhe found she asked fewer questions about the validity of such claims and more questions about how it actually worked.

"So, I have to learn about the pack?"

"Well, let's start with meeting them first. Tomorrow evening, we will have the pack here at the Ranch, and you will see firsthand. And they will meet you, which is critical."

This made Casidhe nervous. She didn't like to meet new people under normal circumstances. She didn't know what to think about meeting a whole lot of magical wolf people.

"Do I have to meet them all at once?" The pitch of her voice rose slightly.

"Well, I think we don't have much time, so we need to move on with it. Also, your acceptance in the pack will depend a lot on how we, the Alpha and I, introduce you. I will speak with Kelly about this."

Casidhe didn't like the sound of acceptance. What happened if they didn't accept her? Did she care? Somehow, she had to admit she did, though unsure why.

"It will be fine, darlin'. You are a Keneally. If anyone can pull this all together in such a short amount of time, it will be a Keneally!" Lesslyn appeared very confident, but Casidhe wasn't sure what she was supposed to 'pull together,' let alone if she could.

"There is something else, although the pack is loyal to Kelly and me, they are still independent thinkers. We don't control them. If you can imagine 24 different people with a strong bond, but with varying degrees of success and affinity within the human population, but who also are part animal–wolves with magical powers and the ability to state change at will, then you can picture the pack. Kelly is a strong leader who keeps everyone in line, but not everyone will be happy to see a Keneally return to the pack. Not to worry, it is not from within that you will be in danger, but some will be less than hospitable on the outside–if you know what I mean."

"I'm not sure I do. I don't know what it means to be a Keneally. It has never been anything other than a last name to me."

"Yes, I can see that. But now, here you are. And I have to think since you have made the journey to us, you want to know more about your heritage and your birthright. Am I right?"

Lesslyn was pushing her to make some kind of commitment, or at least to acknowledge it, one she had not been aware of until that moment. She considered and then answered.

"Yes, I guess you are right. I want to learn more about who I am and where I come from. I am not ready to commit to any more than that yet."

Casidhe wanted to sound firm in her statement, but by the way Lesslyn looked at her, she wondered if Lesslyn didn't know better. Still, she did not verbally challenge her further.

"Of course. Casidhe. There is one more thing I believe you must see to prepare you for meeting the pack tomorrow. This is important when you are considering the challenges ahead of you."

Casidhe was puzzled. What on earth could she be talking about? But before she had a chance to ask a question, Lesslyn began removing her shoes and socks and then stood up.

"It is difficult to state change while in human clothing," Lesslyn said as she unzipped her jeans and removed them. Casidhe sat, too shocked to say anything. She was far too shy to watch someone, especially a stranger, undress completely, but this had taken her so much by surprise she couldn't look away. Lesslyn didn't seem to be shy at all. She removed every stitch of clothing she wore and stood before Casidhe completely naked. Just when Casidhe was about to look away for modesty's sake, something happened. In front of Casidhe's eyes, Lesslyn began changing from a naked, middle-aged woman standing before her to something else altogether. Her nose elongated, and hair grew out of every inch of her body. Next, Lesslyn's eyes and ears shifted into that of a wolf. In one more moment, Lesslyn stood before her on all fours, tail wagging behind her and with what Casidhe thought was a smile on her wolf face. She had never seen a wolf smile before. If she had to guess, she didn't think the entire change took more than ten seconds.

As Casidhe's mind struggled to reconcile what it had just witnessed, Lesslyn, the wolf, came up beside her and licked her hand. Instinctually, Casidhe reached down to pet the wolf's coat behind the ears, just like she had done to every friendly canine she had ever met. Lesslyn didn't seem to mind and licked her hand again. Lesslyn's wolf was as beautiful as Lesslyn the human. She had a dark grey and brown colored coat with a white patch under her chin. Her frame was large, perhaps the size of a German Shepard, with eyes ringed in darker brown circles of fur around bright, golden eyes. Her nose was wet and back. Her ears lay back slightly as if listening but not concerned. She turned and bounced over the couch, over a chair, and ran once around the room. She was quick and back again in a flash of fur. Before Casidhe could even think of what to say beyond the squeak that escaped her lips when Lesslyn leaped away, the wolf changed back into a woman. In the same amount of time it had taken her to become a wolf, Lesslyn was standing naked before her and began dressing again.

In all this time, Casidhe had said not one word. She didn't know what to say. Lesslyn was now fully redressed and called for Blaire, who came from the shadows almost immediately.

"Blaire, darlin', can you bring some tea, please?"

"Yes, of course."

"And let's set up for dinner; Casidhe must be getting hungry."

"Oh, no. I can't stay. I wouldn't want to inconvenience you."

"Nonsense. Of course, you will stay."

Casidhe simply smiled. She wanted to go back to the hotel and sit with everything she had learned and seen today, needing time to process. She had more questions, essential questions, but she was having a hard time remembering what they were at the moment. After the little exhibition Lesslyn had just shown her, not much else would register in her brain.

"Let's take a walk around the house. I'll show you the lady's room, and you may be interested in the library."

"Thank you," Casidhe managed to croak out.

Once she was staring at her reflection in the bathroom mirror, her brain began working again. She wondered what she would look like as a wolf. Do they all look the same? Would the pack like her? She felt nervous to find out. For the first time in her life, Casidhe wanted to be part of something, and she was not used to that feeling. She had spent most of her young life trying to avoid being a part of anything.

Lesslyn showed her the library, telling her about some of the books being as old as the State Changers themselves. Like the great room, the library went up two stories. It was a round room at the center of the massive house and filled with shelves of books from floor to roofline. The light came in through the windows, shining down into the room. There was a spiral staircase allowing access to the second level, where more shelves rose high above. Around the room were several high-backed, overstuffed chairs with ottomans and lamps, giving the space an inviting feel. To one side was a beautiful table that served as a desk with a light and a stack of books neatly piled on the other. In the desk's center was an old-time quill and a bottle of ink, but it looked like it hadn't been used in ages. Finally, Casidhe spied something familiar, a small box with the State Changers symbol on the top. It resembled the wax sealing kit her parents had left her. Under normal circumstances, Casidhe would have loved to sit and peruse the books for long hours, but nothing about this visit was routine.

Lesslyn spoke about some of the books and some of the Fae that had written them. Casidhe struggled to make sense of it. She didn't know what a Fae was or would want with a book. So, she focused on the beauty of the room and hoped to return and spend more time soon.

Next, Lesslyn showed her the garden room off to one end of the house, where the southern exposure could freely offer the room sunlight. It had the distinct smell of herbs, vegetables, and soil. It was not a dirty room, but neat with terra cotta tiles and beautiful ceramic pots and aisle after aisle of living plants grown for beauty, sustenance, and taste. Casidhe wondered who kept up such gardens. It would be a lot for one person, and this person must have a green thumb.

"All State Changers are part Fae, and Fae are part earth." Lesslyn gave by way of explanation to Casidhe's remark about how impressive she found the garden room. Casidhe had no idea what that meant, but it apparently helped make things grow.

By the time they made it to the kitchen, Blaire had dinner ready, and someone else was arriving to join them.

CHAPTER SEVEN

C asidhe looked around the cavernous kitchen, with its stone tile floors, rich cabinets, double stainless refrigerators, and two complete sinks. To one side were the tables–two large long wooden farm tables with comfortable bench seating all around. There was room for a crowd. Casidhe wondered if the entire pack ate here often, considering the number of seats available. She noticed the number of place-settings at one end: four. Then, she heard the voice coming from the other room. At first, she thought it might be Kelly joining them, but the voice was distinctly female.

"We're in here, Dana," called Lesslyn. She turned to Casidhe. "I hope you don't mind; my daughter Dana is joining us for dinner."

"Of course."

Dana was chatting with Blaire about the roads and asking what was for dinner when she entered the kitchen where Lesslyn and Casidhe were waiting. Casidhe was looking out the long window behind the table to the deck outside with its fire pit and seating. Behind that were the trees and hills beyond. It was a fantastic view. She turned as she heard Dana enter the kitchen, her breath catching in her chest as she came fully into Casidhe's view. She recognized the long dark hair and the ocean blue eyes at once. Her heart immediately began beating hard, her mouth went dry, and her face felt like all the blood in her entire body had traveled to her cheeks. Their eyes met, and Casidhe thought for a second a spark of surprise flashed across Dana's face. Casidhe could not look away or speak. Dana came closer, and closer still, until she was near enough to touch. Casidhe did not move, did not breathe. She felt hot. There was something in Dana's eyes . . . was it recognition? *Does she know me as I know her? How many times have I dreamt of this woman? Has she dreamt of me too?* Casidhe could not tell. *Is this real, or am I dreaming now? Maybe this whole house is a dream?* Of all the strangeness and magic she had seen that day, nothing compared to staring into the eyes of this woman.

Lesslyn, now standing behind Dana, noticed the look of surprise on Casidhe's face and knew something was up. "Are you okay, darlin'?"

Dana had reached out her hand and said slowly, "Nice to meet you." Still, Casidhe could not move. In the back of her mind, she knew she was supposed to respond in some way. But part of her brain had jumped the track, and all she could do was stare into Dana's eyes until she lost her balance and almost stumbled over. Lesslyn moved more quickly than an average person could and caught her, guiding her to a seat behind them.

"Blaire, can you bring Casidhe a glass of water, please," she called.

"I'll get it, Mum." Dana broke eye contact and ran to the sink. At that moment, Casidhe finally drew in her first long breath since Dana had entered the kitchen. She looked down, afraid to see Dana's eyes again. "I'm sorry. I guess I am tired," was the only excuse she could think of. She tried to smile, taking the water glass Dana offered but refusing to make eye contact with her again. She worked on the basics, breathing, and thinking. *How can this be? How can she be real? How can I dream of a real person I have never met? Does she know me?* Casidhe wanted to look at Dana but was afraid. Blaire gave her a distraction bringing over bowls steaming with hot food.

"Good, thank you, Blaire. I do believe the girl needs to eat."

"Yes, thank you. I am so sorry. Nice to meet you, Dana. This has been quite a visit." Casidhe said with only a sideways look at Dana, concentrating on filling her spoon with piping hot stew, including potatoes, carrots, celery, and beef. *Beef? I've never eaten meat. Well, I'll just eat around it. It isn't polite not to eat what is so graciously put in front of you.* Blaire put a cutting board on the table with a fresh loaf of bread and a large crock of butter. It all smelled so good, and Casidhe realized she had not eaten since breakfast early that morning, and the sun was now setting.

Lesslyn was filling Dana in on their day and how Casidhe had shown up out of nowhere, not knowing anything about State Changers and the pack. Dana politely asked questions but didn't probe or seem overly curious. *Perhaps she is dealing with her own surprise? Isn't that what I saw on her face – surprise?* Casidhe tried to eat around the beef but found it hard and decided she rather liked it. She was also amazed her senses weren't overwhelmed, and the meat didn't trigger her body to react. She guessed it was the magic of the place but didn't understand how it worked. Or maybe it was too late. *Am I too close to my 18th birthday and past the point of no return?* Casidhe felt a new panic inside her.

They made polite conversation through the meal, and Casidhe enjoyed a second helping of stew with another slice of bread, trying very hard to stay focused. Lesslyn heard the phone ring from the other room and left to answer it. Blaire had already left. An awkward moment of silence followed when she and Dana were alone. Casidhe tried to think of what to ask Dana to keep the conversation going without seeming as uncomfortable as she felt. She came up with, "Do you live here too?"

"Here at the Ranch? Oh no, I live in town. I am a sophomore at Montana Tech."

"Oh, what are you studying?" When Casidhe asked this, she looked up, and their eyes met again. A long pause stretched between them before Dana answered her.

"Uh . . . Um . . . right now, I'm working on a bachelor's in biology. I might go into medicine, but I'm leaning toward research." Her eyes dropped to the floor, and didn't look back up until she asked, "What about you? Will you be staying here in Butte for college?"

"Oh, hm. I don't know. I just finished high school. I haven't thought about what I might do next. I knew I needed to come here and find my parents' people since I don't have any other family anymore." They were doing better with looking at each other while talking. It seemed simple enough, but it wasn't. It was so easy to get lost in her eyes. Casidhe was sure, now that Dana was a real person and was sitting across the table from her, that she was the most beautiful woman Casidhe had ever seen. Of all the changes she was going through, the idea of being attracted to someone, someone real, was the furthest thing from her mind. *But here she is, and here I am.* Casidhe wasn't sure what to make of it.

"Oh, right. I am sorry about your aunt."

"Thanks."

Lesslyn came back in and said she needed to go down to the pub for a bit. Kelly had to run off on pack business, and Brody was running late.

"You can follow me into town, Casidhe, so you don't get lost."

Casidhe got up from the table and took her plates over to the sink. "Thank you so much for dinner; it was delicious."

"You're welcome, lass. We'll see you back here tomorrow night, then?"

Casidhe nodded.

"And you are coming too, Dana. It's a pack meeting."

"Right, Mum. I'll be here."

A whirlwind of activity followed as they all headed out the door. Coats and hats and good-byes and thank-yous to Blaire. They were about to part ways when Dana reached out her hand to shake Casidhe's, saying, "I look forward to seeing you tomorrow night." Casidhe cautiously reached out. When their hands touched ever so lightly, Casidhe felt a warm wave travel up to her shoulder and through her whole body. She couldn't tell if Dana felt it too. She seemed to be very aware that Lesslyn was paying close attention to the two of them and how they interacted. Did that make Dana nervous? It was all so new to Casidhe, but she had to admit she was looking forward to seeing Dana again so soon.

They drove back down the lane and out onto the main road. In no time, they were back in town, and Casidhe drove off in the direction of her hotel as Lesslyn headed to the pub. Dana was going back to her apartment in the city, close to her school. Casidhe tried to imagine her apartment and visiting it. She still had a warm feeling and couldn't help the smile that played around her lips. When she got back to the hotel, she went to her room and took a long hot shower, thinking about all that had happened that day, remembering Lesslyn turning into a wolf. The only thing that could have topped it in her mind was meeting the girl of her dreams, literally.

Remembering Lesslyn as a wolf reminded Casidhe she would meet the entire pack tomorrow evening and how they might not like or accept her. This gave her an uneasy feeling as she dressed in sweatpants and a t-shirt and flopped on her bed. She wanted to find family and someplace to belong. *Have I found it? Do I belong here?* She thought she might want to belong with Dana but wasn't sure Dana felt the same way. What if she had a girlfriend already? What if she wasn't attracted to girls at all?

Casidhe scolded herself. She had to stay focused on this State Changer business. She had to face the pack, and she had to figure out if she wanted to be one of them. They mentioned her going through an initiation, and she had no idea what that entailed. She must stay focused and not on Dana Moore. However, in the back of her mind, Casidhe knew Dana would play a big part in her decision.

That night she had a dream of running through the woods as a wolf, pursuing a rabbit. She could smell it, its fear, its fur, its blood. With the breeze flowing through her coat, she ran faster and faster through the prairie grass, past the trees, and then she saw the fire pit with people sitting around it. She stopped suddenly, listening hard to who was there. She approached carefully. When she was close enough, she saw Dana sitting there in her human form, staring into the flames. She looked at Casidhe. Just when Casidhe was ready to step into the light, she heard noises all around. Within seconds, she was surrounded by wolves, all snarling and baring their teeth. Casidhe knew she was in real danger, and the fur on her back bristled high while her ears drew back against her neck. She couldn't fight them all and feared she would be killed. Before she made a run for it, she looked up to see Dana. Dana's eyes had turned yellow as she began changing into a wolf too. Right before Casidhe woke up, Dana's haunches rose, snarling at her and ready to pounce.

Casidhe awoke drenched in sweat as she went to the bathroom to get a glass of water. She peered at her reflection in the mirror and saw her own golden eyes staring back at her. Fangs were protruding from her upper eye-teeth over her bottom lip. She was part wolf, and she knew it was all true. She also knew it wasn't too late, at least not yet. This gave her a moment of relief until she thought about the dream and wondered if the pack would treat her the way they had in her dream. If Dana was real, are other parts of her dreams real too? This scared her. She didn't want it to be real. She wanted to be part of the pack. She needed to be. At that moment, Casidhe knew she had already decided to stay. Now she just needed the pack to accept her.

Sleep being no longer an option, she turned on the TV for company. How was she going to get through the day waiting and dreading the pack meeting that night? It was going to be a long day.

CHAPTER EIGHT

S omehow, Casidhe made it through the long hours of the day. She went out shopping after lunch, trying to kill two birds with one stone: restlessness and wanting something splendid to wear that evening. She wanted to look her best to meet the pack, but really, seeing Dana again motivated her the most. Each time her mind wandered off in that direction, she scolded herself and refocused on the potential risk at hand.

She bought a new pair of black jeans and an emerald green sweater, which she knew would accent her eyes and look good with her long red hair. When she got home, she was exhausted. She wanted to nap but had too much nervous energy to sleep and gave up, deciding to get ready early. She primped in the bathroom for a long time before realizing she had no idea how to impress a pack of wolves best. She was always a loner, never letting anyone get too close, not caring when others made fun or ignored her. She didn't need them. She didn't need anyone except Aunt Colleen. What would Aunt Colleen say about all of this? What advice would she give me? *'Be yourself, dear.'* She imagined. *But how can I be myself in this situation? And who am I now, anyway?*

She stared back at her image in the mirror. She elected to wear her hair completely down, brushed out, and somewhat tamed. It tumbled in a shiny array of scarlet waves standing out in contrast to the vibrant green sweater. Her eyes reflected the same color, which for now was a relief. Yellow wolf eyes would not help. Maybe later? She went to the desk in her room and pulled out the large envelope from her parents. She reread the letter and wondered what they were like and what their place in the pack had been. She pulled out the Keneally pack lineage, seeing it stopped with her and Cian. For the first time, she realized her parents had been the pack Alphas with Kelly and Lesslyn Moore listed as their Betas. How had she not realized her last name was at the top? It was the *Keneally Pack*. She shook her head. Would they think she wanted to lead the pack in her parent's stead? She certainly had no designs on leading anything, she barely knew what was going on from one second to the next, and she wasn't a State Changer yet.

When she looked up from the letter, she saw the ring box on the table; it had slid out of the envelope without her noticing. She opened the box and marveled again at the ring's beauty. She gingerly slipped it onto the ring finger of her right hand. Once it was secure, a subtle feeling came over her, a wave of confidence perhaps, a bit of bravery, maybe? Casidhe thought her mother could have put magic in the ring, but it didn't make her tingle or fearful; it just made her feel like she belonged. She wondered if it was merely part of her mother's magic, leaving a warm residue for Casidhe. Had it been intentional or an accidental trace left behind? It didn't matter, Casidhe needed it now and gave a quick prayer of thanks to her mother. The idea of her mother, or father for that matter, usually brought on a vacant feeling, like she should know something she didn't. But this time, she felt . . . better; better prepared to meet what lay ahead.

Finally, it was time for Casidhe to start for the Ranch. She piled on her coat and gloves, grabbed her bag and keys, and started for the door. When she saw her reflection in the mirror one last time, she stopped and marveled at how much had changed since she had lived in North Carolina with her aunt a few weeks ago. She had become an adult, traveled across the country, and was now about to walk into the den of strange wolf-people that she hoped would become her friends. She wanted this, more than anything she remembered ever wanting. She took a deep breath and left the hotel.

The roads were clear, and though snow was in the forecast, it had not started yet. She retraced her drive back to the Ranch and pulled onto the dirt road when she found her breathing had become shallower, and her heart was beating loudly in her chest. She had removed her gloves once the car had warmed up and nervously twirled the ring around her finger with her thumb, beseeching whatever magic her mother had left behind for her. When she got to the gate, she saw the wolf symbol over the archway again, but for the first time, she also noticed a large "K" cut out of wood on either side of the pillars. Had that been there before, and she just missed it. Had this been her family's home? Oh, no. Would they all think she wanted it back and was here to challenge them? Her heart beat faster.

Again, after she went under the archway, she saw the crystal-like air, and the sweet smell filled her nostrils. This time, however, she wasn't so surprised, and it felt more like home. The smell was akin to wood fire and fir trees, of fresh grass and pinecones. It was earthy and pleasant, making her think of life blooming in spring, only it was winter!

She pulled up to the house seeing cars and trucks everywhere. Some were parked on the side, some around the driveway, some along the road. The massive house was lit up with a warm light streaming out of every window, low and high. If she weren't so nervous, it would be a welcoming scene. She thought of the ring and exhaled, hoping to release some of her nervousness.

She found a place to park and got out, making her way up the wide stairs to the immense wooden doors. As she approached them, they silently opened before her and the noise and bustle from the people within slowly died out as one by one, they noticed she was standing in the doorway. She had never felt so self-conscious in her life. All eyes were on her, and she didn't see anyone she knew. She stood there for a moment in complete silence before Kelly's large frame emerged from the kitchen, and seeing Casidhe, welcomed her.

"Casidhe Keneally! We are so glad you have come home to us. We have not been complete since we lost your parents seventeen years ago!" He said. When he reached her, he drew her into a huge bear hug that surprised Casidhe. For one second, Casidhe went rigid, but something Lesslyn had said before occurred to her, and as everyone looked on, she forced a smile on her face and embraced him in return with every bit of her strength. The hug lasted a few moments longer until she could see most of those around and closest to them begin to relax and smile slightly. Yes, Lesslyn had been right; Casidhe's place in the pack had a good deal to do with Kelly's acceptance of her, and Casidhe allowed herself to be the long-lost child coming home. This seemed to make most everyone more comfortable. *I'm not here to take anyone on or take back anything.* She knew it was important they know that. Casidhe saw and felt some toward the back of the room sneer. Not everyone was glad to see her, no matter what Kelly said. Before she could take any more notice, she was being introduced to those around her.

"Casidhe, this is Aedan and his mate Claire, and this is Brian and his mate Cara." Casidhe was shaking hands and trying to remember faces and names but soon lost track and simply smiled and tried to repeat the names as she shook hands. She met Liam and Derry and Cormac and Ronan, Kevin and Seamus, Sean, Brendan, and Brody. All the men had full beards. Casidhe wondered if it was the cold weather or the wolf that caused it, but it made it hard for her to remember them. The women stood out in her mind more, Neala and Siobhan and Cathleen and Bronagh, Sinead, Darcy, and Fiona. The lack of facial hair allowed her to see them more clearly.

Her head was spinning with names and faces when Blaire showed up at her elbow and offered her a cup of tea, which she greatly appreciated. She took a moment to draw in a deep breath, then a sip of tea when she noticed Dana at the edge of the room. Their eyes met for a moment before someone passed between them, and in that split second, Dana winked at her. Casidhe tried to tell herself the wink indicated how well she was doing with the pack, but she couldn't help her stomach lurching and a quick and broad smile that broke across her face without any ability to stifle it.

She still had a smile on her face when someone touched her elbow, and she turned to meet Lesslyn. Casidhe thought the exchange with her daughter had not escaped Lesslyn's notice, but she recovered so quickly, Casidhe was unsure. She wrapped her arms around Casidhe's neck and hugged her close. Again, Casidhe was sure this display of affection, though maybe sincerely felt, was more for the pack. And again, Casidhe followed her lead and hugged her warmly back. Lesslyn whispered in her ear,

"You are doing marvelously, Casidhe, well done!" With those words and the look in Lesslyn's eyes, she allowed herself to lighten up a bit. Lesslyn turned to announce dinner was ready and invited everyone into the kitchen. Many others had been milling around helping to prepare the food, and now everyone was lining up on either side of the bar to fix their plates. Soon they were all seated at the tables. Kelly sat at the head of the larger of the tables, and Lesslyn sat at the head of the slightly smaller table, giving Casidhe the distinct impression they ruled the pack side by side. She felt warm and welcomed, and the food was terrific. Wine and beer flowed, but Casidhe didn't partake of anything other than water and tea. She very much wanted to impress these people. Casidhe was still under the legal drinking age, and although she had tasted a drink or two before, she knew now was not the time to push the limits.

Claire asked Casidhe how long of a drive it was from North Carolina when she noticed someone at the other table looking at her intently. She thought his name was Kevin. She had made a note of his cold eyes when they had been introduced earlier. She tried not to look back at him, but she could tell he was not happy about her being here, no matter what the Alpha said. Out of the corner of her eye, as she spoke to Claire, she saw a woman sit down beside him and whisper in his ear. Casidhe thought she might be Sinead. Casidhe couldn't hear them, which confused her until she remembered this place had Fae magic. Perhaps that is why many of her senses were more normal here. They had a quick conversation, during which they both glanced at Casidhe a couple of times, and then they broke away and went to get more food.

When everyone had eaten, Kelly stood and tapped his glass with his fork to get everyone's attention.

"Thank you, Lesslyn, Blaire, and everyone who helped with dinner; you out-did yourselves. I would like you all to join me in raising a glass to welcome Casidhe back to our pack." "Sláinte" everyone said and raised their glasses. Casidhe's cheeks went red at being the center of attention again. Then Kelly glanced over at Lesslyn, who nodded back at him.

"As ye all know, Finn Keneally and his mate Nola were our pack Alphas many years ago, and this here is their long-lost daughter and heir, Casidhe." Silence fell; no one spoke or moved in their chairs.

"Her twin, Cian, is living with the Canadian pack and is quite happy to remain there for the time being. Casidhe here has been raised as human and only recently, with the death of our dearly departed sister Colleen, came to understand she is a State Changer by blood. However, Casidhe will be turning 18 in two months, so she has a lot to learn in that time. It will be up to all of you to help her decide whether she will go through the initiation or not." Kelly's voice had a deep timbre and carried well throughout the room. No one moved a muscle as the anticipation of his every word held their attention.

"Casidhe, what think you of us?" Casidhe, with the others, had been frozen in place. She was now expected to speak to everyone. She gulped hard. This was almost more than she could handle. She had never felt comfortable speaking to a crowd, and a streak of terror traveled from her chest to her brain. In her anxiety, she fumbled with her mother's ring and suddenly felt a warm glow wash over her. With a deep breath, she stood up beside Kelly.

"Thank you, Kelly. As you said, I am new to all of this, and it wasn't, but a few weeks ago, I was sure this could not be real. Aunt Colleen wrote to me in a letter that she was afraid for my life and therefore never told me about all of you. This makes me sad. I wish I had known. It would have changed a lot of things. It would have changed me." The last part, she said quietly, pensively looking down. But then she gathered what strength she could, twirling the ring around her finger, and looked up to speak again.

"I would very much like to become a State Changer and become a part of this pack." Then she turned to Kelly and said, lowering her eyes and bowing her head slightly in deference to the Alpha, "If you will have me and teach me." When she raised her head again, she caught the expression on Lesslyn's face. By what she saw, Casidhe thought her instincts were on target.

Kelly reached over, placed a hand on each side of her face, and kissed the top of her head. "Welcome, my daughter." Then he turned to Lesslyn and she nodded back at him. Casidhe noticed everyone else around the table also nodded, some more than others. But she could feel Kelly observing them, alert and aware of each, watching for any conflicts that might arise. He released Casidhe but put his hand on her shoulder. The gesture said clearly to everyone, 'you mess with this lass, you mess with me.' But what he said was subtler.

"Finn Keneally was my Alpha and my friend. I take in his child with a glad heart. There are forces still that would threaten the Keneally heir; we will protect her with our lives." *Well, that sounded clear*, though she wondered what forces Kelly spoke of. *And would they all protect me?* She didn't think so. Kelly was formidable, but she could tell Kevin and Sinead were not thrilled by her return. Kelly turned to her.

"Preparations will begin tomorrow. There is no time to lose. Many in the pack will take part in your training, and you will get to know each of us. We will be your family, and you will be ours. We will defend you with our lives, and we expect that once you are a full State Changer, you will do the same for us." With that, he raised his glass again, and everyone cheered, "Sláinte." Kelly sat down, and talk resumed around the table. Soon, people began milling about again as the party seemed to be breaking up.

All the strength had drained from Casidhe, and she felt immediately tired, her head spinning with questions and names and implications. Almost immediately, Lesslyn was at her side, gliding her away from the table.

"Well done, Lass. I wouldn't have believed it if I didn't know whose daughter you were. Nola would be proud of you!"

"Thank you," was all Casidhe could say as she twirled the ring around her finger. Lesslyn noticed it.

"Was that hers?" It took a moment for Casidhe to register what Lesslyn referred to as she was not aware she was fumbling with the ring.

"Yes." She said absently.

"I thought so. It was nice of Nola to stand with you this eve. Yes?" Casidhe inspected her sharply. Lesslyn didn't seem to miss much.

"Yes."

"It looks like the party is nearly over; many have work in the morning and children to get home to. If you can wait a bit, I think it will be safe for you to go back to the hotel without seeming like you are ready to leave us so quickly." She smiled knowingly at Casidhe, who smiled gratefully back.

"But you will need to move here tomorrow. Kelly has spoken, and he is right. If you are to become a full State Changer in time, you must begin immediately. I will work out a schedule with the rest of the pack, and we will begin with a tour of the Ranch tomorrow afternoon. That gives you the morning to move your things and settle in here. Okay?"

This last part was an abrupt change to Casidhe, but it made sense, of course. She couldn't stay at the hotel forever. And though she didn't know what was involved with the training and the initiation, it made sense that it would need to occur somewhere out of the way and view of prying eyes. She hadn't known these people long, but she had made up her mind. *What else would I do? Go home to an empty house and life in North Carolina? No, this is what I must do.*

"Yes, of course. I will pack up in the morning and be here by lunch. Is that okay?"

"Perfect. Your rooms will be ready." Lesslyn smiled affectionately and embraced her again. "You are a natural, my dear, a natural!" Someone called her, and she excused herself for a few minutes.

Casidhe stood there dazed but feeling resolute when again she felt someone at her elbow. She turned to face Dana squarely in front of her. Casidhe's overwhelm was nearly complete, and Dana seemed to know it. She reached out and took a firm hold of Casidhe's arm and walked her into the library and over to a small couch, inviting her to sit. She poured her a glass of water and sat beside her. Casidhe felt flushed and was sure her face had turned red.

"You pulled that off better than anyone expected."

"Really? I feel like I am always on the verge of fainting." She took a drink of water, trying not to look into Dana's beautiful eyes. That would be her downfall, and right now, she didn't trust she had enough reserves to not fall into this woman's arms without regret. Casidhe had never felt such a strong attraction to any person, male or female, before.

"There will, of course, be those who will want to make your training difficult as they are not happy to see you, but they will never openly defy Da. That would be suicide."

"What does the training entail?"

"Oh, that is a conversation for tomorrow, I think. Tonight, you look done-in for sure. Can I get you anything else?" Not being able to avoid it, Casidhe's gaze lifted, and she looked into Dana's eyes but said nothing for what felt like minutes, though it probably wasn't long. Dana did not look away but met her gaze with equal intensity. Casidhe held the glass in her right hand, and her left hand rested on her own knee. As their eyes were locked tightly together, Dana reached over with her right hand and laid it over Casidhe's left. She felt like someone had turned the heat up in the room, and Casidhe knew she wasn't the only one who felt it. Dana's ocean blue eyes were so large, Casidhe felt happily lost in them. They didn't move for long moments, and the temperature in the room continued to climb until they heard someone enter the room. Dana quickly withdrew her hand and stood up, looking at her mother.

"Ah . . . I think she's had it, Mum. Should I take her home?"

"No, I can find my way home myself. Thanks, Dana." Casidhe smiled self-consciously, sure Lesslyn had seen the intimate moment. But she could not read if she were happy or upset about this new development.

"Yes, I think it's safe to go; many have already left for the evening. We'll see you for lunch tomorrow then, Casidhe?"

"Yes, thank you, Lesslyn. The dinner was amazing." Somehow Blaire knew she was leaving and arrived with her coat, hat, and gloves.

"Thanks, Blaire."

"I'll see you out?" Dana said. Casidhe tried not to look at Dana, feeling like she didn't want to push her luck this evening in case Lesslyn was not pleased with what was happening between them. *What is happening?* Casidhe didn't know for sure, but she knew she should put off finding out.

"No, stay, won't you, Dana? I want to go over the schedule with you. Blaire can see Casidhe out."

Dana didn't respond, but Blaire led the way out, and Casidhe followed, extending her gratitude once again. As they left the room, she could hear Lesslyn whisper intently, "Dana, really? You can't distract her. Not now." There was an urgency to her voice. Casidhe didn't hear Dana's response.

On the way home, Casidhe replayed the events of the evening, amazed at how well everything had gone. She noticed the ring on her finger, sure it had given her support and confidence. She had never done anything like that before and could not have imagined standing and speaking before a group of people and asserting herself. She silently thanked her mother, whoever she was, for giving her this gift. She thought the change into a wolf person was not the only transformation happening for her.

Then she wondered about Kevin and Sinead and why they were not happy to see her return. Kelly and Lesslyn had made her welcomed, and for just a moment, she felt like she belonged somewhere. Not since her aunt died had she felt that. Then she thought of what she heard Lesslyn tell Dana at the end. Lesslyn was right. Whatever was happening between her and Dana, now was the wrong time. But how could they stop it? Casidhe needed to get a hold of herself.

As she climbed into the bed at the hotel for the last time, she reflected on her life. So much had changed in such a short time. Amanda, those people at her school and work all seemed so far away. Tomorrow, her life would change again, and she would begin State Changer training. She wondered, not for the first time, what that would be like. But exhaustion took over her questions and brushed them aside, forcing her into a deep sleep.

CHAPTER NINE

Casidhe woke with a start; had she been dreaming? It was still dark outside, but the parking lot lights filtered through the slits in the curtains, giving off a muted glow. She surveyed the room, at first, not knowing where she was. She slowly made out the hotel room with its generic furniture, large TV, and bright red numbers on the alarm clock. 2:22. What had awakened her at such an odd hour? She laid in bed, listening for any sound that could have stirred her from sleep.

She was contemplating a trip to the bathroom when she looked over and saw something unbelievable in the long mirror by the door. Frozen in place, she dared not breathe. There in the mirror stood a short, fully-bearded man wearing a suit and top hat. His face appeared somewhat distorted with big eyes, long pointy ears on either side of his head, and a large bulbar of a nose. *I must still be dreaming.* As she watched through half-lidded eyes, he stepped out of the mirror and into her room. She should have been frightened and had to admit; she was a little. But she wanted to know more about this magical little man. Was he a leprechaun? He wasn't green; weren't leprechauns supposed to be green? Even in the dim light, she could see this man was red from the top of his hat, through his hair, and down to the hem of his pants. Even his skin gave off a ruddy color. His black boots and belt were all that stood out against his redness.

She watched him sneak over to her things, pick up her shoes from the floor, and inspected each one individually in the pale light. Seemingly satisfied, he put them back down again. He turned to leave when something on the desk seemed to catch his eye. Casidhe realized the things from her parents were there on the desk, and she knew she had to risk it.

"What are you looking for?" She asked softly, trying not to startle him. She was unsuccessful. He jumped about two feet in the air and back to the mirror in an instant. "Wait. It's okay. What is your name?" she asked hurriedly.

He turned and squinted at her for half a second and, with a high squeaky voice, not matching his hairy face and twinkling eyes, said through a half glint of a smile, "Fergus." And then he was gone, back through the mirror. The mirror looked as if it were made of liquid, and someone had stirred it for a moment and then was still. A simple mirror once more. She laid there a minute more, waiting to see if anything else happened and when nothing did, she sat up and turned on the light. The room was exactly the way she had left it when she had gone to sleep. With the lights on, she wondered if it wasn't some strange vision. She searched under the bed and around the mirror, and in the small closet area. Then she inspected the bathroom, including behind the shower curtain. When she was satisfied no one was there, she went to her desk, packed her most valuable possessions back in the large envelope, and put it at the bottom of her suitcase. She sat on the bed, no longer tired. *Who, or what was that man? I mean, he looked like a leprechaun, but could they be real?* She would ask Lesslyn.

She decided to pack all her stuff now and be ready to check out of the hotel in the morning. By 4:00, everything was ready to go, including the clothes she had chosen for the day, neatly laid across the bed. With packing done, she started to get sleepy again and crawled in under the covers. Would he come back? She turned off the light and laid very still watching the mirror, and in only a few minutes, dozed off to sleep again. She didn't wake again until 8:30.

Pulling back the curtains, she inspected the room, but nothing was out of the ordinary. She showered and dressed and went down to breakfast. She lingered a while over her pancakes and sausage, thinking about what would be involved in State Changer training. And what would it be like to live at the Ranch? Were leprechauns real? All these thoughts made her marvel at her life. When her mind wandered to Dana, she decided it was time to get going. She could not indulge those thoughts right now. She mustn't!

She went to the hotel lobby and checked out; she'd leave the key card after her car was packed. She went back to her room and still saw nothing any different. Maybe it was just a dream. Would Lesslyn think her crazy if she asked about leprechauns?

By 10:30, she drove out of town towards the Keneally Ranch, her new home. The morning hung low and gray, with light snow threatening road conditions. When she traveled through the Ranch gateway, she felt the now familiar thrill of energy flow through her. What would it be like to live in such a magical place?

Blaire stood on the porch, waiting for her as soon as she pulled up and got out. Lesslyn was quickly there and embraced her affectionately, helping her gather her bags and escorted her into the house.

"You will be in the east wing. This way." Lesslyn said cheerfully. "Once we get you settled in, come down to the kitchen. We have lots to discuss."

"Great, thank you." She followed them up the broad staircase made of whole logs cut flat on one side to create a step and a curved branch handrail varnished to a high sheen of light tan wood. Casidhe marveled at the beauty of the stairs as they ascended, past the first landing and up to the left and down the hall to a pair of double wooden doors with a dark inlaid letter "K." Entering, Casidhe took in the large sitting room complete with a small couch, two chairs, a couple of rustic wooden tables, and bookshelves covering one wall. It was all so big and beautiful. Still appreciating the sitting room, she followed Lesslyn through another single wooden door into a bedroom with a large queen-sized bed made in the same log fashion as the stairs. She realized this was the style of many other features throughout the home. Blaire had come in behind her and set down the rest of her bags. "I'll go get lunch started."

"Thanks, Blaire. Here is your bathroom," Lesslyn directed as she led Casidhe into a large bathroom covered in white tile and beautiful wooden counters and shelves. A colossal porcelain tub with a shower attachment stood proudly in the room, inviting any who entered to get lost in its depths. The bathroom was comfortable and pristine at the same time. Casidhe was still admiring the tub when Lesslyn turned to her.

"You settle in and come down to the kitchen when you are ready." Hugging Casidhe once again, she turned and left.

"Thank you; I'll be right down."

"Take your time." She called back.

Casidhe continued to walk around the suite, deciding the tub should wait. The bedroom was completely furnished with a dresser and armoire. In the closet, she found extra pillows, blankets, and hangers ready to be of use. Casidhe decided to pull some of the clothing out of her bags and hang them. Once she opened her bags, she also decided to stash some clothing in the dresser. She had unpacked entirely before she went down the stairs almost an hour later.

"My rooms are amazing. Thank you so much," she said to Lesslyn when she reached the kitchen.

"You are welcome. This Ranch is available to all State Changers and also to those from other packs when they come to visit, but that suite is reserved for family." Lesslyn winked at Casidhe, and they sat down at the table to soup and sandwiches, chips, and tea. Blaire had prepared much of the meal, but she also joined them to eat. After a bit of small talk about the snow and cold and if her room was warm enough, Lesslyn turned their attention to what was most prevalent in all their minds, State Changer training.

"I think we will start with an orientation to the grounds and the other buildings and some nuances of this Ranch. We can do that today. Tomorrow morning, Cormac will come by and go through some history lessons with you. He is the eldest of our pack, and he takes great pride in teaching the young ones our history. Tomorrow afternoon, Bronagh will come by and fill you in on pack safety and secrecy, which is very important." She paused a moment, looking at Casidhe to see if she had any questions.

Casidhe didn't know what she was getting into, so she simply nodded her head.

"You'll get into pack dynamics, your place in the pack, and our relationships with other packs. That may take some time. But our New Year's party is coming up, so you'll see some of that in action." She kept pausing in case Casidhe had questions or comments, but with eyes wide, Casidhe just continued to nod her head.

"We'll also get into the process of becoming a State Changer, how to shift, how to control wolf instincts and how to use them to your advantage, and what is involved with the initiation. I assume your parents gave you a State Changer stone?"

This caught Casidhe a little off guard. "Ah, yes, yes they did. But it shocked me when I first got it, and I fell off my chair. I've been afraid to touch it ever since. What is it for?"

"Yes, I expect it did. Best not to mess with it until you are ready. It will be used in your initiation to help in your first transformation.

"Okaaay." Casidhe wasn't sure what else to say.

"Siobhan will go over the Fae and our relationship to them. She has a great relationship with the Fae, since she is mated to one, and she'll introduce you. Have I forgotten anything?" she asked, turning to Blaire.

"Mates," said Blaire matter-o-factly.

"Right, I think we'll cover that when we are going over pack dynamics and your place in the pack. Sound okay to you?"

"I guess so. I don't know enough to say any different. I am happy to follow your lead in this process."

"Good. The most difficult part of your training will be the physical part. It is challenging to shift back and forth from wolf to human form in the beginning, and it requires a great deal of strength and focus. You will begin working with Ronan to increase your strength and stamina after the new year. We have enough time for you to learn and process before February 4th."

"Isn't that a month early?"

"The initiation always begins on a new moon and is completed on a full moon. The full moon in February is the 19th, just nine days before your 18th birthday. So, everything should work out fine." Lesslyn took a sip of tea, obviously still contemplating what she was missing when Blaire started clearing the table. Casidhe got up to take her plate over to the sink.

"Blaire, do you mind finishing the cleanup? I need to talk to Casidhe for a moment in the library."

"Sure, no problem."

Casidhe's eyebrows raised; what more could Lesslyn have to tell her now? She followed Lesslyn into the Library and sat when Lesslyn motioned her to the comfortable high-backed armchair. Lesslyn sat in the matching one facing it but didn't speak at first. She seemed perplexed, and Casidhe couldn't guess what bothered her.

Finally, Lesslyn spoke. "I would be blind if I couldn't see there is already something between you and my daughter Dana." Casidhe's eyes grew wide, and she began shaking her head in protest.

"No, no, not to worry. Dana has had other female lovers, much to her father's dismay. That is not what worries me, though I think you will understand more of the complications of such a union once you learn more about pack dynamics.

"My main concern is that you really can't afford a distraction right now. I know Dana is . . . appealing. But we are up against a very aggressive timetable to begin the initiation process in time, and any type of relationship, other than friendship, could have negative results. I don't think either of you wants to risk it." All Casidhe could do was nod her head in agreement.

"Good. Now I have also spoken to Dana, and I do hope the pair of you decide to take this warning seriously. It is my duty as the Alpha-She to facilitate your transformation into a full State Changer and I intend to do that."

Casidhe understood Lesslyn's warning. "I don't know what there is between Dana and me yet. We just met, haven't we? But I don't deny there is something . . . however, I understand the importance of staying on task. I will do my best to stay focused on the training."

"Wonderful. There will be plenty of time to decide what is or isn't there between the two of you later, and you will be in a much different position, with a better perspective to make such decisions." Lesslyn smiled at Casidhe, undoubtedly hoping they were on the same page. Casidhe had full intention of keeping on task, but in the back of her mind, she wondered.

"Are there any other questions you have for me now?" Lesslyn asked her.

"Yes. First, does Blaire live and work here, and can I pitch in and help out around here too? I want to contribute in some way?"

Lesslyn looked pleased and, with a half-smile, said, "Yes, of course. Everyone in the pack helps, especially when we all get together. Blaire helps us at the Ranch full time. But we always have chores around here. In between your training sessions, I will have Blaire show you the ropes. Okay?"

"Yes, good. Also, I have an odd question. Is there such a thing as leprechauns, and what do they look like?" To this, Lesslyn sat back in her chair, her eyes narrowing as she stared back at her. Casidhe felt as if she were trying to decide upon something. After a moment, she appeared to have come to a decision and sat up straight again in the chair.

"Yes, there are leprechauns. They are short in stature, usually wear red, and almost all of them look quite old to me, even the wee ones." She smiled. "Why do you ask?"

"Because one came to visit me in my room early this morning and woke me up."

"Woke you up? Leprechauns are quite silent. How did he wake you up?" Lesslyn looked shocked.

"I don't know. One minute I was asleep, and the next minute I was awake watching a short, reddish man step into my room through the mirror. He inspected my shoes and then turned to look at the things on my desk when I asked him what he was looking for." Lesslyn did not hide her shock at this story. "And then what happened?"

"Oh, I guess I frightened him, but as he was about to disappear back through the mirror, I asked his name."

"Did he hear you? Did he answer you?" Her eyes were wide.

"Yeah, he said his name was Fergus before he went back through the mirror. What was he after?"

"Leprechauns are elves that mend shoes, though more often than not, they are sowing a bit of mischief here and there among humans. I bet you surprised him; humans don't see leprechauns, well, hardly ever. Even among State Changers, few have spoken to them topside. They rarely hear and, even more rarely, speak to any other than Fae or very connected State Changers. I have met Fergus, but still, that is curious." She got a far-off look in her eyes as if pondering something. She eventually shifted her attention back to Casidhe but didn't offer anything more.

"So, he was there to fix my shoes?"

"Yeah, probably just snooping. I wouldn't put it past them to play a trick or two on visitors passing through, and what better place to find them than at the local hotel." She seemed to have dismissed it all together now, but Casidhe wondered what had surprised her so much at first.

"If you don't have any more questions, you should get bundled up. Brody will show you around the property."

"I'll go up and get my boots."

"Good, Brody will meet you in the foyer in 10 minutes," Lesslyn said as she left.

CHAPTER TEN

Casidhe returned to the foyer with a minute to spare and was slipping on her boots when Brody came in. She remembered hearing about him the first day at the pub, and she had met him briefly the night before at the all-pack meeting. When he walked in the door, he reminded her of a young mountain man with his long hair pulled back in a ponytail and a large wool sock hat on top, coming down over his ears. His eyes were light brown, and he had a kind smile. She didn't think he was much older than her.

"Hi, Casidhe, ready for your tour of the Ranch?"

"I'm ready."

They stepped out into fresh snow coming down all around them. Despite the precipitation, the air felt light and bright. *Is there always magic in the air here?*

As if Brody had read her mind, he said, "This place is touched by a good bit of Fae magic. No one outside the fence can see what is going on within. Also, most of our wolf senses are dampened, so wolves can interact without over sensitizing to each other's emotions and smells. This allows State Changers to mix together as mostly human. It's kind of funny Fae magic helps State Changers act more human when they are together, but if it weren't for that magic, there would be a lot more aggression and challenges as the animal instincts play a big part in the pack. This helps us preserve the longevity of the pack. It doesn't mean our instincts are gone, just somewhat subdued."

Brody's large feet made tracks Casidhe followed on their way to the large barn. They entered the small wooden door on the side. Casidhe's eyes had to adjust to the lower light conditions as she looked around, trying to see what could be stored in such a large barn. Her nose told her immediately there were indeed animals inside, and sure enough, once

Brody turned on the overhead lights, she could see stall doors lining the long path down the center. The ceilings were low, hinting at a second story above them. As they walked down the dirt floor, Brody stopped in front of the first large stall and whistled to the animal inside.

"This is Cloe; as you can see, she is a winged horse, one of the remaining Horses of Manannán. There are only 7 of her kind left in the world, that we know of, so we take extra good care of ours."

Casidhe only half-listened to Brody as she stared in disbelief at the pure white winged horse in front of her. Cloe was more beautiful than Casidhe could imagine, with long eyelashes and flowing white mane that matched the folded wings by her side. Only her eyes and hooves stood out in contrast to how she gleamed in the faint light of the barn. Brody chatted on about her mate, Clive, who was prancing across the aisle, opposite of Cloe. But Casidhe was having a hard time turning away from Cloe, who she decided was so radiant, it would take a long time to adjust to being in her presence. When she forced her gaze away, she jumped back in surprise as Clive came into her field of vision. As dark as Cloe was white, Clive towered over her, just as gorgeous. His massive muscles quivered beneath his jet-black coat and mane. His wings were folded, but she could imagine the strength and power needed to stretch out and take flight. The pair of them were magnificent, and Casidhe could say little more than "ooh" and "aww" in response to such majesty.

Brody pulled gently on her elbow, and she reluctantly moved forward to the next stall. Casidhe peered in over the door and froze. Her eyes wide, she couldn't believe what stood before her. There in the booth, matching the whiteness of Cloe but with pink around her nose and eyes, stood a unicorn. Her coiled, jet-black horn stuck straight out of her head, coming to a point. She was delicate and precious compared to the winged horse's mass and muscle.

"This is Hanne. As far as we know, she is the only unicorn left in existence, though we keep watching out all over the globe in search of a mate for her. She came to us about 80 years ago from Norway; it was Sven that found her and brought her here to us for safekeeping. Speaking of Sven, I'd like you to meet him." A tall thin man walked up to them. "Casidhe, this is Sveinungr-Bjorn or Sven for short. He has worked with these animals longer than most of us have been alive, and I believe he knew your parents."

Casidhe wrenched her attention away from the unicorn to smile at Sven, trying hard not to stare at the elf in front of her. Of course, she didn't know for sure he was an elf, but if she were to imagine what an elf would look like, it would be Sven. He stood tall and straight, looming over her at full height. He had a greenish tint to his skin, and his eyes were black and beady, his lips rosy pink with a smile that didn't seem to travel to the rest of his face. His eyebrows arched high over his short dark lashes. His dark brown hair flowed around his face and down his shoulders to the middle of his back. But his mane didn't hide his pointed ears sticking out through the strands. He held a hat in his hand and bowed ever so slightly to Casidhe, who returned the bow.

"Sven is Fae. He is a wood elf and has a way with the animals like no other. He does not work for us but works with the animals to care for them. His quarters are at the other end of the barn. So, if you have any questions about the stables or the animals, he is the elf to ask; when he has the time, of course." Brody bowed to Sven in deference to his position. It was apparent Sven was a proud and skilled Fae you did not wish to trifle with.

"It is nice to meet you, Sven."

"And you. You are a Keneally, of course. I recognize your scent. Welcome home." Sven said this with kindness in his voice, but his eyes did not change. Perhaps it was how dark they were, but Casidhe found him slightly disconcerting. Did she have a distinct scent?

"Thank you," was all she could think to say in return.

The rest of the stables held regular horses, which were only average when compared to the three other-worldly animals and Sven. They were all beautiful and healthy and obviously well cared for. Past the stables, they went up a broad set of wooden stairs and through a doorway that opened into a vast arena.

"Is this for the horses to exercise indoors?" she asked.

"Yes, and for us as well, if we choose." This made Casidhe turn her head sharply toward Brody, who smiled. "You will learn more about that soon."

They went through the wide arena to the other side, finding a smaller room. Inside was enough gym equipment, machines, and weights to rival any gym she had ever seen. All the gear ran along the walls leaving a large matted area in the middle. Obviously, it was essential for State Changers to stay in shape. Brody described it as 'the gym,' and they left to walk down a back set of stairs to another door and the outside. They crossed through the snow, which was getting deeper now, passing a building they did not approach.

"That is the butcher shop. We do a fair amount of hunting, and we eat everything we kill. I don't figure you are interested in that yet."

Casidhe, having been a vegetarian all her life, was grateful to bypass that part of the tour. The next building was a small shack. Brody opened the door but didn't go inside. He motioned for her to peer in as he turned on the lights.

"This is the Initiate Shack." Inside was a small single room with a single bed, a chair, a fireplace, and a small table. In one corner stood a small sink and toilet. There were no windows and nothing on the walls or floors. It was the epitome of no-frills, save for the long mirror hung securely on the opposite wall. "You will learn more about this later, but I wanted you to see that there isn't much to it, and it's not scary. Just a simple space to allow the initiate to transform and adjust in his or her own timing."

Casidhe nodded her head and stepped back as Brody shut and locked the door. Next to the Initiate Shack, a woodshed loomed with more wood stacked than Casidhe had ever seen. Next, they came to a garage-type building with five bays. Entering through the door at one end, Casidhe saw an SUV, a truck, and a tractor. At the far end, there were two all-terrain vehicles. Brody motioned that she get into the other side of one while he hopped into the driver's seat, opening the bay door. Once the vehicle rumbled alive and began to warm up, they backed out and began to traverse the snow-covered countryside.

Brody took his time taking her through the trees and along the fence line, giving her details on the Ranch's 300 acres, its trees and topography, the water sources, and the boundaries. Once they had traveled for some time, they reached another gate, much less ornate and welcoming than the front.

"This is the back gate, and usually only Fae come through here. There is a two-way portal to the Sidhe, the Fae's territory, about a quarter-mile that direction." He pointed off into the distance. "Fae can come onto Ranch property only with permission from a pack member, and they don't have a portal inside the fence. This keeps us safe. Not all Fae are friendly." He winked at her at the last part.

"We have our own portals into Fae territory, however. We technically enter the Maze, which is a kind of front door to Tír na nÓg, designed to keep out only those with Fae blood. If you aren't true Fae or a State Changer, you'd lose your life in the Maze."

Casidhe tried to understand all Brody told her, but it was outside of her typical experience. He could see the confusion on her face.

"Don't worry; you will learn more about this from others who are better at explaining it than I am." He smiled and winked at her again.

It felt cozy inside the vehicle as they viewed the trees and back-country, beautifully covered in snow. They turned, heading back toward the house when Brody stopped suddenly. In front of them, a lone wolf trotted along the field. She paused in front of them, showing off her beautiful grey coat with white markings around her underside and along her tail. Her muzzle was a lighter grey, long and narrow down to her black nose. Her yellow eyes searched the area and then looked directly at them. No one moved for a moment. Then the wolf shook her entire body, sending snow and water in every direction, then trotted off toward the house.

"I think Lesslyn wants us back soon."

"Who was that?"

"That was Blaire. She's a beauty, isn't she." Brody said before catching himself and then blushed hard around his beard and eyes. Casidhe smiled back at him as he resumed their trek back.

"The last part of the tour is the outdoor arena. It's much like the inside one."

She peered out at the sizeable split-rail ring. It reminded Casidhe of a horse show arena she had seen at the farm show once. Wondering if this was for the horses, she remembered what Brody had told her about the arena in the barn and knew wolves used it too.

Once they got to the buildings, Brody dropped her off at the house and left to park the vehicle in the garage. As Casidhe climbed out, Brody said, "Blaire will give you the inside tour. I'll see you later."

"Okay, thanks, Brody. It was amazing!"

"You're welcome." He smiled easily, and Casidhe decided she liked him very much.

Once inside the house, Casidhe peeled off her coat and boots, hat, and gloves and hung them on the racks conveniently placed in the foyer, along the wall to one side of the double doorway. Taking off the last of her outer garments, she turned to see Blaire standing beside her. Casidhe wondered not for the first time how Blaire knew to be exactly where and when she was needed.

"Can I show you around the rest of the house?"

"Yes, please."

"You already know the main great-room, the kitchen, dining room, and the library. This part of the house was built around 1800. That would be the kitchen, a small dining room which is now storage and pantry, and the main library. The house has been added to and built on several times. The latest update was in the 1980s with the addition of the west wing and outside court. The house has two main wings. The east wing– where your suite is, as well as two additional bedrooms, is the Keneally wing and was added when your great, great grandfather became the Alpha. Several generations of Keneally's occupied that wing, and the Alpha status got passed down to each new generation. Matter of fact, this Ranch was in the Keneally family for so long, it is referred to as the Keneally Ranch. Kelly and Lesslyn Moore are the first non-Keneally's to reside here as Alphas in over 200 years, and that is only because, well, you know what happened to your parents."

"I actually don't know what happened to my parents," Casidhe said with curiosity. Blaire stopped and stared at her for a long moment before continuing.

"I am sure Lesslyn will fill you in."

Casidhe followed Blaire past the landing and to the right. "Here is the west wing. This is where Kelly and Lesslyn reside and their two children. They built it after your parent's death. You have met Dana. Her brother Jerod died as an infant. He had a congenital disease. Even State Changers, with our boosted immune systems, can succumb to illness occasionally. Anyway, it has only been Dana ever since that time, about 16 years now."

Blaire provided a wealth of information as she showed her around the beautiful house. The décor remained consistent throughout, natural wood and earth colors to accent the beauty of the environment. Between the wings, there were several additional bedrooms. One was Blaire's, and two more were for guests. There was also a third-floor great room that looked more like a recreation room with lots of comfortable seats, a large TV and a couple computers, a lot of windows, and a circular deck facing each direction. When they reached this space, Blaire explained.

"This is the pack room. It is best in the warmer months when the windows and decks are open. In the winter, we use it for special occasions and group gatherings."

They made their way back down to the main floor and the rear of the house. Blaire showed her the 'his and hers' changing rooms with robes and extra clothing hung along the walls.

"When we state change back into human form, we often need clothing on hand. We're not shy about our bodies, but we live in Montana; it's cold much of the time."

Next, Blaire showed her a large room with hospital-type beds, chrome tables, and cabinets filled with medicines.

"This is our hospital. As wolves, we often have minor injuries that need medical attention, and we can't go to the hospital. Neala has been our doctor for a long time, and Sean is now a registered nurse. Being a State Changer can be unsafe with the human population and the Fae. We are like them but not them, so we have friends and enemies. Sometimes our enemies are dangerous."

Casidhe wondered how Blaire could be so unemotional when she said such things, but Casidhe didn't mind. Neither of them knew her parents, so it was just information. Casidhe was becoming more and more curious about who they were.

"I apologize if I am blunt. I have Asperger's, which means I can be overly honest and sometimes socially awkward. I don't mean to offend you in any way."

"Oh, please don't worry. I kind of like your bluntness and honesty." She looked into Blaire's eyes and, seeing the beautiful grey wolf from earlier, thought they could be friends. Awkward friends, but friends nonetheless. A brief smile, then Blaire turned and led Casidhe to another door off the back of the kitchen.

"There is one more floor to show you." She led Casidhe downstairs into the basement, where they found an extensive wine and beer cellar and additional food storage. There were freezers and racks of canned food and bins filled with bulk grains. Dried meats and cheeses hung from hooks on the ceiling. Casidhe felt sure they were ready to survive the zombie apocalypse if such a thing were to happen. She didn't think zombies were real, even though, before today, she would have said unicorns and winged horses weren't real either.

The final door was locked, and Blaire said only the Alpha and the Alpha-She had access to that room. Blaire had no idea what could be in there save for some old antiques and such. They walked past, and Casidhe saw the large padlocks on the door and guessed it had to be something valuable to be locked up so tightly.

They ascended the stairs and made their way back to the kitchen, where they found Lesslyn fixing dinner.

"Oh good, you are done with your tour. Are you getting hungry?"

Casidhe had to admit she was and ran upstairs to her suite to clean up, coming back down soon to help finish the dinner preparation. Kelly came home, and the four of them had a quiet dinner in the kitchen of chicken and potato stew. Casidhe found it delicious and couldn't believe she was eating and enjoying meat.

After dinner, Casidhe yawned unknowingly. Lesslyn caught the gesture, though, and prodded her, "You should turn in early. Cormac will be filling your head with a lot of our history tomorrow morning, and Bronagh will be going over safety and security in the afternoon. You will want to be fresh."

"That sounds good. I am tired. Thank you so much for dinner. Can I help with the dishes?"

"No. You rest. You can help tomorrow." Blaire said.

Casidhe smiled her gratitude, and Blaire stood to start clearing up.

"What time should I be ready for Cormac?"

"He will be here around 8:00 to have breakfast with us, and then you two can have the library for the morning."

She nodded. "Goodnight, and thank you." Casidhe headed to her suite, intending to take a long bath and fall into bed. Sleep didn't come as quickly as she hoped as she found herself contemplating all she had learned and seen that day. She thought she'd begin a journal in the morning to help her process all the facts, ideas, and experiences coming at her. Once she made that decision, she fell into a deep sleep.

CHAPTER ELEVEN

The last thing she remembered before she woke up early the next morning was being very close to Dana's face and falling into her beautiful eyes. When consciousness reached for her, she wanted to push it away so she could stay with Dana a little longer. The harder she tried, the farther away the dream went until she was lying alone, looking up at the ceiling. She resolved to focus on the day ahead.

She rummaged in the drawer where she had stowed her journal. Finding it and grabbing a blanket from the top of the bed, she curled up in the chair by the window. As the sun came up, Casidhe could see that the snow had quit sometime in the night. The winter wonderland out her window sparked the cold air into a cascade of brilliance.

Just when she had settled in, she heard a soft knock at her door. Blaire entered fully dressed and carrying a tray of hot coffee. Casidhe stared at her for a minute.

"How did you know I was up? This is wonderful!"

"Because of the Asperger's, my senses are not as dulled as everyone else's at the Ranch," she said as if this explained everything about her. It almost did.

"Well, thank you, this is really great. I wanted to write down some of what has happened before I get my head all filled up with new facts and ideas."

"Writing helps me process things that don't make sense to others but are clear to me."

"Yeah, I am used to people not getting me either." Casidhe hoped her attempt to befriend Blaire sounded genuine. She didn't have a lot of experience in making friends.

Blaire smiled in return, leaving her to write. She was different, that was for sure.

Casidhe spent an hour sipping on her coffee and writing everything she could remember so far in her journal. She tried to stick with the highlights and essential questions that came to mind. Like why some of the pack wouldn't like her because she was a Keneally, and what pack members do in the arena? She wondered if Lesslyn and Kelly thought she wanted to take over and hoped they didn't believe that. She also wondered about Dana. But after writing her name, she scribbled beside it "later" and circled it. She had to stay focused.

Soon it was time she dress and go down for breakfast. She heard Kelly's deep voice rumbling from the great room and paused on the stairs to listen.

"They know she's here. I don't know how they know, but they know. This complicates things. Saoirse has requested she go to see her." Casidhe could hear another quieter voice speaking but couldn't make out exactly what she was saying. She guessed it was Lesslyn.

"I know. I know. I have put Saoirse off until after her transformation. We'll have to be extra vigilant; she should not leave the Ranch. The other twins are also twisting the bramble a bit, but Saoirse can control them. If I am not mistaken, we may see Cian soon too. Life just got more complicated."

Casidhe heard movement and decided it would not look good to be eavesdropping and ran silently down the rest of the stairs to the kitchen. She knew Kelly was referring to her, but who was this Saoirse anyway? Didn't her parents mention that name in their letter to her? Who are the twins? Casidhe was a twin, but she didn't think Kelly was talking about her and her brother just then. Was she in danger?

Blaire had started breakfast when Casidhe joined her, and together, they had everything ready in no time. It was strange to be in a house full of people, but she decided she didn't mind it.

Kelly joined them for breakfast, not mentioning any of what Casidhe had heard him say from the stairs. She felt safe enough here at the Ranch. After breakfast and cleanup, she went out on the back patio for a few minutes to get some air. She had not seen the ground since Christmas and figured she probably wouldn't for months. She started to get cold, turning to go back indoors when a movement off in the distance caught her eye. A very large, very dark wolf was loping across the backyard. As it got closer, she grew a little frightened by his size, but she did not turn away or run. She watched with fascination as he bounded up and stood before her nearly waist-high. He shook his whole body, and droplets of water and snow flew in every direction, including all over her. She thought she saw him smile as he went past her and into the house.

When she entered a moment behind him, he had already escaped into the changing room. Casidhe found a towel to dry off. In a few minutes, Cormac entered the kitchen dressed in jean overalls and a plaid shirt. His large frame towered over Casidhe, his dark hair with grey streaks at his temples was cropped short, contrasting his bushy grey beard. Casidhe would have been intimidated by him except for the twinkle in his eyes behind dark-framed glasses, which he slipped on as he entered.

"Hello, lassie, do you remember me from the other night? I'm Cormac. Sorry if I got you all wet out there." he said, stretching out his large hand.

"Yes, I remember. Nice to meet you again, and I don't think you are sorry at all," she said good-naturedly. Cormac's smile spread to his whole face as he laughed out loud.

"I think we will have a nice time. Shall we get some tea and begin in the library?"

"Sure."

Once they settled in, Cormac sat back and closed his eyes. "I have told these stories many times, and each time it gives me pause to think of where we have come from and what our ancestors left us. I will tell you the story as it was told to me. Some parts are too fantastic to believe, but so is our very existence, so you'll have to be the judge."

Casidhe didn't interrupt the distinct mood Cormac tried to set.

"Our Irish ancestry goes back many hundreds of years, far beyond the written word. In Irish mythology, they say there were five invasions of the homeland. Some stories are more fantastic than others—tales of giants and gods. The problem with these stories is, they were not written down until many generations later. The priests, priors, and monks took to recording the stories in written form, and of course, their own systems of belief influenced the stories a great deal. We owe them a debt of gratitude, for we may not have an account of these stories without them. But we also have to remember where they were coming from.

"It's the fourth invasion where we join in the story. The Tuatha Dé Danann (people of the goddess Danu) came across the sea in a mist or dark clouds, depending on the storyteller, to the shores of Ireland. When they arrived, they fought and won the first battle of Magh Tuireadh. In the next fight, Lugh of the Tuatha Dé Danann, led them to victory against the Fomorians and became king. A new wave of invaders known as the Milesians later came to Ireland, and the Tuatha Dé Danann lost to them in the battle at Tailtiu. A magician bard and leader among the Milesians–Amerigin was asked to help divide the land between the Tuatha Dé Danann and the Milesians. He, being very clever, assigned everything above ground to his own people and everything below ground to the Tuatha Dé Danann. So, our Fae ancestors were led underground to the magical land of the Sidhe, also known as Tír na nÓg. And to this day, in Ireland, the mounds and caves and portals across the countryside are gateways to the Fae or Fairyland and those magical beings that can be cruel or kind, depending on which Fae you encounter. The Fae are mischievous with humans, so humans try not to cross them.

"There is no need to worry about retaining all of that information, even though that is the shortest version you will probably ever hear. There are stories about each invasion, each king, their families, and their powers. All fascinating, but the part of the story I want you to remember is that the Tuatha Dé Danann were the ancestors of the Fae, and their realm is the underworld, Tír na nÓg.

"Now, when the Tuatha Dé Danann first came to Ireland, they brought four magical treasures, and it is believed they still exist. These would be very dangerous and powerful in this age and must be kept safe. They are the Claíomh Solais–the Sword of Light; the Lia Fail–Stone of Destiny; Sleá Bua–the Spear of Lugh; and the Coire Dagdae–Cauldron of Dagda. As you can imagine, the sword and the spear are mostly for killing, the stone is for telling the truth, especially pertaining to kings and heirs, and the cauldron has the power to produce whatever the bearer needs or wishes.

"The Dagda, also known as the 'good god,' was a king among the Tuatha Dé Danann. Stories tell of his strength and wisdom. He claimed the cauldron, as well as other magical treasures. He had a staff with two ends – one end could kill, and the other revived life. It is the Dagda we want to focus upon, for he is the forefather of the State Changers.

"The Dagda was extremely powerful. One of his wives was Morrigan, the mother of all witches. He took many lovers, and that is our part of the story. The Dagda, like Morrigan and most Fae, are shapeshifters. One day, he went out of Tír na nÓg and took on the shape of a black wolf exploring the wilderness of the high country. He loved the freedom of running in the wild. He loved the smell of the earth through the senses of the wolf. While he was passing through the dense forest, he came upon a lone she-wolf with beautiful silver fur and deep blue eyes. He was immediately smitten, and they frolicked and played in the woods all day. At the end of the day, he didn't want to leave her, so he curled up with her in a dry cave at the edge of a rock cliff.

"The next day, they went hunting and swimming in the river. Again, that night, he could not bring himself to leave her. The Dagda stayed in the woods with the silver she-wolf for three months. At the end of that time, the she-wolf gave birth to four pups. Two of the pups were normal wolf pups just like their mother, but two were different. Mac Tire–a grey wolf and Mac Dearg–a red wolf, each had the ability to shape-shift into a human form and had many of the powers of their father. The Dagda took these two into Tír na nÓg and taught them the ways of the Fae. He also took them into the human village and taught them about humans. They were allowed to visit their wolf-mother when they were young, but soon she and her other two pups joined a new pack, and they could no longer see her. After a couple of years, the she-wolf died in a fight, and her wolf pups, now full-grown members of the pack, did not remember them. Mac Tire and Mac Dearg lived the lifespan of the Fae, which is an extremely long time.

"Mac Tire and Mac Dearg were the original twin State Changers. Since then, there have been sets of twins down through the ages, one male and one female, whose bloodline can be traced back to the Dagda. Each time these twins are born, they become leaders of the State Changers, but tragedy always follows them. It seems in a wolf pack, there are no equals. Everyone has a place. Mac Dearg was seduced by a Fomorian king who sought her power. He convinced her to attack her brother and become the sole leader of the State Changers, who had now become a powerful race unto themselves. You see, State Changers can shapeshift into human or wolf form at any time. But they also are able to enter Tír na nÓg, the Fae realm, without losing time or life. In this way, they became the, not always liked, cousin to the Fae.

"In the battle between Mac Tire and Mac Dearg, Mac Tire was triumphant, but the death of Mac Dearg was a great sadness to the State Changers, for she had been the most liked and revered of the duo until her seduction by the Fomorian king. They both had many children by multiple mates, some human, some wolf, and some Fae. This is how our ranks grew over the generations. Today, we try to mate with only other State Changers, as the human world has become less and less magical, and there are far fewer wolves in the world, thanks to human hunting. Occasionally, there is a union with a Fae, but of those, often the State Changer goes into Tír na nÓg to live.

"There have been many sets of twins down through the ages of course, and always, tragedy or rivalry or some other horrible fate befalls one of them. It is known as the Curse of the

Twins. A couple of hundred years ago, which is a short period of time for Fae, a particular set of twins was born. They were born of two of our oldest families, the Keneally's and Kelly's. The male mated with a Fae and went into Tír na nÓg to live. The female became the Alpha of all the State Changer packs, known as the White Wolf. All was going well until something disturbing happened. The male started sowing contention among the Fae regarding the State Changers. He said they should stay in the human world and no longer be allowed to come into Tír na nÓg, that humans had corrupted the State Changers, and they were far more human than Fae. Some thought he had become jealous of his twin sister, and her power, for even though he was living among the Fae, she was more powerful than he. Some say he discovered a truth regarding humans: their loyalties were never to State Changers or Fae and, therefore, could not be trusted.

"This contention grew and grew, and we had a civil war. The male twin wasn't the only one who disliked and distrusted humans. There are many Fae that feel this way. Even some State Changers think they are above the humans. Of course, some are level-headed in both camps and know the reason State Changers survived for so many centuries is due to the diversity in our makeup. We maintain the connection to the earth and nature from our wolf-selves, and we maintain a relationship with the mass population on the planet and each other because of our humanity. Truthfully, it is our humanity that allows us to care for others who are unlike ourselves. And it is our power as Fae that gives us long life and connection to our past. We have to remain in balance with all three elements to ensure the longevity of our race.

"In the civil war that followed, many died. We lost Fae, State Changers, and humans alike. The male twin revolted against the female, but he was defeated and killed. His death was another great tragedy. After his death, the fighting stopped, but the opinions were not changed. It was a cease-fire, with each side drawing back into hiding. We have had mostly peaceful relations since then until your parents mated. As you can imagine, these two families coming together again was perceived as a bad omen.

"Though Finn and Nola lived peacefully, they were always at risk. Some wanted to kill them before they could have twins, and the cycle of violence would begin again. Some wanted the violence to start again or thought it inevitable, given the complexity of our race. Some just desired power, and others were merely fearful, believing in the Curse of the Twins. All in all, Finn and Nola played it safe and remained low-key until you and Cian were born. When they found out twins were coming to them, they knew you would be in great danger and went to great lengths to hide you both.

"Cian was safe as long as you were no longer in the picture. Fae and State Changers alike looked for you, but Colleen was determined to keep you safe and give you a life. That is why she never transformed into a wolf. If she had, she could have healed herself. But when a transformation takes place, especially out in the world, it leaves traces. Once you are part of the pack, there are ties that bind you together. The pack would have known where to find you both. Colleen loved her sister, and she loved you as her own."

Cormac paused for a moment as tears streamed down Casidhe's face, but he continued.

"You and Cian, being twins from our oldest families and a repeat of our history, will always be in danger. Your parents died when the Fuath, a wicked group of Fae, decided to take matters into their own hands to prevent another war. Or, knowing the Fuath, just to create havoc. Your parents died, of course, but not before they hid you both."

There was a long silence after this. Cormac, perhaps deciding he had told her enough, let the time and space between them stretch out quietly. Casidhe was trying to process it all. She had been caught up in the story, in the history, in her history. Not only did she belong somewhere, but that somewhere was long and involved and complex, filled with love and magic and violence. Her head swam with images of gods and wolves, of Fuath and Fae. An idea came to the front of her mind.

"Are there any other twins among the State Changers right now?" she asked.

Cormac came back from his reverie. "Yes. There is a set of twins, great-granddaughters of the male twin who was killed in the war. They keep to the Fae, but they are vocal about the need for a separation between humanity and those of the magical realm. And I can see the next question already in your mind; do same-sex twins pose the same threat? The answer is no. It seems only when there are opposite-sex twins does tragedy strike."

"What happened to the female twin from the war?"

Cormac didn't answer immediately, but when he did, he spoke slowly and deliberately, "She remained the White Wolf, leader of all State Changers. The female twin was Saoirse, your great, great grandmother. Senan was her twin brother."

Casidhe didn't know how to respond. She had a great-grandmother? And she was in danger. Perhaps a lot of danger. She must train and transform as quickly as possible. She knew without asking that she would have no chance against the forces against her and her brother until she was a full State Changer. Even then, would tragedy strike one or both of them? How could she know; she had never even met Cian? But he must be thinking the same thing about her. Would we repeat history? Were we destined to follow in the steps of our great grandparents? She hoped not.

Though no one spoke, Casidhe's mind was turbulent. She was glad Cormac had told her all of this. She needed to know what she faced.

Something had shifted in Casidhe. A new determination and an overwhelming desire to prove the curse wrong. She would not allow the curse to kill her or her brother or cause a civil war. As soon as that surge of confidence flooded her, it faded. How would she prevent it? She was just one person and not a very strong one at that. All she could do now is train and go through the initiation. That is what she must focus on.

Cormac continued to let Casidhe process her feelings and the situation. Finally, Casidhe's eyes met his, there was a short nod and slight smile exchanged.

"Thank you, Cormac."

"You are welcome."

CHAPTER TWELVE

C asidhe went upstairs after Cormac left and debated if she wanted to go back down for lunch. She was still thinking through what Cormac told her. Hunger decided for her, but she was relieved to find only Blaire in the kitchen. They had a quiet lunch. After dishes were cleaned up, Casidhe waited for Bronagh to show up to go over pack security. After a while, when no one came, she ventured up to the top floor and the pack room.

About half an hour later, as Casidhe was making her way around the room looking at books on the shelves and pictures on the walls, she heard heavy steps coming up the stairs. Kelly entered, making apologies for her wait. "Bronagh won't be able to make it. She's a police officer in Butte and got called away on a case." He got a beverage from the large refrigerator in the back area and joined her on the oversized couch. Casidhe did not know which Kelly would be talking to her today–the gruff guy she met outside the pub not that long ago or the affectionate uncle who had welcomed her to the pack.

"So we don't get behind in your training schedule, I'll get you started with pack dynamics. Aedan and Claire can continue the training tomorrow, and we'll get Bronagh when we can."

Casidhe nodded her agreement.

"Pack dynamics can be complex." With a broad smile, he continued. "In every pack, there is an Alpha, and in most cases, an Alpha-She. There have been several instances in our history where there was a female Alpha. As you know, I am our pack's Alpha, and Lesslyn is the Alpha-She. I have the final say, but she can and often does act as my surrogate since I cannot be all places at once. And truth be told, Lesslyn has a better touch with inter-dynamics than I do." Again, his beard and mustache moved out of the way for his smile. It was apparent he loved and respected Lesslyn.

"I became the Alpha the day your parents died. I was Finn's Beta – meaning, if anything happened to him and Nola or they were unavailable, I was next in charge. The whole pack has a pecking order. A lot of it is strength, but also blood lineage, respect, loyalty, and magical abilities play a part. For instance, Dana may not be stronger than Ronan, who is the strongest of our pack, but she is our daughter, so she has a high place in the pack. At least until she mates. Then, her position could move. Wolves fight for position. For State Changers, fighting ability isn't our only position criteria." Kelly had become very business-like, rattling off the inner workings of pack position and members. At the mention of Dana, Casidhe's heart lurched, but she tried not to show it.

"In every pack, there are those who are happy to be just members in good standing, and there are those who wish to move up the hierarchy. It is my job to remain strong so as not to encourage in-fighting or too many challenges. Some packs are constantly fighting within their ranks. They are not stable, and members do not feel safe. The Keneally pack is not like that. However, there are those who are waiting for the opportunity to find fault with my decisions or actions and challenge me. So far, my Beta, Ronan – who does not want the Alpha spot, has been able to shield me from much of that. Ronan's only weakness is that he is not mated, which is unusual in a pack, especially as a Beta. Besides, Ronan, I have two others that make my position strong. Brody and Bronagh. They are strong and very loyal to Lesslyn and me. I should also mention Blaire. She works here and is a loyal asset to our pack and family. There are, of course, all the others, and I trust them too–Cormac, and Siobhan, Aedan and Claire, Brian and Cara, and all the rest. You have met them all, but you will get to know them better over time. Just like everyone, we all have our weaknesses and strengths, but what I am discussing here is the strength and longevity of the pack."

He paused for a minute, obviously deciding where to go next and looking befuddled for a moment. He was concentrating so hard; he didn't think to ask for questions before he continued.

"This is the way of the wolf pack, which we are. But we are also Fae. Among Fae, it is the level and uniqueness of your magic that distinguished you. I am sure you have noticed Blaire's magic. She dismisses it as Asperger's, but in truth, she has the most acute senses of any wolf or State Changer I have ever known. This gives her advantages in battle and life. I do not often speak of my magic, and most do not. We like to keep the depth and breadth of our gifts a mystery. But I don't mind telling you; I have the ability to shift not only into a wolf– a very large one, but also into a large black bear. This has come in handy once or twice." At this revelation, his smile returned.

"You won't know what your magic is until the initiation, and even then, it may take weeks, months, or even years for all of your gifts to be revealed. The key in a pack is to show enough to discourage challenge, but not too much, so you remain a mystery. Pack members figure that what they don't know can, in fact, hurt them. This helps to keep the status quo in the pack. The more stable we are, the stronger we are.

"This pack has been the Keneally pack from as far back as anyone can remember. Only with the death of your parents did that change, and still, we keep the name and the Keneally spirit alive. Keneally is one of the oldest and perhaps the first family of State Changers and, therefore, one of the most respected and feared packs in the world. Even in the old world, they knew the Keneallys.

"However, since the civil war, our lives have changed. There is much to lose from another war but many on all sides are set in their ways. The Fuath decided it best just to eliminate your parents than to risk another set of twins that could put us all in peril. That was a sad day." He shook his head and stared at his hands for a moment.

"Since their death and your disappearance, things have been quiet. The Fae pulled back the Fuath and scorned their actions. But they remain a threat and have repeatedly shown us that the Ranch's protections have a loophole. We have not been able to find how they get through them. We train and stay on guard. The White Wolf, leader of all State Changers, sits on the Fae council and helps to keep all in check. Everyone knows your brother lives, but they assumed you died with your parents since no one could find you. Therefore, there has been no risk of the Twin Curse."

"Somehow, word of your return is getting out. The White Wolf wants to meet with you right away, but Lesslyn and I have put her off until after your transformation. I hope that is a good idea." He said, more to himself than her.

"Also, Cian knows you have returned and wants to meet you. Again, we have put him off until after your initiation. Right now, you are vulnerable, but you will be less so once you are a full State Changer."

Casidhe didn't know what to say and didn't want him to stop talking, so she limited herself to nods and one-word agreements.

"As the heirs, you and Cian have a right to challenge the Alpha to lead the Keneally pack. Some are convinced you will. Also, as you are Keneallys and opposite-sex twins, you carry the curse. True or not, it is believed and has been proven to play a big part in our history." With that, he abruptly stopped talking.

Casidhe had a chance to respond and knew what she needed to say. "If you want to know if I want to lead the pack, absolutely not. I am not even a full State Changer yet. And even afterward, I will not. I know so little of this world, I could not, nor would not, be of use to the pack as a leader. I don't know the future, but I cannot imagine a time when I would want to lead this pack. It's simply not me. I have been a loner my whole life. I am doing my best to simply be a part of the group."

She dropped her gaze for a moment. "As for the Twin Curse, I hope with my whole heart, it is not true of Cian and myself, but I recognize others will be fearful anyway. I am not sure how to deal with it and look to you and Lesslyn as my Alphas for help."

Kelly looked somewhat relieved. "Good. Of course, we will protect and guide you as our own. It is my promise to you, having failed your parents, to do everything within my power to protect you from harm, from within or without." Large tears filled Kelly's eyes as he said this. The death of her parents had affected him more than her, as he had known and loved them. Casidhe reached over and touched his hand. He grasped it in both of his, and they sat there for a few minutes.

"Yes, well then. As we got a late start, tomorrow you'll spend the morning with Aedan and Claire. They will go over the members of our pack more and a bit about mating, which I am sure you don't want to hear from me." The twinkle in his eyes returned.

"Tomorrow will be another short day. In the evening is the pack New Year's party. Everyone will be here. We'll have lots to do in preparation. It always proves to be a good time." He winked at her.

Casidhe asked, "Is it okay if I explore the grounds this afternoon, then?"

"Yes, of course, this is your home. Just don't leave the boundaries and take Blaire with you. She will be most useful."

Kelly was out the door as he said the last part, his phone ringing in his pocket. Duty called. Lunch came and went, and Blaire met Casidhe in the mudroom at the rear of the house. Casidhe got fully dressed in snow pants, coat, hat, and gloves. Blaire was not. Casidhe wondered if she had changed her mind. She was about to ask when Blaire began removing what clothing she had on. Further confused, Casidhe did not know what to say but soon understood. Blaire proceeded to state change into her wolf form right before Casidhe's eyes.

Blaire's grey fur fluffed up as she shook it hard. Her white underbelly was gleaming like a reflection of the snow. Her long muzzle smelling the air before her, she stretched all fours and then bounced out into the snow. Casidhe tried as best she could to keep up, but having only two feet was a definite disadvantage. Blaire as a wolf was carefree and fun, and Casidhe laughed and bounded as best she could with her. She threw snowballs at Blaire but missed every time. Still, it didn't matter; they had such fun. They ventured into the woods and around the trees. Blaire would lead the way into bushes knowing clumps of snow would cover Casidhe. She barked and howled as Casidhe yelled back and laughed. They were both soaked two hours later when they started back for the house.

Casidhe lumbered along behind when Blaire stopped in her tracks and sniffed the air. Casidhe stopped too and watched. Blaire's hair went up on her neck, she crouched low, and her muzzle wrinkled to expose her teeth. Her low growl rumbled out into the cold air. Casidhe knew at once something, or someone was close by. Off in the distance, a dark grey and brown wolf stepped out from behind a tree and then another light brown colored wolf behind him. They did not growl but crouched low like they would leap forward any moment. Blaire's growl grew louder; the hair on the back of her neck and down her back stood on end. Her body crouched, muscles primed to extend and attack.

Casidhe did not move, barely breathing; she watched how ferocious Blaire had become. Just when she felt sure there would be a fight, the other two backed up slowly, and a light yip came from the male in front. Then slowly, they turned and walked off toward the house. Once there was more distance between them, they bounded off.

It took a minute more before Blaire relaxed her stance, and her lips slid back over her teeth. She sniffed the air and then turned to Casidhe, satisfied. They made their way back to the house. It took Casidhe longer to traverse through the snow, but Blaire stayed with her the whole way.

Once they were in the mudroom, Blaire shook hard, covering Casidhe in more wet snow and water. She was already drenched from head to toe, cheeks rosy, and exhausted from plodding through the snow and laughing hard. It had been one the best times she could remember. Before the wolf scare, that is. She tore off her wet outer clothing and headed for the stairs when she heard voices coming from the kitchen.

Blaire had transformed back into human form and dressed. Casidhe could hear her and two voices in the kitchen talking.

"We were only passing through and didn't mean to startle you."

"You know there is a protocol for coming onto the Ranch in wolf form; besides, you didn't act friendly."

"Sorry, Blaire, it won't happen again."

"No, it won't. I will report this to Kelly."

"Report what to me?" Kelly had obviously just joined them. Casidhe was freezing now and dripping on the rug. She decided to let them handle pack business. She'd ask Blaire later about it.

Casidhe sunk into a tub of hot water, thinking about how much she couldn't wait to become a wolf and explore the snow like Blaire. She smiled to herself and once again marveled at the feeling of belonging that overcame her and how different it felt. She knew she was changing and liked it.

Dinner was filled with warm food and friendly company. Casidhe asked Blaire about the incident in the woods.

"It was Kevin and Sinead. They are fairly new to the pack and didn't follow protocol. I don't think it will happen again. Kelly talked to them."

"You seemed pretty upset with them."

"It is my job to help protect you, at least until you are a full State Changer and can protect yourself."

"Did I need protection from Kevin and Sinead?"

"Well, I think you can never be too careful. Sometimes I wonder about them. They are new, and there have been rumors they are not too excited about your return. But it is just hearsay; I wouldn't worry. Besides, Kelly is intimidating and has already scolded them."

"I wouldn't want to cross him." Casidhe was going to ask more about the rumors, but Blaire walked away, dismissing the subject. She smiled. That was Blaire for you. Casidhe retired early to write, knowing tomorrow would be another full day. As she drifted off to sleep, she remembered everyone was coming over tomorrow evening. That meant Dana. Her heart skipped a beat. She couldn't wait to see her again, and she could not get herself to wish otherwise.

The next morning, Casidhe arose, dressed, and went down to breakfast. Lesslyn and Blaire were bustling around going over party planning. Lesslyn was instructing Brody to pick up supplies, food, and beverages. Kelly was talking quietly at one corner of the long tables with Aedan and Claire, who had arrived for her morning training. They all looked up and greeted Casidhe when she entered. She felt a little self-conscious and mumbled a quick 'morning' and gave a faint smile on her way to the coffee pot. All the activity reminded her she would see Dana again that evening. That thought excited and made her nervous at the same time.

She grabbed some toast and eggs and was going to sit away from Kelly and the others, but they motioned for her to come closer.

"Please, sit with us. We were going over the gaps in your training on pack dynamics." Claire said. Casidhe barely remembered her from the all-pack meeting. She had long brown hair and rather bushy eyebrows that somehow worked for her face. Her eyes were also a chocolate brown color and had flecks of green. She had large lips that hid larger teeth. Still, Casidhe found her uniquely pretty. Aedan, her mate, was less remarkable. He had dark brown hair that framed his face in a shaggy way and blended into his beard and mustache. But he had a charming smile. The only thing that made Aedan stand out in her mind was his height. When he stood to get more coffee, he was noticeably shorter than all the other men and some of the women. Casidhe noticed most State Changers, men and women, were large in stature. Aedan proved it was not a foolproof stereotype.

"Thanks." Casidhe sat down next to them. "Will we be in the pack room upstairs again?"

"Yes, I think so."

"We have some displays to set up, so we'll meet you up there when you're finished with your breakfast."

Casidhe finished and left the busy kitchen, where Lesslyn was piling more on Brody. Casidhe refilled her cup with coffee and ascended the stairs reaching the pack room. Aedan and Claire had put up several charts on the walls with names of pack members neatly listed in sections.

"Great, you're here. Pull up one of the bar stools, and we'll get started. I know you have met everyone, but it's not possible to remember twenty-four people after only one meeting." Aedan began.

"Not unless you're Blaire." Chimed in Claire with a smile.

"Right." Aedan smiled back.

"So, Kelly already told you some of this information, but we thought it would be helpful to see it. The Alpha's inner circle are those that have been with the pack the longest and have proven themselves loyal and dependable to the Alphas. The Alpha always has a second or Beta. He is the pack back-up in case the Alpha and Alpha-She are occupied or incapacitated in some way. You can think of them as the Vice President. In our pack, that person is Ronan. Ronan is extremely strong as a leader–as a State Changer, and physically. He does all the physical training with new pack members." Aedan pointed to the chart hung on the wall.

Claire interrupted. "Pack size is important. Members come and go. Some move to other areas and join other packs, some mate outside of our pack and move to be with their mates, and some are new State Changers who have just come of age. We are only listing here those who have gone through the initiation. Children are definitely part of the pack but not part of pack dynamics yet. Our pack has 24 members right now, not counting children. When you join us as a State Changer, you will be number 25. That is not the largest pack; some go up to 50. That many are hard to manage for the Alpha and can create more inter-pack issues. Some are less than 10. These packs are not as strong and have difficulties dealing with the Fae or humans they interact with. You'll learn more about that over time. But 24 or 25 is a strong and manageable pack size."

"Correct." Aedan continued. "So, the rest of the inner circle would be Brody, Blaire, Dana, of course, Bronagh, Brian and Cara, Cormac, Siobhan, Claire, and myself. We have all been with this pack a long time and are loyal to Kelly and Lesslyn. Some even knew your parents; they have been here that long. Claire and I aren't that old." He finished with a shy smile.

"Right, definitely Cormac and Neala knew your parents, as did Siobhan." Claire stared off in the distance. "Brian and Cara may have been new to the pack at that time and could have known them. I can't remember." Her attention came back at Casidhe. "And, of course, Kelly and Lesslyn knew your parents. Also, Colleen was a member of our pack, as you know, since she was your mother's sister. The pack took a hit when we lost three of our leadership at once."

Aedan took up the conversation again. "So, pack position has a lot to do with loyalty to the Alpha and his mate, but also blood. For instance, Dana is high in the hierarchy even though she is young. Also, strength is important. Ronan is Beta because he is so strong and decisive. Another variable in positioning within the pack is whether you are mated or not. We will get to that shortly. Ronan is not mated, but he makes up for it in other ways. One more factor I would add is the desire to be part of the inner circle. For instance, Cormac is one of Kelly's most trusted advisors. He is mated to Neala, who is a doctor. Although she is trusted to be the pack doctor, and we rely on her, Neala doesn't have time to be part of the inner circle. So, she is in the next group of members, sometimes known as the 2nd string." Aedan smiled sheepishly again, and Casidhe decided he was charming. They continued to ping pong back and forth through the lesson–first Aedan and then Claire. It worked well, and Casidhe could see why they were chosen to perform this task with new members.

"The second group includes Liam, Derry, Sean–our new nurse, and Brendan and Cathleen, who are mated to each other."

"The final group are new to the pack and therefore haven't proven themselves yet. They have either joined our pack recently (coming from other packs within the last two years), or they have gone through the initiation not too long ago. In this group is Kevin and Sinead–a mated pair who joined us from a pack in Minnesota–and the young ones: Seamus, Darcy, and Fiona."

"I know it's a lot to remember, but as you meet them and spend time with them, they will become your family."

"And just like family, you may not get along with everyone, but you know them and love them anyway." Casidhe thought of Kevin and Sinead. Aedan gave her another even more sheepish smile. Casidhe could now imagine Aedan telling bad jokes at the dinner table, causing everyone to groan.

"There is one more pack member we haven't mentioned yet. There is only one State Changer who is over the Alpha in any pack: The White Wolf. Her name is Saoirse, and she is the only State Changer on the Fae council. Technically, she leads all the packs, and all the pack Alphas report to her. She is remarkably powerful and old, and she doesn't leave Tír na nÓg any longer, so far as I know. Some wonder if she isn't more Fae than State Changer, but no one would dare speak of that to her face. She meets every new initiated State Changer at least once, so you will meet her after you have gone through the initiation."

"Yes, I know of the White Wolf." Cormac had obviously not told anyone how much he had disclosed to her about her ties to Saoirse.

"So that is the pack, there is a lot more about them, but we want you to form your own opinions and make your own relationships with each of them. That's all we'll get into for now. We should move on to mating. Never the most comfortable of topics, but we'll make it brief."

Casidhe smiled passively, but her heart picked up a beat on this particular topic.

"Mating is extremely important to the pack, its strength, and longevity. As you can imagine, our pool of possibilities is often limited. That's why we lose people to other packs, and others join us. This helps to keep our ranks fresh but also can be disconcerting."

"State Changers can mate with Fae. Siobhan is mated to an Elf named Thebieas. They have been together a long time, and they not only make it work, but that relationship has helped our pack in overall relations with the Fae. Siobhan has become a trusted Fae advisor not only to our pack but also to other packs around the region."

"State Changers can also mate with humans, though this has been discouraged, as I am sure Bronagh will tell you. It opens us up to risks we would prefer to avoid."

"Mating is critical to the pack for two obvious reasons. One is because two are stronger than one. Can you imagine Kelly running our pack without Lesslyn? No, us either. Together they are formidable. Alone, they would be strong but not strong enough to be Alpha. And even for those of us who are not Alpha and do not wish ever to be, mating bonds provide strength and advantages in the different worlds we navigate. Each of us has our own magical gifts; when we combine them, they exceed their summed parts. The more bonded pairs a pack has, the stronger it is and more stable over time."

"The second reason is children. Without children, our pack would slowly die off. Every pack member is expected to have at least one child, and more are encouraged. It's not mandatory, except for the Alphas, but it is highly encouraged. It is part of our culture and shows your dedication to the pack – your larger family. It may seem somewhat archaic, but if you think about it, how would we survive with such a small gene pool without the importance made on having children."

"Aedan and I have two children. Tara and Patrick are young, only five and seven, but someday, they will become full State Changers and full members of our pack. We have 11 children of all ages in the pack right now and expect more will be added in the next couple of years. You will see all the children tonight as they attend all the holiday events." Claire smiled; a noticeable glow came over her when she discussed the kids.

"Alphas are required to have children. They set the example for the entire pack. The pack is always first and last to the Alpha and his mate."

"To be clear, we do not arrange mating, nor is it required. Save for the Alpha; it is simply encouraged for the strength and longevity of the pack. As you know, Ronan is not mated. He is gay, and I believe he is the only gay Beta in any pack today. If something were to happen to Kelly and Lesslyn, Ronan would only be Alpha temporarily, until a suitable mated pair was found or he found someone to mate with. This has caused some contention in our pack over the years, as a few question Kelly's choice of Ronan as Beta. The mating bond is strong, and everyone knows it would be better if he were mated. To be unmated opens the pack to vulnerabilities. But Kelly is stubborn and won't listen. He insists Ronan knows the risk and is his only choice for Beta."

Casidhe had been listening attentively. Finally, for the first time since coming up to the pack room this morning, she asked a question, breaking the flow of Aedan and Claire's repartee.

"Can't gay pack members mate? I mean, it's legal for humans and accepted, right?"

Claire answered. "Yes, of course. It is permitted, though not common. We live in small groups. I believe suitable mates are harder to find. Additionally, there is the whole children issue. That would get complicated, I think. It's definitely more challenging."

Casidhe did not want to come out and tell them she was gay; it would surface sooner or later. For now, she'd let them guess. She had barely figured out herself. Children had not been part of her life plan so far. *But really, what plan?* This made her scoff at herself. Aedan and Claire did not seem to notice.

"There is one more component to pack dynamics. Once you go through the initiation and you are welcomed into a pack, there is a magical connection that bonds you to the pack. It is also true of mated pairs. Most of the time, this is inconsequential. But during times of intense emotion, like high stress, sadness, fear, or even elation and excitement, your mate and your pack will feel some part of that emotion. Also, there is a slight tremor in the pack when a member state changes. After a while, it's hardly noticeable. But it's always there."

"Well, that is about it on pack dynamics. There is so much more to it than what we can convey in a conversation. You just have to live with us for a while, and you will pick it up. Do you have any more questions?"

Casidhe's mind was spinning, and she couldn't think of anything at that moment. She shook her head.

"Very well. You can ask anytime. We will be around. This evening, in fact." They were all rising from their seats and heading for the door when Aedan turned and said thoughtfully, "There is something we forgot to mention. You are a Keneally, and this is the Keneally pack. You have certain rights and expectations that go with your name. I don't want to give you more to think about right now, but we would be remiss if we didn't mention it."

"I have already told Kelly, I have no designs on leading this pack at any point. I simply want to belong here, to be part of the pack."

It seemed like Aedan was about to say something else when Claire put her arm through his and said instead. "That sounds great, Casidhe. We are happy to have you join us."

Casidhe looked at them both and decided to let it go. She didn't want to know any more about the expectations of her. She wasn't even a State Changer yet. She'd cross that bridge when she came to it. Also, she did not want to get into the whole Twin Curse conversation again, which she suspected was where Aedan could end up. As they went down the stairs, Casidhe thanked them as she side-tracked to her room for a quick reprieve from everyone and everything. She'd go down soon and help with the party. For now, she wanted to think about all she had learned.

CHAPTER THIRTEEN

C asidhe helped in the kitchen all afternoon. She, Lesslyn, and Blaire prepared soup, salads, and hors d' oeuvres, organizing incoming trays of food and coolers of drinks and ice coming from others within the pack. It was a whirlwind of efficiency and organization. This was clearly not their first party. Brody showed up with a van full of trays and boxes. Kelly came back with two kegs. Blaire was cleaning glasses and pulling out plates, napkins, and silver. Casidhe chipped in everywhere she could.

By 5:00, all arrangements were completed, and they were ready to have a party–all except for themselves. Everyone was arriving around 6:30, so they each made their way to their quarters to get dressed. Casidhe showered and primped her hair. She pulled the bulk of it upon her head in a loose bun with long red tendrils framing her face on each side. She put on a little makeup to smooth out her skin and accent her emerald eyes. She combed through her closet for some time before settling upon a pair of sleek black slacks that clung to her thin legs and a green and gold tunic-style blouse that billowed over them. Her shoes were gold flats—*no sense in being uncomfortable for hours*. The whole ensemble gave a flowing, elegant look she didn't hate when she reviewed herself in the mirror. Before she went down the stairs at 6:40, she slipped her mother's ring onto her finger. Crowds were still difficult for her. Any power the ring possessed, she would welcome tonight.

As she exited her room, she heard the din of voices coming from below. She took a deep breath and made her way down to the foyer, where there were already a dozen people hanging up coats and embracing. Several children ran through on their way to the great room or somewhere beyond. Squeals of joy and laughter followed them as they went.

When Casidhe reached the first landing above the foyer, heads turned in her direction, and some of the chatter quieted. This made Casidhe uncomfortable, and she now wished she had come down earlier as she absently twirled the ring on her finger. She saw Blaire off to one side, assisting those who entered, and their eyes met. Blaire smiled at her encouragingly. Casidhe tried to hurry so the attention would shift elsewhere, but she didn't want to stumble. Funny, she never remembered there being so many steps on this stairway. Just before she reached the bottom, she spied Dana standing alone at the rear of the room. She had been watching Casidhe the whole trip to the bottom step. She wore white slacks and a blue tailored blouse that accented her eyes. She smiled at Casidhe, but there was something in Dana's look that made Casidhe's heart pound. Dana's eyes were bright, with a wild, gold tinge shining through. Casidhe's face flushed.

She made it to the bottom of the stairs and turned the other way, not trusting herself with Dana at this moment. She needed to compose herself, especially if Dana was going to look at her with that hungry look in her eyes. Could everyone see it? She went through the kitchen, to the door, and stepped into the back entryway, trying to cool off. How could someone make you feel that way with a look? And how was she going to make it through this evening without falling into that woman and never wanting to emerge? She took deep, cold breaths to remind herself she needed to stay focused. *How had this happened?* Somehow, Dana had crept into her heart and mind so profoundly, Casidhe barely recognized herself or her own body.

It wasn't long before she was freezing and ventured back into the kitchen. She grabbed a bite and a glass of sparkling cider from the kid's table—no alcohol for her tonight. There is no way she could manage it and Dana in the same house. She made her way back to the great room, greeting others as she went. Brody had cleaned up nicely; his ponytail was pulled back in a ribbon, and he had trimmed his beard. Wearing a denim shirt over black, pressed jeans, Casidhe thought he looked handsome and hoped Blaire would notice for his sake. He whistled at her teasingly and then pulled her into a bear-hug. She smiled up at him, wondering if Cian would feel as much like a brother to her as Brody felt.

"You look good, Brody. Have you seen Blaire yet?" she smirked at him. He blushed.

"I saw her, and I hope to see more of her later." He said, smiling broadly.

"Good luck." She said sincerely.

Casidhe saw Bronagh talking to someone else whose back was turned. She smiled and waved but didn't interrupt the conversation. When she reached the great room, she found Aedan and Claire with their two children, Tara and Patrick. She greeted them all, and the parents ran the children off to play with the others. Claire offered to introduce her to Ronan, who would be working with Casidhe next. They made their way over to a tall, bulky man standing by the window.

"Ronan, have you met Casidhe? I believe you will be work-ing with her soon."

"Nice to meet you again, Casidhe. How's the training com-ing along?"

"Well, thank you. I have been learning so much. I look for-ward to working with you."

"Yes, indeed." Ronan was the only male State Changer she had met who didn't have a full beard. He had a dark, meticu-lously trimmed mustache and the whitest teeth she had ever seen. His smile was stellar. Ronan looked like a movie star, one of those action-figure types with huge biceps and a mas-sive chest. He was beautiful; even Casidhe had to admit. She could not imagine he couldn't find any guy he wanted. But then again, the pickings had to be slim among the State Changers.

"What will the training be like? I have never been very ath-letic." Casidhe said, excusing her slight frame.

"Yes, you will need to build some muscle mass, I see." This made Casidhe feel self-conscious, and Ronan understood.

"Don't worry. I have trained all types of people. You will do fine. It might be a little tough in the beginning, but you'll be surprised at how good it feels to get stronger. You'll find a whole new level of confidence."

"Okay. I'll trust you to get me into shape." She thought this sounded scary, but what else could she do. She knew this was part of the training. She only hoped Ronan was as good as everyone said.

"That's the spirit. I'm not sure when we start, but I expect it will be soon. I travel with my work, so we'll have to figure out a schedule. The demands of shifting are hard on the human body; you must condition it. Otherwise, the transformation could tear your body apart."

Casidhe's eyes grew wide in fright. Ronan put a comforting hand on her shoulder. "Don't worry. It's my job to get you ready."

Casidhe gulped hard and nodded her head. Perhaps she should have started this part of the training already. She was trying to talk herself down. *The transformation is months away, right? I have time to train and prepare. I have time.*

Lesslyn came up to her elbow. "How are you doing, darlin'?"

Ronan greeted and embraced Lesslyn and then got called into another conversation, leaving Lesslyn and Casidhe alone for a moment. "I'm fine. Though I am a little frightened of what Ronan just told me."

"Don't worry. Ronan is a pro. He'll get you ready. We do need to get on his schedule, though. He sells ski equipment up and down the Rockies in the U.S. and Canada, and this is his busy season."

"He looks like a skier."

"Ronan is unquestionably an athlete. Have you had anything to eat yet?"

"Only a bite."

"Well, let's get you some more to eat. I don't want you getting too overwhelmed, and there is plenty of evening left before the New Year toast at midnight." She had been slowly guiding Casidhe through the crowd, introducing her to Liam and Derry, who were talking together. They seemed nice, though

Casidhe had a hard time remembering which one was who. They looked alike, but she didn't think they were brothers. When they reached the food table, Casidhe filled a plate and found a spot to sit on a small loveseat when someone called Lesslyn away. Casidhe was happy to have a moment to sit quietly. She felt someone watching her from across the room. She glanced over her glass when she took a sip of her cider. Kevin and Sinead. *I should have guessed. What do they have against me, anyway? The Twin Curse?* She had half a mind to go up and ask. But just then, the whole room shifted and became a blur. Only the woman standing in front of her existed.

"Hi there," Dana said and sat down very close.

Casidhe's mouth went dry, even though she was drinking cider. *Why do I feel so hot when she is near me?* "Hi." She managed to croak out.

"How is the training going?" *Am I expected to have a conversation with this woman while our knees were touching?*

"Good. I have learned a lot." Casidhe would be happy if her heart rate would slow down so she could breathe easier.

"When do you start with Ronan?" *And how can she be so calm?* Casidhe met Dana's eyes for the first time since the foyer, grateful the golden gleam was no longer present. But with Dana so close to her, she could smell her shampoo, recognizing it from her nights at the drug store. On Dana, it smelled enticing. She never had that reaction from the boxes.

"Soon, I think. Maybe next week if he's not traveling. How is school?" Casidhe was proud she got a question out.

"I don't start the new semester for another two weeks. I've been working on campus during the break." The more they talked about mundane things, the more time Casidhe had to pull herself together. But as Dana told her about her job at the lab and the professor she worked with, Casidhe had to look at her. Dana's long black, silken strands begged to be touched. Her blue eyes were bright, somehow conveying feelings that were far more intimate than the words coming from her rosy lips. *No, don't look at her lips. Anywhere else.* Casidhe quickly took a bite off her plate. This allowed her to look down and occupy her mouth, which she was afraid would betray her, leaning into Dana's at any second. The air felt thick. Casidhe was sure Dana was attracted to her; there was no way this could be happening without both sides pouring emotion into the space between them. Dana had stopped talking. Casidhe could not help herself; she looked up into Dana's eyes.

"You feel it too, right?" The question sounded innocent, but it was far from it. It was an invitation. As her eyes met Dana's, she allowed the longing to show for a split second, holding her breath for Dana's response.

"Ohhhh . . . yes." That was all Dana said, but within those words, Casidhe could feel Dana's desire as her eyes turned a golden yellow again, and the wild attraction almost knocked Casidhe off her seat. She was burning up, and her heart beat wildly in her chest. She gripped her glass so hard she was sure it would break.

Their intimate bubble popped the moment Lesslyn came up behind them.

"Hello, gals," cut through the haze like a knife. Dana and Casidhe both straightened. "Your father has been looking for you, Dana. I think he is in the kitchen."

"Right." Dana got up, obviously put off, but resigned. She winked at Casidhe and turned to leave.

Lesslyn took Dana's spot on the couch. Casidhe didn't know what to say. She had been in a trance. All her self-control had evaporated in Dana's presence. "I'm sorry, Lesslyn. I don't know if I can control myself around Dana. I want to stay focused on my training, but all of my best intentions seem to go right out the window as soon as I see her." Casidhe was not sure why she had said that out loud. She had never been open about how she felt before, except maybe with Aunt Colleen. Lesslyn seemed to understand and patted her on the hand.

"You are not familiar with the passions of the wolf, or Fae magic, but I believe you are learning. And Dana is . . . special. It seems prudent to keep you two apart, at least until after the transformation. Not to say you can't see her at all, but we should try to limit your interactions. Okay?" It was a question, and Casidhe appreciated she asked instead of demanding.

"Yes, I think you are right. I am going to go get some air." Casidhe went out the side door to the back patio, and within moments, Blaire was there. It was uncanny how she showed up every time Casidhe needed her.

"You and Dana, huh?" She asked.

"Yeah."

"I see. But you should wait until after your initiation."

"I'm pretty sure everyone can see it. And I know. I know. I try. But as soon as she is around, I lose all of my resolve."

"Dana has that effect. I'll help you. Whenever she comes over, I'll stay close."

"I think it will help. Thank you!" Casidhe felt desperate and kind of pathetic now. How could she not control herself? She had never felt anything so intense before, except the need to hunt on those few occasions when the instinct had over-whelmed her. *Ah, so that is what Lesslyn meant. The wolf instincts and passions are very strong.* Casidhe took a deep breath and turned to Blaire.

"What about you. Are you interested in anyone?"

"Oh, you mean Brody," Blaire said matter-a-factly.

"Well, him or anyone else?" Casidhe tried not to be so obvious.

"I expect I will mate with Brody soon. He is handsome, and I do like his long hair. Also, he is loyal to Kelly and Lesslyn, which is important to me. They took me in when other packs would not. My gifts can be threatening. Brody will have his hands full for sure." With the last bit, Casidhe was sure she saw Blaire blush a little.

"Let's go inside. You are getting cold out here, and the toast will be soon. I should make my way over to Brody so he doesn't have to kiss anyone else at midnight." Again, Blaire said this so flatly it took Casidhe a minute to take in what she said. Once she did, Casidhe giggled a little, and that caused Blaire to giggle too, which for Blaire was something.

Once inside, everyone started assembling in the great room. Some were coming down from the pack room upstairs, while others came in from the kitchen. They were milling in from every corner of the house. Casidhe felt the warmth of friends, family, and pack–this group of people who were becoming important to her. So much had changed. How and when did it all happen? But Casidhe knew. It was when she discovered the wolf inside. It was when she allowed that wolf to be somehow real; to be her future; to be herself. That had shifted something fundamental in the person she had been her whole life. *Aunt Colleen should not have kept it from me. I love you, and I miss you, but you should not have kept it from me.*

She stood in the open patio doorway, on the periphery of the crowd. Blaire had gone to get Brody and promised to return once she found him. Kelly was talking about the year, new pack members, and new births. He spoke Casidhe's name, and all turned to her for a moment before he continued. Lesslyn was at his side, her arm affectionately around his waist. Couples had found each other, and the kids were running underfoot. Several champagne bottles were being passed around. Everyone was preparing for the toast at midnight. Just before the countdown began, Casidhe backed out of the doorway, which was open for air. On the patio outside, tall kerosene heaters lined the stone walkway, putting off heat and light. Watching the crowd inside, she felt someone come up behind her. She turned to see Dana smiling at her and offering her a glass. Casidhe reached out and took it but scarcely moved otherwise. Even outside, the temperature around them had begun to warm up, and Casidhe's heart was now pounding hard in her chest. *Where is Blaire? With Brody, no doubt.*

Casidhe could hear the countdown, "10, 9, 8, 7, 6." Dana was so close now; they leaned into each other. "5. 4. 3. 2. 1. Happy New Year!" Everyone yelled. Dana and Casidhe just whispered to each other, and then it happened. Dana leaned in and lightly brushed her lips against Casidhe's. Feeling the impossible softness, Casidhe, losing all resolve, leaned in for more. Desire washed over her so strongly; she was sure it would consume her. In that moment, Casidhe decided what her lips were really meant for. The kiss launched a cascade of emotions that spiraled out from her body and wrapped them both up in a tightly bound cocoon. It did not matter where she was or who might spy on them through the glass windows; she wanted to melt into the heat that was Dana. Still holding the glass in one hand, her free hand went up into Dana's hair and pulled her closer. Dana's arm encircled Casidhe's waist like a hot iron band, clamping them together. They were attached. In that moment, Dana became Casidhe's person, now interlocked, never to find the key. The flames were burning hotter, and Casidhe no longer cared about training, or Lesslyn, or the pack, or anything else. She only wanted to be with this woman: her lips, her tongue, her smell, her skin. Time was unknown; it could have been a second; it could have been an hour.

Something off in the distance clamored for Casidhe's attention. She didn't want to hear it; she wanted to stay here in Dana's arms. It grew closer. Then there was a commotion, and Dana was wrenched from her embrace. In what seemed like slow motion, their lips parted, and Casidhe saw two very tall beings covered with hair in their space. One tossed Dana aside. Casidhe watched her fall to the ground. *What is happening?* In a passionate haze, her mind struggled to catch up with reality. She pulled free of someone, trying to reach Dana. Just then, she felt a hard and painful blow to her head, heard a loud crack; then everything went dark.

CHAPTER FOURTEEN

C asidhe's head was pounding so hard she could only see shades of grey when she could open her eyes a little. She noticed one of the tall, hairy beings was next to her. As soon as he realized she was waking up, he struck her hard across the face. She flew backward and felt blood spill from her nose and tasted it in her mouth. She was frightened, and her head hurt, but she was also confused and angry. *And where is Dana?*

"You can't kill her here. We are still on the Ranch. The magic protects her."

"I know that." Her attacker snarled.

"Get to the Maze. We can jump to the Sidhe from there."

"She is easier to carry if she is unconscious, but she has a hard head." He growled.

"We can't use magic to transport her either. So, we'll have to drag her."

And drag her they did. When she tried to fight back, they kicked her hard in the ribs. This knocked the wind out of her, and Casidhe had trouble breathing after that.

"We're almost there." The other one said. "Damn the protections on this place. If we could use magic, we'd be gone by now." The first one only grunted in response.

Casidhe was cold, shivering, and her whole body hurt, especially her head. She could feel they had entered a cave; the air changed, as did the smell. She could no longer see as both eyes had swollen shut. Her hands were bound, so she couldn't stop the blood from flowing down her face. She struggled to breathe, the pain in her head and chest excruciating. *Who are these people, and why are they attacking me? Where is Dana? Where is the pack? Aren't they supposed to protect me?*

Once they entered the cave, they dropped her to the ground, leaving her for a moment in pain and confusion. She went in and out of consciousness.

"Where is the entrance? I have never gone through this portal."

"Weren't you supposed to be prepared?" They were fighting amongst themselves.

"I am prepared. Didn't we get away from the whole pack and kidnap their precious heir, right from under their noses?"

"Yeah, that was great. Now let's not get caught on their land. It won't take them long to catch up."

"Here it is. Grab her, and let's get out of here!"

Just when she expected to be picked up and dragged again to wherever they were taking her, she heard another noise. There was a high-pitched, whirling sound, like a fast spinning top. Casidhe heard a grunt and thought it came from one of her attackers. One yelled something Casidhe didn't understand, and she could hear several bangs and grunts, followed by the spinning noise again and a thump like someone hit the cave floor. Finally, quiet. No sound at all for a minute. Casidhe could not make out what happened, and when she tried to move and get up, a searing pain stabbed her side. She collapsed to the ground again.

"Take it easy. We'll get you fixed up." She knew that voice but had trouble placing it. Her head hurt so.

"Who is it? What happened?" She mumbled, but her words came out garbled. Still, somehow, he knew what she wanted to know.

"It's me, Sven. A couple of Fuath tried to do you in. But I was on guard this time. They won't be after you again. At least not those two. Let's get you to the house." Sven touched her hands, and the ropes fell away. He lifted her gingerly in his arms, being much stronger than he appeared. They glided along for only a minute or two, but Casidhe lost consciousness. She was not sure how long it took but didn't think the whole incident had taken long. She sensed they entered the back of the house by the smells of food, but the pain was too much, and she welcomed the loss of her senses again.

When next she awoke, she felt a bed beneath her. Was it her bed? There were others around. She thought she heard Lesslyn and Kelly. She tried to speak. "Dana?"

"Yes, darlin'. She's here."

"Casidhe, I'm here. I'm okay. Rest now." Dana whispered in her ear, and she felt a light kiss on her cheek. Casidhe calmed down after that, and soon, she drifted off into a more restful sleep.

She woke up sometime later and could see the room around her. She was in a bed in the hospital room at the Ranch. There were tubes and wires around her. Neala, the pack doctor, stood nearby. Her head still pounded, and when she tried to adjust in the bed, a stab of pain went through her torso.

"Casidhe, don't move, if you can help it," Neala said, coming closer so she could see her without moving. "You have a concussion and two cracked ribs. You also have several contusions on your face and around your rib cage. All in all, not as bad as we feared when Sven brought you in."

Casidhe wondered how much worse it could be, and then she remembered one of her attackers talking about killing her, and she realized she was lucky. Lucky Sven was there. She owed him her life. She tried to smile, but her face hurt.

"Fuath are vicious creatures," Neala said.

With that, Kelly and Lesslyn both entered.

"It's good to see you awake. We were so frightened we'd lost you, and we would have if Sven had not been on hand," Kelly said through gritted teeth, his anger barely contained. "We should not have let our guard down. We almost repeated the same tragedy as what happened to your parents. Clearly, we still have a security issue." He shook his head and clenched his fists.

"Casidhe, you must rest and recover as quickly as you can," Lesslyn said, obvious concern in her voice but also an urgency Casidhe didn't understand. Maybe it was the concussion.

Neala spoke up. "Not today, you two. She won't be able to comprehend today. Give her until tomorrow."

"Okay, but we can't wait any longer than that. Ronan will need time with her beforehand."

"I know, but she wouldn't be any good now."

"Right."

Casidhe didn't know what they were talking about and had trouble concentrating. The world was fading, including the pain. She'd worry about it later; for now, she wanted to sleep. She heard words far away without any comprehension.

"I gave her a sedative. She is a State Changer, so she will heal fast, but you must give her at least 24 hours. She'll need longer before you put her in the ring with Ronan."

"We don't have that long; she'll have to try."

"Come back tomorrow; then, you can talk to her."

Kelly and Lesslyn left the room as Dana entered.

"Dana, you should be in bed." Lesslyn insisted.

"I know Mum, but I have to see her. I'll rest. I promise." Kelly pulled Lesslyn out of the room.

"Come on, Les, give her a minute. Neala won't let her stay."

Once they had gone, Dana came over and took Casidhe's hand in hers.

"She's out, Dana. She'll not be conscious for a while," Neala said on her way out the door.

"I know; I just want a minute."

Dana leaned down and kissed Casidhe on her purple cheek. "I almost lost you, and I only just found you. I don't know what all of this means, but I know I don't want to lose you. Get better soon." She squeezed Casidhe's hand.

Neala came back into the room.

"I'll be back," Dana said before she left.

Casidhe woke up many hours later, noticing her head had cleared a little. Neala was no longer in the room; instead, she saw a young man she remembered as Sean, the nurse. "How are you feeling?" he asked.

"Thirsty," she croaked.

"Yeah, the medication can do that. He brought her a cup with a straw, and she sipped hard, making her face hurt. She cringed.

"Take it easy. It will take a little bit for your wounds to heal, but State Changers heal fast, so that's good. Are you hungry?"

"No."

"That's okay; it's only been a few hours since the attack. You'll be hungry soon enough; probably in the morning, you'll be ravenous. I've seen it before." He smiled knowingly at her, and she decided to take his word for it and drifted back to sleep.

The next time Casidhe woke up, the sun shone in her window, and her head felt much clearer. She cautiously tried to shift in her bed, and though her side still hurt, it wasn't as piercing as it had once been. She reached up to feel her face. She could tell her lip was cut, and her cheek was still swollen and tender, but she could move. She shifted a little more when Neala came in, smiling.

"I never cease to be amazed at the healing powers of State Changers, especially since I work with humans all the time. You are looking better. I want to get another x-ray of your ribs to be sure they are healing properly, but you are on the mend. How does your head feel?"

"Much better, there is still a dull ache, but not the pounding I had before. How do I look?"

"Well, you will be purple and sore for a day or two, but you'll make a full recovery. Can I get you anything?"

"I think I am hungry. Sean said I would be, and he was right, I'm starving."

"That's normal for a wolf. You need protein to help heal. I believe Lesslyn is already on it."

Sure enough, Lesslyn came in with a tray of food. Steak and eggs, hash browns, and toast. Casidhe couldn't believe how much she wanted all of it.

"Well, you are looking better, and by the way you are eyeing this plate; you're hungry too."

"Yes, please." Casidhe started right in on the food without any more conversation. It hurt a little to chew, but she didn't care.

As she was finishing, Kelly came in too. "Well, that's more like it," he smiled at her and the almost empty plate. Neala left for a little, and Lesslyn handed over the cup and straw for Casidhe to wash it down.

She could tell they wanted to talk to her but waited for them to start.

"Casidhe, we are very sorry you were abducted and hurt right here at the Ranch. We were not expecting the attack, but we should have been. The Fuath managed to get onto the Ranch and nearly get you into the Sidhe. If that had happened, we would have lost you forever." He paused, letting that sink in a second. "We are worried another attack could happen soon. The Fuath are brutal, as you have experienced first-hand. They won't rest. We have to take further precautions to keep you safe." Kelly shifted his weight, obviously nervous to continue.

"You have to go through the initiation as soon as possible!" Lesslyn blurted out. Casidhe just stared back at her wide-eyed. She turned and looked at Kelly questioningly. He nodded in agreement.

"But how? I'm not ready. I can't now, can I?"

"Well, it is not ideal, but we don't have a choice. We can't wait two more months or even one, for that matter. We can't take the risk. Of course, even after you become a full State Changer, you will be in danger, but you will have a chance. As a human . . . every day you are human, you are at great risk."

"But Ronan said if I wasn't conditioned, the transformation could tear me apart." Her voice had risen higher.

"You will have a few days to get ready. The new moon is on the 6th. Today is the 2nd." Lesslyn pushed.

"But. How can I train with Ronan? I was just attacked and hurt."

Neala had come into the room quietly. "Casidhe, I know this is difficult to understand since this is your first experience with injury and healing. But as I told you before, State Changers heal very quickly, even those who haven't gone through the initiation yet. In 12 hours, you have healed more than most humans do in a week. If you eat well and continue to hydrate, you will be back to full health in three days."

Casidhe stared. Lesslyn got closer and touched her shoulder. "We don't want to cause you more pain, dear, but we can see no other way. We almost lost you, and Dana was hurt. The only chance we have is for you to become a full State Changer. Once you enter the initiation process, no one and nothing can touch you until you emerge on the full moon, which is January 21. The initiation is a full 15 days, beginning at midnight on the 6th and ending at midnight on the 21st. It takes that long to give each initiate time to come to terms with being a State Changer. Everyone's experience is different because every State Changer's gifts are different."

Casidhe couldn't believe what she was hearing and was sure her face showed it.

"You can recover today, but tomorrow–the 3rd–you will begin with Ronan. You'll still be sore, but you'll be well enough. You'll have four days with him. It will be hard work, and you will not like it much, but it could save your life," Lesslyn tried to convince her.

Kelly spoke up. "We cannot force you, of course. It is your decision. But we have sworn to protect you, and this is the only way we believe we can. You'll have today to think it over."

"There is one more thing that could play into your decision. The full moon in January is called the Wolf Moon. For State Changers, it is our most powerful moon. This year, two additional astronomical factors come into play during the Wolf Moon. There will be a full lunar eclipse that night. This will create changes in the light reflected on the moon from around the earth. The result is a Blood Moon. It means the moon will appear red in color. And if that were not enough, the moon will be close to the earth in its orbit, making it look larger. It's called a Super Moon. Together, the full moon on January 21st is a Super Blood Wolf Moon. This is rare and auspicious. I cannot say I know the full ramifications of becoming a State Changer on a Super Blood Wolf Moon, but I can say few have done so."

Casidhe didn't know what to say. She laid there, a blank look on her face. Neala stepped in.

"Let's give her some time, okay?" and she started shoo-ing them out of the room.

"Yes, of course. Rest and think it over," Lesslyn said as they left.

"Can I get you anything else?" Neala asked before she left the room too.

"I'd like to sit up more if I can manage it."

"Let me adjust the bed first." Before Neala had the bed upright, Casidhe was lifting herself enough to allow Neala to prop the pillows behind her. The effort was uncomfortable but not entirely painful. This surprised Casidhe. She had heard them say she would heal quickly, but she was beginning to believe it.

"Thank you, Neala. I appreciate all your care."

"No trouble at all. It is my job." She smiled and left.

After Neala left, Casidhe moved her legs around, then her arms. No trouble there. Her ribs were tender and her face sore, but she was shocked at how much better she felt. She touched her cheeks and jaw with her fingers accessing the damage when she heard the door open. Dana came in dressed in torn blue jeans and a red sweater; her dark hair pulled up in a ponytail. Casidhe was happy to see her but then felt self-conscious about her face. Dana instantly guessed what was happening and went to her side.

"You look great." She leaned in to kiss her quickly on the lips. It was so innocent, just a peck, but a hot glow spread over Casidhe, blushing her cheeks immediately.

"Are you okay?" Casidhe asked, reaching up and touching the light bruise on Dana's forehead.

"Who me? I'm fine. It's you they wanted. I was only in the way. Very conveniently." She winked.

Casidhe's blush deepened. Dana grabbed and held her hand.

"Cas, Mum, and Da told me about you going through the initiation process sooner. Do you think you can?" Casidhe had not moved past the new nickname Dana had just given her and knew she was falling hard for this woman.

"Um . . . I . . . I don't know. They think I can. The Super Blood Wolf Moon sounds important. What do you think?"

"I only know that Wolf and Super Moons are potent. I imagine if it is all happening at once, it would be a boost. But I really don't know what it means.

"It's not what anyone else thinks anyway; it's up to you. You must know your own resolve because that is what it takes, no matter what role the moon plays. For me, there was no thought about being a State Changer. As the heir to the Alpha, there was not much question. But the initiation is personal and demanding. You must know if you are ready. Which is hard since you don't know much about us yet." She trailed off for a second, contemplating their hands together.

"I will tell you what I do know." She looked up and leaned in closer to Casidhe's face, her eyes serious but a slight smile on her lips. "I know I don't want anything to happen to you. I know this is all new between us, but I don't want to lose you, and I almost did." Her smile faded, and a cloud of fear came over Dana's features. Casidhe reached up with her other hand and brushed Dana's cheek.

"But you didn't. I am still here."

"Yes, and I want you to stay, for a long time." This time Dana blushed a little, which Casidhe thought was not usual.

"I am not planning on leaving."

"Good." Dana's smile returned.

"What does the initiation entail? Why does it take so long?"

"Well, at first, your body has to adjust to shifting. It is physically demanding, and in the beginning, painful. But after you get used to it, then the real fun begins. You must learn to live as a wolf–hunting, killing, eating–all as a wolf. You'll have wolf instincts and appetites. Then after you get used to it, you must become human again. The back and forth is uncomfortable. Some don't want to be human again, and there have been those rare few who have not completed the transformation because of that. But we warn against this because those wolves end up going mad. The human mind can't exist in an animal form forever, and if you don't complete the process, you won't receive your Fae gifts – one of which is the ability for your mind to stay human even while in the form of a wolf. Fae gifts come at the end of the process after you shift back and forth between forms without effort or remorse. Then the Fae part enters, and our magical natures fuse with the rest of us. By the final night, we have become all three aspects of ourselves: Fae, Wolf, and Human. This is the complete transformation."

Casidhe was trying to imagine it. She had no idea what any of it would feel like; she had to take the word of others. Dana let her sit with the information for a few minutes, sitting close to the bed, holding her hand.

Casidhe looked into Dana's face, surveying her features, and she knew she wanted to look into this woman's eyes forever. She didn't know how they had come to such deep feelings in so short a time. Perhaps it was the dreams; maybe it was their destiny or fate. Whatever it was, it didn't change the fact that Casidhe knew for sure she would do anything to be with Dana.

"I would start today if it meant being with you." The look of shock and then pleasure on Dana's face was worth the risk of being honest with her. Casidhe tried to lighten the mood. "Besides, your parents seem to think I'd be done for, if I don't, so . . . self-preservation." She shrugged with a wide smile. Dana was grateful for Casidhe's joke but didn't want her to think she'd missed anything. She stood up and leaned in, kissing Casidhe softly on the lips, sealing their commitment to each other.

She could tell Dana intended it to be a quick kiss, being careful not to hurt her face further. But once soft lips touched soft lips, they neither would pull apart. Feather-light at first, their lips gently brushed each other's, getting to know one another. Then the wild desire flared from deep within them, and the kiss deepened with urgency; lip's parting, tongues tasting. Casidhe groaned into the kiss; Dana's taste was intoxicating. She couldn't understand her need to touch this woman.

The sound of Casidhe's groan fueled the exchange even more. Casidhe forgot about bruises and ribs, initiations, and attacks. She wanted only Dana.

Blaire found them this way several minutes later. She cleared her throat several times but without effect. Casidhe was vaguely aware of Blaire standing in the doorway, waiting for her presence to register through the passionate fog they were enveloped in. Blaire cleared her throat a little louder, but still no response. Not getting through to them, she came a little closer and banged her tray down on the table. That did it; they broke free of each other, looking up sheepishly at Blaire.

"Hello. I expected to find an attacked woman here in the hospital, but she seems to be missing. Have either of you seen her?" They laughed while Dana extracted herself from Casidhe's embrace and sat back in her chair again, trying to calm her breathing. Casidhe knew she was flushed and felt somewhat embarrassed at being caught in such a compromising embrace. But when she glanced at Dana, who didn't look embarrassed at all, she shrugged. *I mean, look at that woman, who could control themselves around such a beauty? At least it was Blaire who found us and not Lesslyn, or worse, Kelly.*

"I thought I'd bring you an early lunch. Lesslyn said you ate all your breakfast, and Neala said you would need plenty of food." Plenty was right. The tray was weighted down with two hamburgers, chips, salad, and fruit. To her surprise, Casidhe wanted it all and cleared the tray in no time.

Dana asked Blaire what else was happening around the Ranch.

"Kelly met with Sven, Ronan, and several of his most trusted pack members. Both Kelly and Lesslyn are supposed to talk to Saoirse later this afternoon. She is very concerned. New security measures are being placed around the property. I am not sure what they are, probably secret and magical, knowing Kelly. Lesslyn is on pins and needles, awaiting

Casidhe's decision. They have spoken to Ronan to be sure he is available the next few days in case you decide to go through with it. I think there is to be an all-pack meeting later tonight. An attack like that hasn't happened in 17 years." Casidhe knew Blaire was speaking about the attack that caused her parent's death. She wondered if Cian was safe. She decided to ask Kelly or Lesslyn when she saw them.

"Sounds about right. Mum and Da aren't taking any more chances."

That seemed to be a cue for Lesslyn to show up. She walked in and saw the empty tray and was pleased Casidhe was eating well. "You are looking better and better, Casidhe. How are you feeling? You look a little flush; is it too warm in here?"

Casidhe blushed more, knowing her rosy cheeks had nothing to do with the ambient temperature in the room. "No, I'm fine." She didn't dare look at Dana, sure Lesslyn would catch on if she did. She changed the subject.

"Lesslyn, I wanted to ask you if anyone has contacted Cian? Is he in any danger?"

"Yes, Kelly called Colm in Calgary this morning and told him what happened. Their pack is staying close to Cian. He is already a full State Changer, so I expect he is not the easiest target. But I am sure if the Fuath are determined enough, then you are both in danger. Colm's pack is strong. I trust they can keep Cian safe."

"I would like to meet my brother soon, but I can see right now would not be a good time." She only half-smiled. Casidhe wanted to meet her twin, having a lot of questions for him and about him. But putting both Keneally heirs in the same place would be too much of a risk. No, they should stay far apart for now. She also knew that she needed to be a full State Changer before they met, although she couldn't put her finger on why.

"Lesslyn, I would like to speak to Ronan before I make my decision on when to go through the initiation, if that is possible."

"That seems reasonable. He'll be here tonight, is that soon enough?"

"Yes, I'd like to get out of this hospital room and go to my room and take a bath. Is that okay?"

"Let me check with Neala. I'll be right back." Lesslyn left the room.

"I can take you upstairs and help you." Dana offered. And although Casidhe thought her intentions were mostly good, she decided that would not be the best for her recovery.

"Dana, as much as I would love that. I fear I would relapse almost immediately and end up back in bed – with you." She smiled broadly. "I think Blaire better help me if you don't mind, Blaire?"

"Not at all. Having seen you two, I would agree with Casidhe. She needs to rest, Dana; you know she does." Dana looked stricken, but for only a second. She threw up her hands, gave Casidhe another hungry look, and then got up to leave. "I have to call work anyway. I'll come to see you later, Cas." She blew her a kiss and made a quick exit before her mother returned. Lesslyn entered a moment later.

"Neala says it's fine. Try to limit yourself, but proceed with anything that doesn't cause you pain. If you do feel pain or dizziness, let one of us know right away. Okay?"

"Yup, I promise." Casidhe swung her feet over the edge of the bed and prepared to stand. Blaire and Lesslyn both stood on either side and assisted. She didn't feel as weak as expected. She took it slow, walking toward the door. Then she realized she was wearing a hospital gown.

"What happened to my clothes?"

"Ruined, I'm afraid. We had to throw them out."

"Damn, I loved that outfit. Oh, well." She was happy it was only her clothes that were ruined.

Blaire draped a robe across her shoulders to give her another layer on the trip up the stairs. Lesslyn stayed with them the entire trip, but seeing Casidhe doing fine, she left the two of them to manage at the door. In the end, Casidhe felt well enough to bathe and change alone, but Blaire stayed close by in case she was needed.

"I don't remember having any childhood illnesses. So, I have nothing to compare with this rapid healing." She called from the bathroom.

"The reason you didn't have any childhood illnesses is because of your heritage. Most State Changers do not have illnesses. If they do, they tend to be severe. That is why I am such an anomaly, and why many didn't want me to be part of the pack. No one has ever heard of a State Changer with autism before. Even though it could be worse, it was outside of anyone's experience."

"Wow. I didn't think of that. So that is why I didn't miss any school days. I was never sick. Huh. Well, I don't know much about autism, but you seem normal to me."

"Maybe you don't know what normal is."

Casidhe had to look around the door to see that Blaire was kidding with her. "Haha."

After Casidhe was clean and dressed in sweats, she curled up on the couch opposite Blaire and asked, "So aside from me getting attacked, what else happened New Year's night?" She raised her eyebrows at Blaire, hinting at what she wanted to know.

"Brody did kiss me, and it was very nice. He asked if we could go out tonight, but that's before everything happened, so it's postponed."

"Oh, I'm sorry. I don't want my issues interfering with everyone else's lives."

"But that is how it is with the pack. We always adjust based on others. That is how we live."

"Yeah, I can see that. Well, I hope you two get to go out soon."

"I am sure we will." Blaire was always so matter-a-fact. Casidhe appreciated that about her. She went into a giant yawn.

"You should rest. I'll check in on you later. Or someone will. But maybe not Dana."

"Oh, come on," Casidhe said but only half-heartedly. As much as she would love to see Dana again, she secretly hoped she wouldn't come by yet. She needed to keep her wits about her, and that proved impossible around Dana.

Casidhe napped for a couple of hours, waking up famished. She didn't understand how she could eat so much. They weren't kidding when they said she needed food to heal. She got up, washed her face, and changed. By the look of the light coming in the windows, it was late afternoon, and she wondered if they were making dinner yet. As soon as she walked out her door, however, Blaire was there, staying with her down to the bottom of the stairs and into the kitchen. Lesslyn came over when they entered.

"You are looking better. Another day and you will be good as new. Are you hungry?"

"Yes, somehow, I am starving."

"Well, sit at the table, and I'll bring you some stew and bread."

After she polished one bowl, Lesslyn brought her a refill. "Ronan will be here soon, so you are just in time. The rest of the pack won't be here for another hour."

"That's great."

She didn't have to wait long. He entered, looking as handsome as ever. Compared to Ronan, Casidhe felt a wreck. *How can he always look so good?*

They went into the library, and Casidhe got right to it. "Kelly and Lesslyn think I need to go through the initiation right away to give me the best chance of survival against another attack. They feel sure there will be another. Since I am still healing from the last one, I am concerned I won't be ready for the initiation process in only four days. I want to know what you think."

Ronan did not speak for a full minute as he considered his answer. "Physical training is first and foremost . . . mental. You must be ready and committed. Your body can do much more than you think it can. That is true of humans and State Changers alike. State Changers have special powers, of course, but the truth is, when we decide we want to do something, we almost always can. I'm not going to lie to you. It is going to be difficult. Probably the most challenging thing you have ever done. The first day of training will be the worst. But each day will be hard. You must be dedicated and focused. Once you enter the initiation process, there is no going back. You have to see it through to the end.

"I will do my best to prepare you. At the end of the four days of training, I will know if you are ready to make it through the initiation. If I think you cannot handle it by then, I will tell you. But, no matter what I say, it is up to you. In the end, only you will know."

Casidhe was quiet for a long time. He did not interrupt her thoughts. Finally, she said, "Problem is, I don't know yet either. I have never pushed myself that hard before, not physically. So, I guess we'll both have to decide at the end of the four days."

"That's honest. Then you are committed to training as hard as you can with me until the end of January 6th?"

"Yes." Again, the silence stretched between them. Casidhe would see Dana later, but she would not see her again until the end of her training. She knew she couldn't focus if she did. *Then what? We'll see, I guess.* She smiled at Ronan.

"Okay, then. I will be here at 7:00 tomorrow morning. Be ready. The type of clothing you have on now is suitable. Meet me in the barn arena."

"I'll be there." *Oh, shit. What am I doing?* She was more than a little frightened of what Ronan had in store for her.

That evening, they had the all-pack meeting that Casidhe did not attend since she was not a full State Changer yet. She didn't care; she had other things on her mind. She retired to her rooms early after dinner to rest up. She tried to write in her journal, but she had trouble concentrating. When she was about to give up and go to bed, she heard a faint knock at her door.

"Come in."

Dana entered. "I wanted to see you before you begin training tomorrow." Casidhe was about to tell her that they had to keep their distance for a few days after tonight when Dana interrupted.

"You don't have to say it, Cas. I know. I don't want you to be distracted by anything, including me. You have to give it your all, and I know what happens between us is . . . overwhelming." She smiled provocatively. Casidhe could feel the now-familiar warmth begin to rise within her. She was about to move into Dana's arms when Dana put out her hands to stop her. "Wait. I just want to tell you, I believe in you. I think you can do this. I know you'll handle whatever Ronan dishes out. And in my mind, you are already a State Changer, though I can't wait for you to embrace the passion of the wolf." Casidhe took a step closer. "Anyway, I think you'll go through Ronan's training with flying colors. But, if at the end of the training, you don't think you're ready, I'll support you in that too."

Casidhe had continued her advancement into Dana, and with each word of encouragement and support, Casidhe had moved slowly closer. By the time Dana finished her speech, Casidhe was directly in front of her. When Dana shut up, Casidhe closed the gap, and they embraced. It was a turbulent kiss, each trying to convey their feelings without allowing their desire to take over. A kiss of the heart, tender but poignant. Pulling apart slightly, they let their foreheads touch.

"Thank you." They were so close their voices were barely above a whisper.

"Always, Cas."

"I like that, the way you shortened my name."

"I can't wait to find out what else you like."

"You, everything about you."

"You don't know everything about me."

"But I want to."

They were heating up fast again and knew it. It took all their resolve to pull apart.

"I'm gonna go. I will see you in four days."

"Okay." Casidhe didn't want her to leave but hoped she would before she asked her to stay.

Dana kissed her quickly, turned, and shut the door behind her.

Casidhe took a deep breath and went to her bed, collapsing. *What on earth have I gotten myself into?*

CHAPTER SIXTEEN

For the next four days, Casidhe only spent time with Ronan. Blaire was in the kitchen early, prepared her breakfast, and brought food periodically throughout the day. Otherwise, it was all Ronan, all the time.

He pushed her, pulled her, barked at her, and encouraged her. He was her trainer, coach, torturer, and friend. He hurt her and then hurt her some more. They ran the rink inside and even outside when it wasn't snowing. They did lunges and pushups and pull-ups and lifted weights. She was on the ground, on a large ball, on ropes, bars, and on the ground again.

They did deep, slow breathing and long stretches to start. Then they did the circuit of machines. He increased the difficulty and strapped weights to her arms and ankles. They walked. They ran. Then rested and breathed and stretched again. All the while, Ronan talked to her. Casidhe had never been around anyone like Ronan–strong and beautiful, but also hard and determined. He spoke to her of things she had never heard anyone say to anyone, let alone to her.

"You can be all you want to be . . . You can do anything you want to do . . . You are the best you . . . You are one of a kind . . . You are strong . . . You are stronger than you think . . . You can do it . . . You can do more . . . Look how strong you are."

The first day sucked so badly. Her rib cage felt tender, and her head started pounding again after two hours, but she didn't speak of it. He was so sure she could do it, she believed it too. She pushed through the pain. At the end of the day, Ronan explained why he said such positive things to her all day.

"Never put yourself down, Casidhe. It always weakens you. Acknowledge your strengths, and you always have strengths, even when you don't feel them. Genuinely give yourself credit whenever you can. Tearing yourself down will defeat you before you even get started. Speak kindly to yourself about yourself. It strengthens you." She slept hard on the first night after a huge meal, dreaming only of what Ronan had told her all day.

Day two started early, and the stretching session went longer; the running extended further; the weights got heavier, and the rests were shorter. She felt tired by midafternoon, but Ronan saw it coming. He told her a story about a Fae princess.

Aislinn was taken from her Fairy parents and placed in a human home. She felt so different; no matter how they cared for her, she felt like she did not belong. They loved her, and she tried to be happy, but when she was old enough, she left, leaving behind a gift for their kindness. Since they were a poor farming family, she left them a golden chalice. They couldn't believe it and blessed her, though they would gladly have given it up if she would return. She searched everywhere for her real family, over the sea and into the mountains. She searched deep within Tír na nÓg for many years.

Never finding them, she returned to her human family but was too late. They had died when robbers came to kill them for their gold. She was sad for a long time, but in the end, she decided to farm their land and take care of what was theirs. One day a traveler came through and asked for food and water. She made him dinner and gave him a place to sleep for the night. In the morning, he was gone. She was sad to see him go but wished him well. In nine months, she bore a male child that looked like the traveler. She thought she should be angry but wasn't. She loved the child and raised him on the farm. When he was full-grown, she got sick and died, but she had found peace and happiness on the farm. Her son soon married and had children of his own. For many generations, the farm has thrived, and still to this day, bares the descendants of the fairy princess. Aislinn learned to make peace with her fate and appreciate what she had.

Ronan told the tale with such detail and passion Casidhe lost her pain to the story. When he finished telling it, another day had ended. She couldn't believe how time had passed and how much she had endured.

Ronan explained. "What you focus on will always dictate your experience. If you focus on something exciting and new, you will feel that excitement. If you focus on the pain, you will feel the pain all the more. This is true in all of life. Remember this when you are going through the initiation." She considered this through her long bath and a hot meal. Drifting off to sleep, she was still contemplating the fairy princess.

On day three, they began as the two days before–breathing and stretching. They sat for a long while with their eyes closed, exhaling long and deep. Each out-breath, Ronan would remind her to let go of the pain, or let her muscles relax completely, or feel the perfection of this moment. "Don't go anywhere else. Stay right here in this spot, listening to what your body says to you. Feel the strength of your muscles and the sharpness of your mind. Feel the life in your breath and the beat of your heart."

Then they got up and ran for five miles. She felt stronger and faster. By the end, she was breathing hard but wasn't exhausted. Not yet. They went to the machines, and she lifted more weight than she had ever thought possible. Again, and again. Rep after rep, until her muscles felt like jelly. All the while, he would ask her, "What are you focusing on?" She would tell him, and he would show her level of strength or weakness in response to those thoughts. "Focus on the feeling of laughing with a friend. Or a carefree walk in the woods. Focus on anything that feels good to you–that feels happy." She would try it, and before she knew it, she was pushing and pulling more and more. They did this all afternoon. Focus then lift. Focus then lift. She marveled at what she could do. She found the source of her strength inside her mind and her ability to focus on whatever she wanted.

By the end of the 3rd day, she was exhausted but exhilarated. She could barely move, but she didn't mind.

Day four dawned altogether differently. She woke up so sore she could not move without her body screaming at her. She had no idea how she would work out another day. She dragged her body to the kitchen for breakfast, then put on her coat and headed for the barn. Once inside, she found Ronan waiting for her. He looked at her hard and nodded.

"I expected as much. We will have a short run to warm up today, and then I have something else in store."

Great. A run. Casidhe was not excited. Her body rebelled. No focus, no happy feelings, no stories, no strength. She was just plain tired. She didn't know how she would train today and then go into the initiation tonight. She felt defeated.

Ronan acted like he didn't notice and started around the track. She followed slowly, shuffling her feet along. He did not stop but didn't go too fast either. She kept pace behind him, stumbling along at a slow jog. After circling the track a couple of times at this pace, he picked it up a little. At first, she couldn't tell but soon realized he had increased the pace slightly and that she had followed his lead, maintaining the same distance between them. It was such a tiny increase. Two laps later, he again picked up the tempo. This happened again and again for three hours. Every two laps, he would run just a little bit faster, hardly enough to notice. Each time she would follow suit, thinking it wasn't that much difference. After a few laps, he started humming a tune. By the end of the second hour, he sang a raucous song full of vulgarity and profanity. He would laugh and continue. It wasn't a complicated tune, so she joined him, and soon, they were both laughing at the song and moving along at a good tempo. By midway through the third hour, Ronan picked up the pace once more, and this time, she noticed they were running hard. But she didn't seem to mind, and her body acquiesced. The singing stopped after two more laps when Ronan began sprinting. Casidhe saw him shoot off, running full out to cross the invisible finish line. She tore off after him. At the end of the second lap, he collapsed, laughing hysterically, and she beside him.

"How?" was all she could get out between gulps of air. He didn't answer right away, catching his breath. Once he could speak, he explained.

"Sometimes, you must fool your body a little bit at a time. The only way to eat an elk is one bite at a time, right? And the only way to accomplish a big task is one little bit at a time. Step by step, until you cross the line. You did it. You didn't think you could, but you did. Do you know you ran over 15 miles this today? If I had said you would run 15 miles or for over three hours when we started, you would have rebelled and given up. But, by staying present and only increasing slightly, you were able to do it. Now that you know my secret, you can use it for yourself. You just do a little bit at a time, increasing ever so slightly, and before you know it, you have completed the task. Even impossible tasks."

Casidhe stared at him. Ronan truly was a master trainer. "Now what?"

"Now, you rest. Have a nice long bath, lunch, and a nap. In my opinion, you will make it through the initiation process. I'm not saying it will be easy, but I believe you can do it. I have seen your strength and your stamina, and what is in your heart. You can do this. That is my expert opinion."

"You are sure?"

"Yes. It still depends on your state of mind. But yes. Just remember what you have learned in the last four days, and you will make it."

She sat quietly for a few minutes. Then she got up and gave him a sweaty hug. "Thank you, Ronan."

"You're welcome, Casidhe."

When she entered the house, Neala was waiting and asked her to come back into the hospital room. Casidhe followed her, a little confused.

"I'd just like to check you out before you make any decisions, if you don't mind."

"Yes, of course. I'm exhausted, but I don't feel any residual pain from the injuries."

"That's good."

"I don't understand how I was able to build muscle and progress in the training so fast."

"It is part of your body's abilities. Since your muscles can heal so fast, they can grow fast too."

Casidhe sat on the bed, and Neala listened to her chest and heart. She asked about her head and if she had any head-aches. She inspected her eyes and touched the spots on her head and cheek where bruises had been. Casidhe felt limp and sweaty, but okay.

"You need to rest. Here, drink this." Neala handed her a cup of hot liquid.

"What is it?"

"It's an herbal remedy from my great grandmother, who was a druidess. Not all medicine is western." She said, wink-ing at Casidhe. "It will allow you to rest the afternoon and help restore your aching muscles."

"Great." But when Casidhe tasted it, she squeezed her eyes shut tight and screwed her mouth. "It doesn't taste very good."

"I know. Sorry about that. I am not sure why medicine is always unpleasant, but it works. Drink it down."

Casidhe tried hard not to gag as she swallowed the bitter drink, but she drained the cup.

"Now, off to the showers and bed with you."

"Thanks, doc."

Casidhe left the hospital room and went looking for Less-lyn. The large bathtub was calling, but she needed to give Kelly and Lesslyn a decision. She didn't find either of them. But she did find Blaire.

"Hi, Blaire. Do you know where Kelly or Lesslyn are?"

"I'm not sure. How are you feeling?"

"Exhausted. I am off to the bath. Can you please tell Less-lyn or Kelly to prepare for the initiation tonight? I am moving forward."

"Sure," She said and left.

As the hot water washed away the sweat and dirt, she be-gan to feel drowsy. She dried off, threw on a long cotton t-shirt, and climbed into bed.

She thought the drink Neala had given her must be powerful because she could no longer keep her eyes open. She saw the clock numbers reflect: 1:00. *I should be hungry, but I don't have the energy to get food.*

CHAPTER SEVENTEEN

The sun had gone down long before Casidhe stirred. In her sleepy haze, she felt a warm presence join her under the covers.

"Cas, it's me."

Casidhe vaguely became aware of Dana's smell as she reached for consciousness and the warm body beside her.

"Mmmm," she murmured as she wrapped her arms around Dana and nuzzled into her. She was sure this was a dream, and she didn't want to wake up. Casidhe laid there wrapped up with Dana as contentment permeated her exhausted body. She was in that in-between state of sleep and wakefulness. Dana's arms held her tight and stroked her hair, and Casidhe didn't move.

"Cas, I would be delighted to stay here with you like this, but you have to eat. It's getting late, and there are preparations." Casidhe didn't hear the rest, then she heard, ". . . going through with the initiation tonight."

Lack of consciousness muted Dana's words, but the last part caught her attention. As she slowly woke, Casidhe knew she needed to get up. She groaned. In her next wakeful moment, she felt Dana reposition herself and lean in to brush their lips together. Almost without volition, Casidhe responded. The kiss quickly became a long exploratory encounter. Casidhe moaned, but this time she was fully awake, her body leaning into Dana's. Her hands wandered over Dana's back, tangling in her hair. Casidhe kissed Dana with abandon, her desire escaping the bonds she didn't know she had on it. Dana tried to protest and pulled back. Their lips barely apart, Casidhe could tell it took great effort to withdraw.

"Cas. We can't. Not yet." Dana whispered desperately.

"Why?" Casidhe whined.

"The initiation. Remember?"

"No." Casidhe knew she was being difficult, but right now, she didn't care. She leaned into Dana's lips, trying to kiss her again. Dana backed up a little more.

"My god, woman, if you kiss me like that again, there is no way you will make the initiation tonight. Then you'll have to wait a whole month for the next new moon."

Casidhe dropped back against her pillow, trying to clear her head. *Initiation. Ugh.* "I know. I'm sorry."

"Oh, please don't be sorry about this." She leaned over Casidhe, kissing her lightly on the nose. "I just don't want you to be sorry later."

Casidhe smiled weakly. "It will be a while before we can get back here."

"I know, but you're worth waiting for."

"How do you know?"

"Instinct." Dana smiled wickedly.

Neither one could move yet. Casidhe closed her eyes so she could focus, trying to coax herself. *You must do this, Casidhe. You must become a State Changer. It's what you want, remember? Dana won't leave. She'll be here when you finish.*

Casidhe opened her eyes again. "I do want to do the initiation." She said softly, her eyes pleading.

"I know Cas. So, let's get you moving." Dana extracted herself from Casidhe, rolling over and climbing out of bed. She straightened her clothes, which were very much askew. Casidhe watched, wondering how she had found this woman. *Really. How did I dream of her, and now here she is?* She shook her head and got out of the bed, her muscles not as sore as they should be after the beating of the last few days. Turning the corner into the bathroom, she looked back at Dana.

Dana grinned. "Get dressed before Mum shows up and wonders why I haven't brought you down to dinner yet."

"Be ready in a minute." She called, not believing how much better her body felt. That potion Neala had given her was magical. She could tell she had pushed herself hard in the last few days, but she was no longer exhausted. She felt stronger than she had ever felt. Looking at her reflection in the mirror, she saw new muscles forming. Then, her stomach grumbled when she came out into the sitting room where Dana waited. Casidhe had put on a pair of comfortable jeans and a navy sweatshirt. She pulled on socks and shoes and tied her hair up in a ponytail with the rubber band from around her wrist.

Dana watched her every move, but made no comment or motion in her direction, which was best.

"I'm ready." Casidhe finally said. "And I am starving."

Dana grabbed her hand and pulled her out the door. "Well then, let's get some of Mum's amazing food in ye." Casidhe laughed at Dana's attempt at her mother's Irish accent.

They arrived hand-in-hand in the kitchen. Kelly, Lesslyn, Blaire, and Brody were there, but they had eaten some time ago. Neala and Ronan had both gone home. Kelly frowned at the closeness of his daughter with Casidhe. Dana saw the look, let go of Casidhe's hand, and went up to him. "Da, don't be cross." She said as she kissed him on the cheek. He looked at her smiling face, and the frown faded away. She clearly had a way with the Alpha. He turned and addressed Casidhe.

"How are you feeling, Casidhe?"

"I am feeling good. Much better than I expected to feel after Ronan's training."

"And you still want to proceed with the initiation?"

"Yes. When does it start, and how does it work?"

"Since the new moon is always at different times, the initiation process starts at midnight on the day of the new moon and ends at 12:01 on the morning of the full moon. As stated, this is a Super Blood Wolf Moon." Kelly shook his head in amazement.

"There is a protocol. Get some food, and I will run through it."

Casidhe filled up her plate to the rim with all the food left out for her and began eating while Kelly continued. Everyone else sat around and listened. Dana stayed close.

"You will need the moonstone your family left you. It is handed down from generation to generation and has Fae

powers to aid in the shifting process. Also, there's a liquid potion Neala has created that helps with the pain during the first
state change. You will enter the Initiate Shack a few minutes
before midnight, and we'll lock the door. When you feel the
time is right, you will drink the liquid and hold the stone in
your non-dominant hand. This activates your wolf instincts.
The rest will happen naturally. The only way to leave the
Shack in the next two weeks is through the wolf door, and it
is also the only way to get back in. You are encouraged to shift
into your wolf form as often as you can and stay in that form
as long as you want, in the beginning. You will get hungry;
you will hunt and drink and run as a wolf. No one can touch
you during this time. The Dagda himself put strong magic over
this process. Once you touch the stone on a new moon, no
one can harm you until the next full moon, not even the Fuath."

This was good to know. Casidhe didn't want to be accosted
in the woods as she ran around as a wolf. Her stomach gave
a quick lurch. *Am I really doing this?*

"After you are comfortable with your wolf and have accepted and aligned with that part of your nature, you will feel
as if you are ready to emerge from the Shack. However, there
is still the Fae aspect of your being to come forward. This
transformation is unique to each person. No one's experience
is the same. I cannot say what will happen during this part. I
can only tell you that you will know when it is complete. At
12:01 on January 21st, you will emerge a full State Changer."

No one spoke. Casidhe thought she should have questions.
Would she kick herself later for not asking them? She couldn't
think of one. It all seemed too surreal.

"I have made it out to be very simple, and it is simple. But
it is not easy. In fact, it is quite difficult."

"I guess I will just have to go through it."

Lesslyn spoke, "You will do fine. You are much stronger
than you realize, and Ronan has prepared you well. I want to
stress; we cannot be of any assistance once the process has
started. There can be no interaction with anyone else. It is
your own nature that must guide you and see you through."

"I understand," Casidhe said but knew she didn't. What did her nature have to show her? The idea that she would soon be a wolf . . . She cleared her throat and nodded.

"Very well. Then eat up as much as you like. Brody has heated the Shack, so you do not have to worry about freezing in there tonight. You have a couple of hours before it begins."

Casidhe smiled slightly to put them all at ease. She and Dana helped with the cleanup, and then they retired to the great room around the fire. Dana and Casidhe sat on the couch together, holding hands. Casidhe was a little skeptical at first, showing affection around Kelly and Lesslyn, but Dana was so comfortable with it that Casidhe relaxed.

Casidhe was fidgety. She watched the clock, and when 11:30 came, she excused herself and went upstairs. She decided to change into comfortable, warm sweats again. She grabbed the bag with the stone from her parent's and looked at the ring. She decided against taking it too. Not even her mother could come with her on this adventure. She grabbed an extra pair of socks and her toiletry bag. She thought a toothbrush might come in handy when she wasn't a wolf. She shivered at that thought. She gazed around one last time and couldn't think of anything else, hurrying back down to the great room. Blaire and Brody were not there.

"Is it time?"

"Yes," said Kelly and Lesslyn in unison.

Dana got up from the couch, hugged her tight, and then kissed her quickly. "I will be here when you return." She winked and turned and left the room. Casidhe silently thanked her for making the separation easier.

Blaire entered with a sealed bottle of liquid. "You will want this later." She said, handing it to Casidhe.

"Thanks."

Kelly and Lesslyn each embraced her and kissed her on the head, and wished her well. Brody came in the door and said he would escort her. She put her coat on and headed out with him, not turning to look at the others as she left.

When they reached the Shack, Casidhe saw a small lamp on, giving it a cozy look. As Lesslyn said, it felt warm inside. She set down her things on the small side table, shivering, despite the temperature.

"Do you have your stone?"

"Yes."

"Good. Just follow your instincts, Cas, and remember what Ronan taught you."

"Right." Casidhe noticed Brody used her new nickname too.

Brody gave her a big smile and then closed the door. Casidhe could hear the lock go into place and noticed for the first time that the door had a smaller wolf door at the bottom. If you were a little person, you could fit through it, but it was clearly made for wolves.

Casidhe went over to the bed and sat on the edge. *Now what? Should I pull the stone out now? Or should I rest? I am going to be here for two weeks; perhaps I should sleep.* She laid back on the bed and thought about Dana and their most recent experience. Casidhe marveled, not for the first time, at how much she was attracted to Dana. She had never felt anything so intense before. *Is it her, or is it the wolf?* Casidhe didn't know, but the pull was undeniable.

Casidhe was grateful that, for a long while, nothing but Dana filled her mind until she drifted off to sleep. An hour later, she woke with a start, but she could tell it was still dark outside. What had roused her? She listened intently, lying completely still. Nothing. She relaxed and dozed off again.

Past dawn, she woke up and had to take a second to remember where she was. It reminded her of the time she had spent on the road in hotel rooms. Each night a new place. She got up and stretched. *It must be early; it's quiet.* She got a drink of water and sat back down on the bed. She started to relax a little but worried she shouldn't.

She wasn't hungry yet. This was good since she had no food. She decided to do some exercises to warm up and get her blood flowing. She stretched as Ronan had taught her and exhaled, trying to clear her mind when she heard the unmistakable sound of a wolf howl. Her head jerked toward the small door expecting a wolf to enter. Nothing happened. After a few moments, her heartbeat regained its regular pace.

Then, she heard the howl once more. This time it sounded closer. And again. Still closer. Her heart was beating fast. Was it a friendly wolf? Would it attack her? Kelly had said she was safe, but maybe he meant from Fae interference. Was she supposed to be a wolf by now? Maybe he figured she could hold her own against other wolves. But she wasn't a wolf yet, and she still didn't know how. She walked over to the table and held up the end of the bag that contained the moonstone. It rolled out and stopped just at the edge of the small table. The howls were close now; the hair on the back of her neck stood up. She didn't know what to do. 'Follow your instincts, ' they had said to her. *What are my instincts? Mostly to run.* But she couldn't go anywhere, so she reached out and grabbed the stone.

CHAPTER EIGHTEEN

P ain shot through her arm and up into her head, causing her to cry out. She squeezed her eyes shut and pushed her palms into the sockets as her mind struggled with too many pain sensations at the same time. A roaring hot furnace ignited from inside her body, making her blood feel as if it were on the verge of boiling. She stumbled toward the small table where the bottle of pain reliever sat, but she fell to the floor, screaming out in agony. Electric spasms shot through her, convulsing her limbs and chest. She squinted, blindly reaching for the table, afraid to let any light in through her eyes. On hands and knees, grunting and gasping, she reached out and caught the leg of the table, but a stronger wave of tremors flooded her body, causing her to scream out again. Tears streamed down her face, but she hardly noticed as she lost all control and vomited on the floor in front of her, unable to reach the toilet nearby. She gripped the leg of the table, causing the container to topple over and roll under the bed. She dove for it, but it rolled out of reach as her arms and legs refused to work properly.

Another wave of unbearable agony hit her hard, causing her to shriek as it pulsed through her body. The heat now felt like hot marbles rolling under her skin, attempting to push their way out. She tried to pull her arms in and wrap them around herself, trying anything to make the pain ease. Suddenly, the muscles in her face seized as if her mouth were being ripped open. Her hands flew up to grip her cheeks, hoping to keep her face together, but the agony continued to rip through her. With what little logical mind she had, she thought only, "*bottle.*" She braced herself for another wave, and sure enough, her skin prickled and began to pulse. She screamed again and again. Finally, when she could take in a ragged breath, she lunged under the bed and grasped the bottle with one outstretched hand. Breathing hard, she curled up in a ball, bracing herself for another wave.

This time, she knew for sure her head would pop as her senses exploded with colors and shapes, smells, and noises, so many, so loud, she could not withstand them. She tried to cover her ears, but her hands were full. She laid on the floor, grunting and groaning. When she could take no more, the wave subsided enough to allow her to unscrew the cap on the bottle and gulp down the liquid. She doubted it would stay down, but to her surprise, it did, as a low-pitch hum began ringing in her ears. The liquid didn't taste pleasant, but it seemed to dull her senses just enough. In another moment, she could uncurl and sit on the floor, her head resting on her fists, her hands still occupied. She drank the rest of the liquid and dropped the bottle. In her other hand, she still held the stone. At no point did she consider releasing it, never really knowing why.

After sitting there for a moment, another wave came over her, but the intensity had slacked off. It still hurt like hell, but after what she had already endured, she could handle it. Then the pain increased once more, and she knew if she hadn't drunk the liquid, she would not have survived. She pushed herself up on all fours and screamed. She didn't stop screaming for a long time. As her voice went horse, her bones and skin rearranged themselves. Her back arched, and she ripped her clothes off while she still could. Soon she no longer had arms, only front legs, and hind legs. Her mouth protruded and grew into a muzzle while fangs extended from her top and bottom jaws. Her skin stung with a million pinpricks as she sprouted hair over every inch of her body. As the transformation continued, Casidhe's incessant shrieks filled the air of the tiny Shack.

Then the screams stopped. And the howls began. She felt a tail sprout from her backside, redistributing her weight. She felt her ears perk up high on her head, extending her range of hearing. She felt her eyes change, and with them, her perception of the world around her.

Finally, the howls stopped too, and only whimpers remained. Casidhe knew without looking; she was fully transformed into a wolf. She could feel the stone under her left paw. She had not lost contact with it. She did not dare move, being wholly depleted. Silence. Only it wasn't silent. She could hear so many sounds. The scampering of tiny feet. Cars off in the distance. A dog barking miles away. She could hear muffled voices from the house and the animals stomping and chewing in their stalls in the barn. Her ears moved this way and that, taking in the noises, trying to identify them.

Just as she got used to her new hearing, new smells entered her nose and filled her brain. The instincts and processing of the wolf-mind were working in tandem with the human mind as if a struggle for dominance was taking place. While identifying smells, part of her wanted to investigate. But she knew it was too soon to leave the safety of the Shack, even as a wolf. Still smell after smell assaulted her, challenging her, enticing her, and occasionally alarming her. She noticed she did not feel fear the same as a wolf. It presented more as an aversion than fear to her wolf mind. The exhaust of the trucks, the smell of a bear, and most assuredly, the scent of humans gave her a tangible 'stay away' feeling.

Contrastingly, the smell of a hare family nearby made her nose twitch and her fur tingle. She wanted to go after them. *Not yet. Soon, but not yet.* Her strength greatly diminished by the transformational process; she knew she needed to hunt and eat soon. She weighed the balance between the need to rest and the need to eat and decided to rest a little longer.

She laid on her back haunches, front legs straight out before her, stone still beneath her and her head down on the floor. Sounds and smells were slowly being adjusted and filed in her mind so as not to overwhelm her. She closed her eyes and opened them again. Colors were different, muted. But her field of vision was broader, shades and shadows revealing more than before.

She pushed up her hind legs, keeping her front legs down, extending her back into the air, creating a long stretch. Afterward, she rose up on all four legs. She shook her whole body, starting at the head, and felt a vigorous shiver move along her neck, torso, and back, all the way to her tail. *Wow, a tail.* She felt it move up and down, back and forth. Her center of gravity shifted with the addition of the tail. At the end of the shake, all her fur extended, she felt warm. Then she yawned, a huge yawn that pushed her mouth open, her lips back, exposing her teeth and fully extending her long tongue. This effort not only relaxed her but also heightened her senses. She slowly walked over to the mirror, for the first time losing contact with the stone, to survey her new body.

She expected to see a wolf in the mirror, but nothing could prepare her for the shock of staring at her own reflection and seeing something so dramatically different than what she had seen her entire life. Golden, orange eyes stared back at her. She moved closer until her black nose left a wet mark on the mirror. At that moment, she could smell the faint scent of the wolves who had been there before her. She was not the first to use this Initiate Shack, nor would she be the last. She backed up a little and turned her head from side to side, examining her fur coat, which appeared to be a mix of brown, black, and white with ruddy patches on either side of her muzzle, on her ears, and along both sides of her body and down her tail. The combination gave her a rusty appearance. The fur around her neck and down the center of her back was long, and unlike human hair, it responded to her thoughts. She could make it stand on end or bush out in every direction. She yawned once more and was astounded at how long her tongue, and sharp her teeth appeared. After another full-body shake, she decided she had seen enough. It was time to experience what this new wolf body could do.

Padding over to the small door, she put her head down and pushed hard through it until emerging on the outside of the Shack. She felt the temperature difference but did not feel cold. It was early in the day, and the Ranch still sounded quiet. She trotted toward the woods. It felt strange to be on four feet instead of two, but not unpleasant. She noticed how the joints in her legs bent back and then flung out, extending her legs and splaying her paws as they met the ground. *Weird.* Despite the events of the last few days and the horrible pain it took to be in this body, she felt amazingly strong and agile.

She took a detour to the east edge of the vast field, not far away. When she reached the open area, she stretched out and began to run. She marveled at how her body flew through the air, often with none of her feet on the ground at all, followed by all four feet meeting the earth in succession, alternating left and right, front and back, propelling her further and faster. She was free, more than free; she felt complete abandon as she glided across the snow-covered field. The pads of her paws barely touched the cold, wet snow beneath them.

The breeze moved through her fur as her muscles extended and contracted, pushing her forward. She smelled the dirt and the trees in a way she never had. She was no longer human. She was an animal, part of the natural world. She spotted a stream trickling along a path through the trees, trotting to a stop next to it; she paused to taste.

The mundane experience of taking a drink was all new. Casidhe's long tongue extended into the water and entered the stream, wrapping around a few droplets and quickly bringing them back into her mouth. She repeated the process again and again, mesmerized by the practice of lapping up water. Once her thirst was quenched, she sat on her back haunches to look around—colors registered differently, less variety but more detailed and with a broader range of vision. A slight flutter caught her attention, while, at the same moment, she smelled the musky aroma of a female deer just before it came into view. She watched it for one beat of her heart, then the wolf instincts overcame all thought, and she sprang into action, on its heels in a matter of seconds. The dear darted this way and that. Casidhe followed. The deer jumped over a fallen log, and she did the same, sailing through the air, once again flying. Her tongue dangled out of her mouth, flapping. She let go, experiencing the most exhilarating freedom she could imagine. Soon the deer did a double jump and darted right. Casidhe lagged and soon had to give up the chase. But oh, how fun it was to chase freely, full-out, and without care.

She stopped and looked around, her human mind lost, but without panic, her nose sniffed the air and placed the direction of the house and humans immediately. She panted, still catching her breath while taking in the forest around her. Then the familiar smell of a rabbit caught her attention, and her instincts surged as her stomach grumbled. It was time to find and eat that rabbit. She stalked toward the scent. When she knew it huddled close, she froze, anticipating its next move. It sat just beyond the patch of brush directly ahead. She moved closer, so slow it was hard to tell she moved at all. Her nostrils flared, placing the rabbit only a couple of yards ahead. Inch by inch, she approached, not making a single sound. In the instant the rabbit sensed a wolf; it sprang from its hiding place and made a run for it, darting back and forth. Casidhe was ready, and when the rabbit lurched, she did too. In a flash, she pounced on the rabbit with her full weight. *Caught.* She bent down with her mouth and gripped its head in her strong jaws and then shook it vigorously back and forth.

With the rabbit's neck broken and her hunt successful, she trotted back toward the stream, the limp body hanging to one side of her clenched jaws. She tasted blood. Sitting the rabbit by the stream, she watched it for a full minute. When it did not move, she bit into its underside, and holding the rest of the body with her paw, she ripped it open, exposing the tender meat within. The process of eating a full rabbit with only her teeth and paws took some time. But she managed it. At the end of her feast, all that remained was the fur and feet, and they just weren't worth it. She walked over to the stream again and lapped away until satisfied. Her belly full, she laid down on a large sunny rock to take a nap. Without fear or remorse, she found complete contentment on that rock. She felt no hatred for the rabbit nor love. It was food. It was instinct.

After a little while, she heard a noise in the woods. She did not sense nor smell danger. She got up stretched the usual front legs out in front of her, back legs up and back arched. Then she yawned twice and shook all over. She discovered this was her natural way of transitioning from one position to another. She trotted along the stream before venturing off into the woods. She didn't find the source of the sound, but it didn't matter. She noticed several sparrows fluttering around some berry bushes. She pounced in their direction without expecting to catch anything. She tried a berry, but it tasted terrible. She spotted and lunged at sparrow after sparrow, not catching, just playing. The sparrows appeared to understand the game and would get close and then flutter away. It was great fun.

After a while, she smelled something curious deeper into the woods. She cautiously trotted in that direction. When she could make out the smell clearly, she decided to go in the opposite direction. She knew ahead, hid a cave, and other types of beings had been there.

Several times throughout the afternoon, she knew for sure she smelled other wolves, most often in the direction of the house. As the sun set in the sky, she thought about food again, but Casidhe wasn't sure if she were hungry or simply allured by the smell of a pheasant in the brush ahead. No matter, she wanted it and began the patient stalking and then pounce process that she had used with the rabbit. Once again, she had her prey dangling from her teeth. She did not wait. It seemed she liked bird better than rabbit. She pulled out enough feathers to get to the juicy belly and consumed most of it. She also ate some snow and dirt in the process. It wasn't terrible.

After eating, she rolled around in the snow a little, just because she felt like it. She jumped up and shook off, flinging snow and water in every direction. Some part of her mind suggested going back to the Shack, but she decided against that idea.

She didn't want the pain that being human offered. As a wolf, she had no regret, no need to earn her place, no shame. She did not question herself. There were no doubts, no question if she were enough–pretty enough, smart enough, talented enough, good enough. As a wolf, she fit into her environment perfectly, without those questions. She belonged here and decided she loved being a wolf. She found a small rock outcropping along the ridge that offered protection from the wind and took another long nap.

It was fully dark with bright stars in the sky when she yawned, stretched, and went trotting around the forest again. She relied on her sense of smell and hearing but found her night vision still effective, even with no moon.

Casidhe spent six days as a wolf. She did not return to the Shack, did not transform back into human form, and did not think of anything other than hunting and eating food, frolicking, and exploring the snowy forest, and taking long naps, of course. She found warm, dry places to rest during the night and slept in the sun during the day. She had not a care. As her human mind got pushed far away, she did not miss it.

On the morning of the seventh day, she expected the same carefree day of running, pouncing, and enjoying the forest as the air shifted. She awoke from her mid-morning nap with a new smell drifting in on the breeze. It caused the hackles on the back of her neck to rise. She smelled another wolf nearby, she was sure. She leaped down from the rock and backed behind a bush, watching, listening, and smelling. It wasn't long before she saw her: a dark she-wolf trotting close by. She was so close, Casidhe's sense of smell immediately identified her. Dana. Multiple thoughts scattered across her mind at the same time.

Suddenly, she remembered who Dana was and what she was supposed to be doing during this time. She watched Dana closely, fascinated with her wolf form, having never seen it before. Dana had black fur with silver bushing around her head and belly to tail. Dana was a fantastic wolf, a black beauty. Without thought, Casidhe followed behind Dana, her feet acting of their own accord. She soon realized that if she could smell and know it was Dana, the reverse must also be true. Dana had to know Casidhe was there and perhaps had been watching her while she dozed on the rock. Casidhe remembered she was not supposed to interact during the initiation, not human, wolf, or Fae. That was the rule. *Why had Dana risked it? Was she checking on me? Had she been worried? Was the Ranch in trouble?* Casidhe followed Dana but did not approach her. Dana did not look back but kept the same steady pace through the woods, circling back to the house. Casidhe watched as she entered the rear doorway. *Why did she come so close?*

Casidhe's human brain was back online. She decided to go to the Shack. How long had she been in the forest? A couple of days, she guessed. She entered the Initiate Shack through the small door. Nothing had moved since her departure, including her moonstone, still lying on the floor. She went over and sat down next to it. How was she supposed to turn back into a human? Should she touch the moonstone again? Would it be painful like before? She braced herself and put her paw over the stone. Pain shot through her canine body. She whimpered and writhed but did not remove her paw.

It took far less time to transform back into human form, and it was much less painful. *Is that because it is easier to transform into a human? Or maybe it just gets easier?* Hadn't someone told her that? Casidhe couldn't remember, but she hoped that was right. Soon she was on the floor, naked, feeling cold without fur. She stood up clumsily and gathered the clothing she had torn off days before. *How many days?* She didn't know. She wasn't hungry, so she laid on her bed and rested. *Why had Dana risked contact?* She still didn't know. She thought about Dana and the idea of running together as wolves as she drifted off to sleep.

Casidhe woke after dark, still not knowing how far along she was in the initiation process. She poked her human head out the wolf door just enough to see the moon. It was half full. *How can this be?* Could she really have been in the woods for so long? With the appearance of Dana and the return of her human senses, she realized that she had allowed the wolf mind to have control for too long. *How can it be more than a week since I entered this shack? That means the initiation is half over. What else should I do? I know what it is like to be and live as a wolf. Perhaps, I need to get better at transforming back and forth. And I must not get so lost in the wolf like that again.*

With the moon half full, the hunting would be good. She braced herself and reached for the moonstone again. She would state change, hunt, and then come back here. But nothing happened. She did not transform. No shooting pains entered her body. She squeezed the moonstone in her fist and tried to make it happen, concentrating on the wolf. Still, her features did not change. She sat there for a long while, trying to remember if there was anything she had missed or forgotten. Did anyone give her a clue of what to do next? She remembered nothing she thought would help. Feeling a little hungry, she curled up on the bed and pulled the blanket up to her chin. The night was much colder without fur.

She laid there for several hours, trying to figure out what to do. Sometime after midnight, she drifted off to sleep. In her dream, she could hear a wolf howling. Then the answer of many other wolves, too many howls to determine the number. She felt anxious, unsure of what she should do. Suddenly she heard a whimper and ran to find the sound, realizing she was running on four feet instead of two. She trotted toward the commotion and heard a loud yelp and another whimper in the distance. It was Dana, and she sounded hurt. Casidhe ran full out, trying to get to her in time. She heard the yelps getting louder, then the howling and growling from others. Casidhe knew Dana was in danger. *I have to get to her and save her.*

When she was near a clearing in the forest she now knew well, she heard a noise behind her. She threw her feet out in front of her and spun around, growling loudly between curled lips and bared fangs ready to fight. But before she saw her attacker, she suddenly woke up. She stood on the bed on all fours, entirely her wolf self. The bed linens were all over the place, half hanging on the floor. It took her a moment to remember where she was and what happened.

It had been a dream, but it seemed so real. Dana was in danger, and they used Dana to lure her into the woods. It was an ambush; she felt sure. *Could it be real? Was Dana really in danger? Had it been the intense emotions of trouble and a potential fight that had evoked the wolf?* She'd think about it later. Right now, Casidhe ran out of the door and started for the clearing, hoping Dana was okay. She listened hard while she approached the clearing. There were no wolves, no howls, yelps, or whimpers.

She cautiously approached the area watching this way and that for any attackers, listening. Nothing. At the edge of the trees, she peered into the snowy expanse in front of her. No one. She was relieved but also confused. It had been so real. She stayed on the edge of the trees and circled the long way around the clearing. She heard the heart-pounding of a rabbit nearby. Her stomach gurgled its need. Should she dismiss the dream and hunt? There was nothing to raise the alarm. She let the dream fade and allowed her predatory nature to take over her mind. Food, she needed to eat. She soon arrived on the other side of the clearing, tearing into another rabbit.

After finishing her meal, she made her way through the woods, the half-moon now lower in the sky. She found her favorite little stream and lapped up the cold, clean water. After a while, she started back to the cabin. If intense emotions conjure the wolf, how did she evoke her human form? She entered the cabin. It was a mess. She looked for the stone and found it under her clothes, now torn and of little use. She touched the stone with her paw, but nothing happened. She was still a wolf. It seems the moonstone is only active for one use in each direction. She went over to the mirror and squinted at herself. How do I become human again? No answer came from her golden eyes and furry reflection. She laid down on the floor, her front paws out in front of her, and put her head down, tail circling and wrapping around her. If strong emotion could bring on the wolf, would the opposite be true of her human form? She tried to slow her breathing and be calm. That wasn't too hard; she felt no danger here. Something played at the back of her mind. Ronan's voice said to her, "What you focus on dictates your experience." Did she need to focus on being human, and in a human body? She closed her eyes and tried to imagine her own body: legs and arms, feet, and hands. She imagined wiggling her toes and fingers. She envisioned her long red and sometimes unmanageable hair and her green eyes reflecting back to her. Then she imagined her slightly freckled cheeks and full lips. When she got to her lips, she remembered the feeling of kissing Dana's lips and how impossibly soft and warm they were.

As she replayed her and Dana's past kisses, she could feel her limbs take shape. She could feel her human body forming around her, but she didn't stop. She stayed in her memory, replaying every moment of her time with Dana until she felt completely human again. She opened her eyes to see her naked body in the mirror. Reaching for the blanket, she wrapped it around herself.

Sitting curled up on the bed, she thought about what had just happened. She had dreamed of Dana in trouble, which had triggered her wolf. She had recalled the memory of kissing Dana and regained her human form. Everyone else who had gone through this process didn't have Dana to trigger their transformation. *Why do I?* She remembered Lesslyn changing state into her wolf form and back again with ease. *Perhaps I just need to practice?* At least for now, she had a way to shift without the stone.

CHAPTER NINETEEN

She laid there a while, trying to figure out the significance of Dana in her life. She dreamed about her long before she met her. When they did meet, it felt as if they already knew each other, and there was an impossible attraction between them, which was nearly overpowering. During her initiation process, she had followed Dana back to the Initiate Shack and her human mind. She dreamed Dana was in trouble, and now thoughts of Dana triggered the shift back and forth from wolf to human. For someone who had always been a loner, she had become very connected to this person. *How did this happen?*

And why Dana? Why not her twin brother. Hadn't they been together in her mother's womb? If she needed to attach to someone, wouldn't he make more sense than this beautiful woman, daughter of the Alphas?

Even if the reasons why eluded her, Casidhe knew for sure that Dana had become the one person she wanted to be with. *I hardly know her, but I know that is true. How is it possible?*

She heard comings and goings from the house, but they were in a different world from her now. She could not interact with them and so withdrew her attention from them. Even if Dana were there, Casidhe, mine as well be miles away from everyone while in the initiation process. *What else should I be doing here? Aren't I supposed to receive my Fae magical gifts? How will I receive them?* Descriptions of this part of the initiation had been vague at best. The day wore on, and only questions filled Casidhe's mind until her head hurt, and she felt lost. She snuggled down into the blanket and fell asleep again.

Dreams of Dana in trouble filled her sleeping mind. Running through the woods to reach Dana replayed. Hearing the same sound behind her, she turned growling once more. Only this time, someone else showed up. A young man with short auburn hair and light eyes came out behind a tree. He was not tall, but his shoulders were broad, and muscles pushed out against the fabric of his shirt. She stood her ground and growled from deep within her belly. Her eyes were bright with danger. This man would not stop her from getting to Dana. He did not move or approach, but he didn't back down either. She watched his eyes shift to a golden orange showing her he too was a State Changer. Then without knowing how, she knew who he was. It was Cian, her twin brother.

With that shock, she woke up and stared up at the ceiling. Was that really her brother? He had not attacked her, but he didn't speak to her either. She felt no harm from him, but neither was there love. Of course, why would he love her? They had never known each other, not since they were infants. The circumstances of the dream created more questions, and his position in them caused her to wonder about his motives.

More questions, that's just what I need. She tired of being inside her head. She wanted to run through the woods again. As a wolf, the questions faded away. Sitting on the edge of the bed, she did not know what time of day or night it was, but she wanted to run. She closed her eyes and tried to think of running on all fours through the snow and trees. She demanded her nose smell far and wide, friend and foe, prey and wolf. She extended her ears to hear the crackling of a nut from a squirrel many yards away. As she pushed her senses, she felt the transformation begin. She was getting better at it. She hadn't received her magic yet, but she was learning how to transform at will and without too much pain this time.

When she was entirely wolf, she yawned, throwing her mouth wide open and curling back her lips, and extending her tongue. Then she shook her body, flaring her fur, celebrating the warmth it provided. She didn't wait, taking off out the door into the waning light of dusk. The smells of the forest invited her, and she accepted, running in to join them.

She spent the night hunting and playing while noticing the moon waxing into full. The moonlight provided new shadows and reflections off the snow, which she learned to use to her advantage as she hunted for her next meal. Towards morning, she laid on her favorite rock in the moonlight, not wanting to go into the cabin again. She didn't want to wrestle any longer with the questions for which she had no answers.

Listening to the night sounds, she had another dream. But this time, she was sure she was not fully asleep. Her eyes were closed, but she still felt aware of her surroundings. She could hear the owl hooting in the distance. She could hear the mice running under the brush, the moles burrowing under the ground, and she could smell the aroma the human house gave off at dinner time. But even while all of this seemed real, she also saw the repeating dream scene unfold as before in her mind. It continued until Cian stood there, his eyes turning golden orange before he transformed into a wolf in front of her. His fur resembled hers, black, white, and rusty, but his muzzle appeared much darker–nearly black, and so too, was his underbelly. He approached her on all fours. She had stopped growling but did not move. She stood alert, the hair on the back of her neck involuntarily raised. Still, he advanced until their noses were inches apart. Her nose filled with his scent, and she knew he was adjusting to hers as well. They paced slowly around each other. Each wary, but curious. He felt dimly familiar to her, but she did not know him.

Just when she thought she could relax some, they each heard a loud yelp in the distance. Both their heads jerked in that direction. *Dana!* With that, she left her brother standing there and ran off towards the sound. Then she felt herself back on the rock in the moonlight, and the vision faded away.

More questions flooded her brain, and she knew she could not escape them. It would require all her human capacity if she were to understand any of this, and that would be impossible with the allure of the wolf's senses. She jumped down from the rock and headed back to the Shack.

Once inside the Initiate Shack, she went over to the covers and tucked her head under them, crawling in. She thought of her human body, considered her questions and Dana, hoping there was no real danger, and it was only a dream. Within moments, fur and fang were gone, replaced by chilled skin and clenched teeth. She pulled the blanket tightly around her and sat in the corner of the bed. What had Ronan said? Small increases were necessary for impossible tasks? Well, the whole transformation had seemed impossible, and now here she was, able to shift at will. She had grown comfortable with her wolf but felt confused by her dreams and visions. The one constant was Dana. Even in the dream, she had left her brother–her own flesh and blood–to save Dana. That much was clear, even though she did not understand why.

Casidhe tried to figure out how many days she had been in the Shack. By the position of the moon, she thought she only had two or three days left. The dreams were coming at her fast. Was this her gift–to see people before they came into her life? Did this mean Cian was about to show up? If not, how was he in her dreams? But what of Dana? Was she really in any danger? This is the part that caused her the most concern. She had to know if Dana was in trouble and if she could save her. She racked her brain for anything else Ronan might have said that would help. "Speak kindly to yourself about yourself." But that didn't seem to help. Her mind remained puzzled, so she sat on the bed and tried to relax and do what he said. She spoke kindly to herself.

I'm okay. I'm doing it. I've successfully found Lesslyn and Kelly in Montana. I've joined the pack; I have trained hard, and I have been accepted. Now I have successfully changed state into a wolf and learned how to survive and thrive in the forest. I have learned how to shift back and forth, and I have nearly completed the arduous initiation process. Casidhe Keneally, you are a State Changer!

As this last part fully formed in her mind, she said the words out loud again. "Casidhe Keneally, you are a State Changer!" And immediately, her mind was no longer in the Shack.

Casidhe stood in the middle of a grassy meadow looking out over a lake. Small foothills surrounded her, and towering mountains loomed from further away. Heaving grey boulders jutted out of the deep green carpet of grass and moss that covered the ground. There were few trees in any direction. The air felt crisp and salty but not cold. She turned around, taking in the scene, not knowing where she stood. She noticed for the first time a small boat gliding across the lake in her direction. As it came closer, she could see there were two people on board. It came to a halt along the shore, and she watched them climb out. The woman wore a floral top and a blue skirt. Her hair was the color of Casidhe's, but her eyes were blue. Next to her, the man wore a faded t-shirt and jeans. His blonde hair reflected the sunlight, but his full beard was red. His emerald green eyes mirrored her own. She felt no fear, only curiosity.

The woman smiled warmly and spoke. "Hello Casidhe, it is so good to see you. We are your parents, Finn and Nola Keneally."

"But you are dead," Casidhe said flatly.

"Yes. We are. But as State Changers, death is just another state of being."

Finn spoke. "We are so sorry that we could not be a part of your life, but we're happy to see how far you have come."

Casidhe didn't know what to say.

"You have some questions for us?"

Casidhe had a lot of questions, but . . . *I mean, they aren't real, right? Maybe this is my unconscious mind trying to help me out.*

"What are these visions about, and is this my Fae gift?

Nola spoke. "Yes, you have a similar gift as I. You see events before they happen. But I caution you; the future is fickle. It can change in a moment. What you do to change it can have unintended outcomes. I saw my children were in danger. We tried to protect you and your brother, but we were killed in the process. I knew you'd be safe with Colleen, but I did not see what the effects of not changing state would have on her body. In the end, she died protecting you, which left you unprotected. I did not see the whole picture. You may never know all that can and will happen and must judge wisely where and when you interfere. It is a capricious gift and sometimes a curse. Keep it to yourself if you can."

Casidhe wasn't sure she liked this gift or found value in it, especially if the visions could not be trusted, and she could only see bits and pieces. She decided to ask another question.

"What of this Twin Curse? Is it real?" Casidhe asked.

"Others believe it is real, so yes, the danger is real. You must try to befriend your brother. If others see there is no animosity between you, perhaps their fears will dissipate."

"Are you saying then, there is a chance that there is no curse?"

"We can only say there has always been a curse. Bad things have happened when two heirs have been born, one male and one female. Whether it is always fated to happen is unknown. Only that it always has. Be careful, if the curse is real . . ."

Casidhe knew if the curse was real, then her brother would not be her friend. She didn't like that idea. She hoped they could be friends. Looking closely at the woman, she realized how much she resembled Aunt Colleen, which made her miss her aunt. She liked the look of them both but did not feel close to them. Was that because they were not alive or because they were strangers to her?

"You may also have some of your father's power, which is to reshape events. If this power finds you, you may also find a talisman to help control it."

"I had a small wooden staff," he said. "It curled around on itself like a twisted root. I hope Saoirse, the White Wolf, retrieved it after my death. Ask her about it at some point. It would not be good for it to fall into the wrong hands, as it is a potent talisman. You may use it, or another may come to you."

"Casidhe, you must remember you are a Keneally. Others may fear and hate you for it. This is important for you to be aware of."

"But what does that mean, to be a Keneally? And why do they hate me for it?"

"It means you are a descendant of the Dagda himself, and as such, you have powerful gifts–certain rights and position among the State Changers and even among the Fae. But as you can imagine, this creates fear and jealousy. Also, you are an opposite-sex twin. That means there is even more for others to fear from you. You must be cautious."

Her mother saw the concern on her face. "But you can trust Kelly and Lesslyn Moore, and Saoirse will guide you."

Casidhe wanted to ask about Dana but shied away from the answer. What if they didn't think Dana was right for her? She didn't want to hear any explanation that would create a distance from Dana, so she decided not to ask.

"There is one more thing. The ring I left you will help you understand your visions and dreams. It is ancient and comes to you from many State Changers before us."

"It has already helped me."

"Be well and safe, our daughter, and Happy Birthday, you are the true heir to the State Changers, whether you ever accept that position or not."

Casidhe watched them climb onto the boat again. As they drifted out into the middle of the water, a mist rose and engulfed the boat, and they were gone.

As the vision faded, her eyes adjusted once again to the Shack as she sat on the bed, naked and wrapped in a blanket.

So, my gifts are these damn visions and dreams. Casidhe thought it a lame gift, one that caused her a lot of confusion. She shook off the blanket and began the process of transforming into a wolf. She needed to run.

When she exited the Shack, it was dark. But it didn't prevent her from running hard through the woods, past the trees, and across the clearing. She ran until she was panting hard and began to feel hungry. She found a small fish swimming in a shallow pool by the stream and caught it easily. It wasn't enough, but it helped.

Casidhe spent the rest of the night running through the trees, chasing rabbits and rodents alike. She thought she had a beaver at one point, but it dove into the water and disappeared. By night's end, she had eaten her fill and grew tired. She came around the back of the Shack and prepared to disappear through the door when she heard the wolf howls.

The hair on the back of Casidhe's neck went up immediately. The sounds were coming from the west, through a denser patch of forest. She turned and headed in that direction. She was no longer running but darted from brush to brush, staying hidden whenever possible. The howls were louder, and then she heard the yelps and whimpers. It was Dana. Her dream had come alive, and Casidhe knew Dana was really in trouble this time. She trotted faster but kept stopping to listen for any other wolves around her. *Is this a trap?* As she got closer, according to her dream, this was the moment Cian should turn up. She waited, her heart beating in her chest, her fur on end. But Cian did not come. *Damn visions aren't trustworthy.* She crouched low and half crawled toward the small clearing where she heard the howls.

In the distance, Casidhe could make out several wolves. They were circling Dana and nipping at her as they went past. Each time, Dana would yelp or whimper. Casidhe recognized Lesslyn's fur coat and her smell on the periphery of the circle. This confused her and made her angry. How could Lesslyn let them torment her own daughter? Another wolf circled Dana, snarling as it grabbed the back of Dana's leg, and they both went down. Dana yelped loudly. Casidhe couldn't prevent the low growl that escaped her own throat. Her hackles raised; she was ready to fight.

She knew if she ran into the melee, she would defy the State Changers rules. But she was a wolf; they couldn't take that from her now. Right? No matter, she couldn't let them hurt Dana. Another loud yelp and more snarls came from the clearing. Casidhe responded with another growl, this one louder than the last. But no one heard her because, in that same instant, Dana howled long and loud.

In a reversal from the yelping, Dana snarled at those who were biting and nipping at her. Casidhe watched, so shocked she did not jump into the fray. She saw Dana come alive and fight off her aggressors. She ran at them and dug her teeth into the leg of one until they yelped in response. She let go and pounced on another full force, causing them to fall and then scamper away.

In the end, Dana triumphed, racing around the others, growling and holding them off. This happened until there were no other attacks, and each of her aggressors rolled onto their backs, surrendering to her. Casidhe watched in amazement, proud but confused. Had this been a test? But for who? Dana or herself? If the attacks on Dana had continued one more moment, Casidhe would have joined in and forfeited her initiation.

Casidhe slowly backed up and left the shadows of the fight. When she had ventured far enough away, she began to run back to the Shack and didn't stop until she was safely inside. She quickly changed into her human form and fell on the bed, grabbing the blanket for comfort.

Not only had Dana brought her out of her wolf mind earlier in the initiation, but now she had exposed Casidhe's weakness for her and nearly caused her to fail. As she started to get perturbed with Dana for the last part, something occurred to her. Dana's timing on turning from a subservient wolf to an aggressive wolf was too perfect. Had Dana known when to turn the tide? What was it with this woman anyway? Now Casidhe wished she had asked her parents about Dana when she had the chance.

Dana made her feel a stranger to herself. Emotions stirred in her she did not recognize. She had been a loner as a child, and then Aunt Colleen had really left her alone. But now, this woman had invaded her solitary life, occupying her mind and arousing her body. It was new and unfamiliar, but as confused as she was, she wanted Dana to stay. In all of the uncertainty, she never doubted her desire to have Dana in her life.

Casidhe walked around the cabin in her bare feet. In a flash, she realized today was her last day in the Initiate Shack.

Tonight at 12:01, she would complete the initiation and be a State Changer. Before she fell asleep, she thought of how close she had come to failure.

When evening came, Casidhe awoke and changed state into her wolf form. She would end this process as the wolf, she decided. For the last time, she peered at herself in the Shack's mirror and knew she had become very comfortable with her animal self. She was not as comfortable with her Fae gifts. That would take more time. There were many questions to be answered, but she didn't expect to see her parents again.

She left the Shack, not knowing what would come next but elated this step was complete. She ran. Oh, how she loved the wind in her fur. She loved the feeling of her paws hitting and then digging into the snow-covered earth, pushing forward and flying across its surface. She loved the smell of the trees and moss and dirt. She loved the thrill of the hunt and even the kill. She had come to terms with being a wolf. It felt natural; it felt right. It would take much longer to understand her Fae-ness.

That evening, she did all the things she loved doing as a wolf, even finding a little time to bask in the bright moonlight on her favorite rock. She hoped she could come back here again soon and bring Dana with her. While lying there, she gazed up at the moon hanging large and bright in the sky above her. It darkened on one side as the colors changed. Her wolf eyes did not see the brightness of the reds, but she noticed the change. She laid there an hour watching the moon get darker and the shadows around her deepen. When the eclipse was complete, she felt a darkness come inside her body. Something sad and unavoidable. Suddenly, she felt a searing pain on her right hip, causing her to yelp. She smelled her fur and flesh burning. She jumped up and ran in circles, whimpering at the pain. She laid in the snow and rolled over, trying to ease the burning sensation in her hip. Nothing relieved the discomfort. She nearly took off running, but just as the moon's glow began to peek out on the other side of the shadow, the darkness left her, and the pain subsided. She was unsure what had happened, but she felt better and better as the moon slowly came back into view. She'd figure it out later. Midnight approached as she trotted back toward the Shack.

When she got close, she could hear and smell the pack. They were all wolves. This surprised Casidhe; she hadn't expected it. But there they were, and she had to figure out who was who, based on their smell rather than looks. It wasn't hard. She recognized Kelly and Lesslyn right away. She made out Dana, as beautiful and black as she remembered. She recognized Blaire and Brody's smell as they approached. Ronan's smell was also familiar. But when she saw him, she thought his sleek brown fur and white undercoat made sense. He was beautiful in any form. The others were all there too. Cormac, she recognized his silver patches. Bronagh was mostly grey with black around the eyes and mouth. Kevin and Sinead were there at the rear of the pack. She kept an eye on them.

One or two of the pack began to howl, and then they all joined the chorus in response to seeing her, and they ran around, circling her. To be welcomed to the pack in this way made Casidhe's heart beat wildly in her chest. She jumped and rolled around and among the other wolves. It was a happy reunion as they ran around each other and howled. At one point, Kelly took off, Lesslyn right on his tail. The rest of the pack bounded after them. Casidhe did not hesitate. Soon the entire pack raced through the forest. They ran, tumbled over each other, howled, and pounced. They played as wolves long into the night. Dana always stayed by her side.

At one point in the celebratory romp, a long and loud howl gave them all pause. One by one, all were still. Casidhe turned with the others to see a lone wolf at the top of the nearby hill. She was tall and completely white from head to foot, reflecting the bright light of the super moon. Only her eyes, which were a deep golden orange, stood out in contrast to her white coat. Kelly answered her call. A cacophony of howls followed, and Casidhe joined in. The White Wolf had acknowledged her, and the pack responded. Before the howls were quiet, the White Wolf was gone. But she had been there.

Later, Casidhe remembered the White Wolf had not been out of the Maze for many years. She suspected it had to do with the Super Blood Wolf Moon, but maybe it had something to do with her too.

They picked up the smell of a mule deer and hunted as a pack. Soon, all were waiting for their turn to eat. Casidhe knew for sure this was where she belonged. She was carefree and playful; she was powerful and fast. She was part of the pack. Her pack, the Keneally pack.

Just before dawn, they went back to the house, and each state changed into their human form. After dressing, they met in the pack room at the top of the large house. Kelly and Lesslyn stood side by side. They toasted Casidhe and cheered. Each pack member congratulated her. Welcoming a new pack member was a joyous occasion for all.

Long after dawn, Casidhe fell into her bed in her room. Dana had been close to her side all evening as a wolf and in human form. But she did not stay, needing to go to work soon. She kissed her lightly on the nose and left for the day, promising to see her later.

Casidhe fell to sleep immediately and had no dreams to speak of, which was fine by her. With all the excitement, she forgot to inspect her hip.

CHAPTER TWENTY

C asidhe woke up in the afternoon, along with the rest of the house. It seems partying all night with a pack of wolves will wear you out. She spent a good thirty minutes in the tub, not having had a bath in over two weeks. When she stood in the bathroom naked and clean, she inspected her body. She had muscles on muscles. It appeared her wolf body translated over to her human body. All the running, jumping, and pouncing created a lean and toned body, she barely recognized. Of course, Ronan had started the process, but after two more weeks as a wolf, she was very fit.

She also felt much older. She had always been more mature than others her age, sometimes so much so, she didn't fit in with her peers. She had accepted it. From ten or twelve years old on, inside her head, she was an older woman. She didn't try to prove it; she just felt it. But now, she felt ageless.

Then she noticed the burn on her right hip. She got up next to the mirror to get a closer look. To her amazement, the Celtic wolf symbol was branded into her hip. *Do all Keneally's experience this? Did Cian have a matching one? No one has spoken of it to me.* The mark no longer hurt, but she marveled at how a symbol could mysteriously burn itself into your body. She knew much of her life had turned magical, but it was still surprising.

It wasn't only her body that had changed. She felt a new power within herself. She wasn't sure how it would translate into her life, but she liked it. She had merely to think like the wolf, and her eyes began to turn a golden bronze color and a growl formed in her chest. It no longer frightened her. On the contrary, it thrilled her and gave her comfort. She felt at home in her own skin for the first time since . . . well, ever.

She would soon turn 18, and one thought came to mind. Formidable.

She dressed in a pair of jeans and a deep purple, long-sleeved t-shirt. She pulled her hair back into a thick ponytail, looking at herself one more time. "Not bad, Cas. Not bad at all," she said out loud. There was a knock at her door.

"Come in."

Blaire came into the room to tell her the family was having a late lunch if she was hungry. "You look good, Casidhe. Being a State Changer agrees with you."

"Thanks, Blaire. I feel good, and I am starving. Let's go eat."

They went down to the kitchen to find Lesslyn and Kelly filling plates and pouring tall cups of coffee. Casidhe helped herself and joined them at the table. Most of the pack had gone on to their homes and lives. Dana was still at work, and Casidhe was grateful. They had a lot to talk about, but Casidhe needed a little more time to adjust to her new self. She feared all the exuberance would fuel the fire between them in about three seconds. It was not the time for that just yet. She needed to get used to this strength and vitality. She needed to learn some control, or they needed to be in a private place. This thought made her smile. Yes, she liked that idea best. Someplace private. Perhaps she could go to Dana's apartment?

Brody walked in and greeted everyone on his way to the food. They were eating more than talking. When their stomachs were full, Kelly turned to Casidhe.

"You will need to speak to the White Wolf soon. I have put her off, but now that you have gone through the initiation, she will want to see you. Besides, you need her blessing as a State Changer. It's a formality, but we follow her lead. Would you be willing to go tomorrow morning?"

"Yes, of course. Where do we go?"

"I will take you into the Maze. It is the first level of Tír na nÓg, the land of the Fae. As a State Changer, I fear for your life less than before. You must still be careful, but no one would dare attack you in Saoirse's chambers."

Casidhe wanted to ask how they got there but decided to wait and see. She wasn't frightened and felt like she could handle herself. Besides, Kelly and the White Wolf would be there. She was curious about Saoirse and began forming questions for her.

"Great. What time do you want to go?"

"Let's meet here for breakfast at 8:00 and head over after that."

Casidhe nodded.

The rest of the conversation was packed with questions about her experiences as a wolf. No one asked about the process; she figured it too personal a topic to ask or share. She was in no hurry to do so. But she didn't mind talking about how wonderful and carefree it felt as a wolf, and they each reminisced about their own first time.

The conversation continued through clean-up. Brody and Blaire retired to the great room, and Casidhe followed them. Kelly had a phone call, and Casidhe didn't see where Lesslyn went. Once they were settled in comfortable chairs, Brody made an announcement.

"While you were hanging out in the Shack or the woods, Blaire agreed to become my mate." The smile on his face was so broad he could barely contain it. Blaire sat beside him, her feet up under her and leaning into him. Casidhe looked up in surprise, questioning Blaire.

"Is that right?"

"Yes, it is," Blaire said, almost defiantly. But the smile on her face said much more.

"Well, I am very happy for you both. Will there be a ceremony?"

"Yes, in two weeks, on Valentine's Day. All the pack will come, and Kelly will do the service. He can do that. It's legal and everything, that way, we cover all the bases, human and pack."

"Wonderful. I can't wait to celebrate with you both." She hugged them both.

Brody was visibly beside himself with happiness, and Blaire looked it too, though, if you didn't know her, you might not be able to tell. After they chatted for a while about what the ceremony would be like, Casidhe excused herself to give them some privacy. She wasn't ready to head up to bed yet, so she went to the library. She was scanning the shelves for interesting books when Dana walked in. Casidhe could feel it was her immediately, though she did not turn around right away. The anticipation of being alone with Dana had built up, and Casidhe, with her newfound body and powers, was unsure how they would contain or manage the attraction. Dana did not come close.

"Cas, we have to talk."

"I know."

"I knew we were heating up fast, and I knew you would come out of the initiation strong, but I did not anticipate the sheer power that is radiating from you right now. It excites me but also scares me a little. I don't mean I am afraid of you, just of what will happen."

"I know." Casidhe still did not turn around. She knew her eyes were golden, and she knew the wolf in her was very present.

"But I would also like to talk. I am not sure if we will be able to, at least not at first." She said this last part with a seductive smile on her face that Casidhe did not have to see to know. "But, not here."

"Agreed."

"Tomorrow night, my place?"

"Yes." Casidhe turned slowly. She felt a power inside her she could not describe. Sexual tension was one thing, but this felt volatile? They stared at each other from across the room.

"We'll have to go through this to get to the other side."

"Mmmhmmm." Casidhe grinned. Then she closed her eyes and took a deep, ragged breath, followed by another calmer breath. Control the wolf, she told herself. She opened her eyes again, and the golden hue had faded. Her smile was kinder and less hungry. Dana grinned back.

"I'll pick you up?"

"No need. I'll drive to your place. I go see the White Wolf in the morning, but I don't believe it will take long. What time should I come over?" *There, see. We can have a normal conversation.*

"How about 6:00?"

"Great." Casidhe decided she would go into the woods as a wolf earlier in the day to shave off some energy. She didn't think it would work, but she would try.

"Did you hear about Brody and Blaire?"

"Yes, such great news. I am happy for them both."

"Yeah, Mum and Da are ecstatic. It makes the pack stronger; besides, they are great together."

"Dana, you have to go now. Okay? I don't think I can contain this for long, and here is not the place."

Dana nodded her understanding. They were dangerous around others right now.

"Right. Tomorrow night then."

"Right." Casidhe smiled, trying to maintain control, knowing she wasn't wholly successful. Dana didn't seem to mind. She pivoted on her heel and left. Casidhe exhaled and sunk into a chair. She was there only a moment when Lesslyn walked in from the rear. Casidhe knew she had seen the exchange.

"My, oh my. Well, I must say that was . . . something."

Casidhe did not know how to respond, putting her head in her hands.

"Don't break anything in the process."

Casidhe's eyes flew open, and she stared at her, startled. She didn't expect Lesslyn to tease her. "Lesslyn, it's combustible. I'm not sure what will happen when so much . . . sexual energy meets."

"You will figure it out, and your instincts are good. You'll have to expend some of it before you can proceed with a normal relationship."

"How did this happen so fast?"

"I am not sure. I know Dana has a certain . . . shall we say magnetism, but you two were on a collision course since you first met. There is a force beyond my knowledge going on. If you have a chance, you might ask the White Wolf. She is old and knows much." With that, Lesslyn patted Casidhe on the shoulder. "It will be okay, darlin', I promise."

Casidhe was too keyed up to read a book or go to bed, so she went to the rear of the house and into the changing room. She disrobed, and state changed into her wolf. She was out the door and loping towards the woods before anyone saw her go. She ran in the full moonlight for a while, doing a little hunting but wasn't very hungry. She enjoyed the feeling of running, the smells of the forest, and the wolf blood coursing through her fur-covered body. After a couple of hours, she made her way back inside, changed back into her human form, dressed, and went up to her room. Looking out the window, she noticed the moon was still bright, causing her to rub her hip. *I should ask Saoirse about this too.*

The next morning, she dressed in a green wool sweater and black jeans. She combed her hair out and let it fall about her shoulders. She put on a little makeup and decided on her hiking boots. She wasn't sure if they would travel far but wanted to be ready. Kelly stood in the kitchen, drinking coffee, waiting for her. She grabbed coffee and a bagel and followed him out the door.

They climbed into the all-terrain vehicle and drove through the backwoods. Just before they reached the large clearing where Casidhe loved to run, they detoured off into the hills. Another couple of bumpy minutes, and they reached a large outcropping of rocks. Casidhe remembered being here a time or two when as she roamed the woods as a wolf.

Kelly parked the vehicle, and they got out, Casidhe following him up past a few smaller rocks that had fallen from larger boulders. Casidhe was glad she had put on her boots. She didn't see a clear path, though she imagined there might be one beneath the snow. Up they climbed until they reached what appeared to be a black rock, but instead was a dark hole that entered into a cave beyond.

"Sorry, this trek is a little easier without the snow," Kelly said. "But, we purposely keep this portal hidden."

"No problem. I understand." Casidhe wasn't sure she did understand but played along. She might have had trouble with the climb before her new body. Now, it was merely a matter of footing.

When they entered the cave, the passageway led to the left along a low, rough tunnel before opening into a large cavernous room that echoed somewhat when Kelly spoke again.

"Let's stop a minute before we go further. This is one of two portals on the Ranch; they are both one-way portals for Fae. Meaning, Fae can only go back into Tír na nÓg from here, but they cannot enter the Ranch from these portals. State Changes can come and go from both into the Sidhe. On the other side of this portal is what is known as the Maze. Technically, these portals are part of the Maze. It is the transition space between worlds. Should a human find a portal and enter the Maze, they could get lost forever. A human should not enter Tír na nÓg as time passes differently in the Sidhe. It is expansive and intricate, and there are many different kinds of Fae who live there. Most have never ventured into our world, nor have they any interest. Some come and go like us, though even most State Changers stay in the human world most often. Leprechauns can come and go through portals of their own making. Elves – there are too many varieties to list, use portals. There are portals across the globe, some in caves like this one, some in burial mounds, some are even underwater. The Fae world is quite different from ours. Even natural laws are different in Tír na nÓg. So, stay close. We won't be venturing in far. Saoirse is meeting us in the Maze, which is where she lives.

"Speaking of Saoirse: she too is a State Changer but very old and dare I say, more Fae than most State Changers; some believe she is your great, great grandmother. I'll let her tell you if that is true. She mostly stays in the Maze, which I assume is due to her age. One day in the Sidhe is like 100 days in our world for a human. The only way State Changers can come and go is because enough of the Dagda's blood still flows in our veins, and he granted us transference to and from as one of his gifts to our kind.

"The White Wolf is the leader of all State Changers, all Alphas report to her. She is queen Alpha, as it were. She also sits on the Fae council and therefore, is always looking out for State Changer's interests among the Fae. I don't know what we would do without her. She is fully aware of the Fuath's attempt on your life, by the way, and wanted to meet you, as a Keneally twin, even before you went through the initiation, which is unusual. Perhaps she is family. I convinced her it was too dangerous. In the end, she agreed. But she is anxious to meet you now. She made an appearance at your pack welcome on the Super Blood Wolf Moon, so there is something more going on. I have not seen her topside in many years.

"She meets with each new initiate, and technically, you are not a full State Changer until after you have her blessing. I would tell you what she is going to say, but each message is unique. Occasionally, she will take in pupils who wish to know more of the Fae ways so they can someday aid her in the work she does between worlds. Siobhan trained with her for a while, which is why she is such an expert of Fae now, well that, and the fact that she has mated with an elf. Are you ready?"

Casidhe nodded. Kelly turned and walked to the back of the cave and through a dark, damp wall. For a moment, it looked like he just disappeared. But then his hand reached back and grabbed her and yanked her through the invisible doorway. Ahead, she saw what appeared to be a long hallway in an old house. They were standing on a wooden floor with wooden walls on either side. It was narrow but wide enough for two to walk down, well enough. The ceiling was low, and there were no lights that she could see, though it was not dark. Hung on either side of the walls were gold-framed pictures with images of people, or Fae, to be more precise, because some did not look human at all. Sometimes there were landscape images, grassy knolls, lakes, rocks, mountains, and the like. Kelly led the way, and Casidhe stayed close behind. Every few feet, there were closed doors on either side of the hallway. Sometimes Casidhe thought she heard noises behind the doors but couldn't be positive. Kelly kept walking until they came to a fork; one branch of the hall went left and one right. They took the left. Still, more closed doorways and strange pictures on the walls welcomed them. They followed a stairway that went down. Then two more forks followed as they took a right and another left. A stairway led them up one level to another hallway and more closed doors. Eventually, Kelly stopped in front of the 3rd doorway on the right. He knocked briefly and then opened and stepped through.

As they had walked, Kelly told Casidhe he had chosen this portal, even though it was further from Saoirse's chambers, so she could experience the labyrinth that is the Maze and get a sense of how complex it is. She knew for sure she could not find her way back alone.

They entered a large, brightly lit chamber with huge sun-filled windows on all sides. Casidhe could barely see the top of massive ceilings. It looked like the foyer to a cathedral. She thought they were underground, so she was unsure how such a room could be possible. In between each of the floor-to-ceiling windows stood chairs large enough for giants to sit in. In the center of the room, sprawled a gigantic wooden table with heavy claw feet. It had to be over ten feet across and thirty feet long. At one end, a normal-sized over-stuffed chair sat at the head, and several others were beside it.

Once Casidhe focused on the table and chairs around it, she noticed the woman sitting in the head chair. *Didn't they tell me she was really old? She doesn't look any older than Aunt Colleen, maybe sixty at the most.* She had shoulder-length, blonde-white hair in a flowing style, pulled up on top of her head, like what she'd expect to see on a movie star, not an ancient State Changer. Her eyes were piercing blue, her creamy skin flawless, and thin red, glossy lips added to her loveliness. The real surprise was her ears; they were elongated and pointed at the top like Sven's ears. She wore a long deep red tunic over black leggings down to her black boots, accented with a red and black tartan scarf around her neck. She had a brilliant smile and was beautiful. Casidhe couldn't hide her shock.

"I love the look on the new initiate's faces when they see me. They always expect a shriveled old woman. I mean, I am old, but part of being Fae means you can always look good." Casidhe thought her speaking style was different, not Irish like the Moores, much more foreign, though she understood everything she said. Saoirse's smile seemed genuine, and Casidhe liked her immediately.

"Hello, Casidhe Keneally, I have been looking forward to meeting you, but Kelly wisely thought we should wait. I'm Saoirse." She grinned and reached out her hand to shake Casidhe's.

"Nice to meet you." Once Saoirse had her hand, she did not let go but pulled Casidhe in, examining her intensely, her face, her eyes. Then she let go and walked around Casidhe, evaluating her up and down. It was a little awkward, but Casidhe didn't mind.

"I see the training, even shortened, has done well for you, as is being a wolf. You are wise beyond your years, I think."

Casidhe did not know how to respond, so she didn't.

"Come, sit down. Let us talk. Kelly, will you give us a few minutes."

"Of course." Kelly walked over to one of the large chairs around the wall and sat in one. He looked small in it, which said something about the size of the chair.

Saoirse motioned for Casidhe to have a seat next to her in the comfortable chairs.

"I am sorry to hear about your aunt. I warned Colleen that forsaking her wolf would have dire consequences on her health. But she insisted it was the only way to keep you safe." She shook her head back and forth.

"Now the question is, who are you? You became a State Changer on a Super Blood Wolf Moon. Quite auspicious, don't you think?"

Casidhe started to ask her about the burn but was cut off before she could speak.

"I know who you are," Saoirse said. "What I want to know is who are you going to be? You are a Keneally twin, an opposite twin, the scourge of State Changers. Are you destined to be our ruin or our future?"

Casidhe didn't think these questions were for her to answer.

"A woman of few words, I see. Well, that is better than empty proclamations, I suppose. What I see is quite fantastic. You are beautiful and strong. Very strong. You remind me of Aoife. And you are gifted with the sight, I believe?"

The interaction with Saoirse had become disconcerting, but the fact that she guessed Casidhe's gift was, well, baffling. Maybe it wasn't a guess.

"Oh, I can usually tell Fae gifts in a minute or two. Gifts leave signs if you know what you are looking for. Besides, your mother had the sight, so it makes perfect sense, though it doesn't always happen that way."

Casidhe finally responded. "You are correct, though I am not sure what signs you see. By the way, my father said to ask you about his staff."

"Ah, excellent. You have spoken to them. Then your gift is strong."

"But not always accurate. It doesn't always happen as I see it in my dreams or visions."

"No, and it won't. It will take practice to understand where the subtle differences are. You will have to figure out when you are adding events to the dreams with logic or merging insights together that have no relationship. Gifts still take practice. You need to be trained in the ways of Fae sight. I will take it upon myself."

"But won't that be a dead giveaway if you start training me? Aren't I supposed to keep my gifts secret from others who would wish me harm or use them against me?"

"Good, your parents warned you, and you were listening. But do not worry; no one knows what I teach my students. It all remains quite personal. Also, I have a plan that may help throw off your enemies for now."

Casidhe raised her eyebrows. "My enemies?"

"You know you have enemies; did not the attempt on your life from a couple of low-life Fuath prove it?"

"Yes, I guess. I just never thought I was important enough to have enemies."

"Well, you should know it now. You are important. Much more than I can tell you, even I cannot see everything."

They were silent for a second as Casidhe took this in. Did that mean Saoirse had the gift of sight, too? But what did she mean?

"How can I be so important? I am new to all of this. I understand there are those who think I will fight with my twin and cause a war, but I haven't even met him yet. I am only one person. I don't understand why someone would want to kill me." She knew she wasn't being rational. Of course, her parents were dead. So, it must be true, and everyone had told her it was true. *But have they met me? I am not that scary. Well, unless you are Dana.* That made her smile a little.

"Ah, yes, Dana."

Damn, can she read minds, too?

"This can be good or bad. But I think you have been given a secret weapon in her. Has she not already facilitated your process?"

"Yes, at least twice, possibly three times, if you count the initial dreams of her."

"Right . . . Hmm. Mating with Dana Moore will give you a good position in the pack, not aggressive but close to the Alpha. You become a Pseudo Beta without challenge. This is good, wisely positioned. But there will be those who do not agree with two females, and of course, someday you must have children. This is your duty as a State Changer and to your pack."

"But isn't that only if I am Alpha, and I am not interested in Dana because she gives me a good position in the pack."

"Maybe not, but it happens anyway, and Alpha, you may be one day."

Casidhe did not know what to say; she did not want to be Alpha. She liked Kelly being her Alpha and protector, having never had a father.

"You have much to learn before that time, so don't worry yourself with it now." She pulled out a curious-looking book from under her tunic. It looked ancient, with many crinkled pages and odd drawings, and the writing was another language entirely, one she did not understand. Saoirse scribbled words down in the same script as Casidhe watched. Then she shut the book and tucked it quickly away. "Do you have any other questions before we get into my plan?"

"Yes. Can you tell me anything about this?" Casidhe pulled her jeans' waistband down just enough to reveal the State Changers symbol burned into her flesh.

Saoirse did not move to touch it; in fact, she sat frozen by the sight. Casidhe thought she noticed Saoirse draw in her breath a little quicker than normal, and her nostrils flared ever so slightly when she did so. But in the next second, there appeared nothing different in Saoirse's face. Any surprise or concern was hidden as if it were never there at all. "I will have to consult the Book. I'm sure it is of no consequence, but I would keep it to yourself for now."

Casidhe thought that a curious answer. If it were of no consequence, then why should she keep it to herself?

"Do you have any other questions?" Saoirse wanted to move on.

"Yes, why is there such a strong attraction to Dana? It feels out of control, like the heat will consume us.

"Heat, you say? Hmmm." She studied Casidhe's face as if looking for some sign, which made her feel uncomfortable. "Then, do not control it. Give in to it. It will not burn you. Once you let the firestorm happen, I believe you will get to a relationship that is easier to manage. As to why, I think time will reveal that answer to us all."

"And my father's staff?"

"Yes, I have it, and should the gift of altering event paths present itself, I will give it to you. Now, what of your birthday party?"

"What birthday party?"

"You and Cian's birthday party, of course. Kelly, will you join us, please."

Kelly came over and sat in the third chair next to Casidhe.

"I propose we have a birthday party for Casidhe and Cian. We bring together your two packs and celebrate the Keneally twins. I feel no animosity between them at this time, and a united front could be just what we need to help everyone relax about this Twin Curse thing. If the curse is only a result of the fear it invokes, we will get on the other side of it and move forward. If it is real, and I do not know that it is not, then we will have a closer look at how it will unfold. What do you think?"

Kelly contemplated for a minute. It was his job to protect his pack, and Casidhe was now a member. But he could not find fault in Saoirse's plan. "Yes, that could work. Where will this party take place? I would prefer someplace neutral."

"Yes, but I don't believe it would be prudent to have it in the Maze. There are too many Fae with far more power than I like. One wrong move and two packs could be wiped out at once. We need to invite as many Fae as want to come, but many will not. Of course, Fae will make it more dangerous but also gives us some protection as many are aligned with us. If you agree, we will have it at the Keneally Ranch.

Kelly nodded his reluctant agreement slowly.

"Good. I will speak to Colm, Cian's Alpha, and get his agreement. We have time to get the word out and plan. I suspect even anticipation and curiosity will keep all parties safe until the day."

Kelly agreed. "I will speak with Lesslyn and begin preparations on our part. Please tell Colm to contact me after you have spoken to him, and we can coordinate."

"Good. Good. One more thing, Casidhe will begin training with me."

Casidhe didn't think either she or Kelly had a say in this decision, but she was not opposed to it.

Kelly nodded again.

Saoirse stood, indicating the others should also. She turned to Casidhe. "Casidhe Keneally, firstborn daughter of Finn Keneally and Nola Kelly, you will submit to your Alpha and protect your pack?"

"Yes."

"Then I welcome you to the State Changers." Saoirse kissed her on each cheek and the top of her head. She smiled, turned, and left the room.

Kelly smiled. "It's official now. Welcome, my daughter." He kissed her on the top of the head too, and they left. They retraced their steps back out of the Maze. Casidhe was glad she was with Kelly. She felt sure she would be lost in the Maze forever.

When they reached the all-terrain vehicle, Casidhe looked at the clock on the dashboard. She thought they had been in there about an hour, two at most. It was 1:30 in the afternoon. She knew it could be 200 hours later if she were human. But she now understood how time could be lost in the Sidhe.

When they returned to the house, Kelly found Lesslyn in the kitchen and filled her in. She seemed thrilled Casidhe was now officially part of the family. Lesslyn had a curious expression after learning she would be training with Saoirse from now on but didn't ask any questions. Casidhe began to understand when it came to the White Wolf; things remained mysterious.

CHAPTER TWENTY-ONE

Casidhe got back up to her room around two o'clock. Now that she was out of the Sidhe, time seemed to be slowing down to normal again. Casidhe thought about what had happened that morning but grew distracted by the anticipation of seeing Dana. She wrote in her journal then paced around her room. Saoirse told her not to control the heat, but she was nervous. She had never been with anyone before. Lunch did not sit well in her stomach as the evening drew nearer.

At 3:30, she decided to run through the woods to burn off some steam. She state changed into her wolf and ran for the trees. An hour later, when she returned, she knew it had been a good idea. She felt more confident, and much of the nervous energy had been left in the forest. She bathed, dressing in blue jeans and a teal blouse that clung to her nicely, accenting her lean form. She liked her new figure, and why not?

Leaving her hair down, she worked to tame it. She put on a little makeup, especially around her eyes, allowing them to stand out more than they usually did. She slipped on short black leather boots before examining herself in the mirror. She thought she looked attractive, which surprised her, as she had rarely thought of herself that way. Grabbing a black leather jacket, she headed out the door at 5:30.

The car was cold, but she was not. She had not driven off the Ranch since she had started the training. Now, she dared anyone to accost her. She felt ready for anything. *Well, maybe not anything.*

Parking close to Dana's apartment building, she walked down the sidewalk, her heart beating wildly in her chest. Wolf confidence or not, too much anticipation surrounded this. She was apprehensive and exhilarated at the same time.

Her heels clickety-clacked on the concrete as she made her way to apartment 211. The red door contrasted with the grey building. At the entrance, she checked her watch, and it was 6:05. She knocked. She heard Dana approach the door, turn the lock, then the knob, and swing the red door open. "You're late."

"Fashionably?"

"Quite. Please come in."

Casidhe entered, trying hard to act calm. The apartment was sparsely furnished but lovely. A dark brown leather couch and a matching chair filled the room, along with a small coffee table, an end table, and two small lamps giving the room a warm glow. The main living space was open to the kitchen area with a bar and several stools dividing the two. Off to the right, Casidhe saw a doorway, presumably leading to the bedroom.

"Would you like a drink?" Dana asked.

"Yes, please. Just water. It's very hot in here."

Dana went over to the kitchen and opened the fridge, finding and pouring a glass of cold water from a container within. She brought it over to where Casidhe still stood by the door and handed it to her. They were being polite. Casidhe took a long draw from the glass, nearly draining it, and set it down. Then she took off her leather coat while allowing herself to pay closer attention to Dana for the first time.

Dana's silky dark hair fell about her red satin blouse. It was unbuttoned at the top, revealing a V of soft skin. Casidhe did not move her gaze from that spot for a second before forcing her eyes to travel back up to Dana's beautiful face and the startling blue eyes staring back at her. Casidhe felt the heat rise higher. She knew her own eyes were taking on a golden tinge after peering into Dana's.

"Dana." It came out horse, more like a growl than she had intended. In less than a second, Dana was directly in front of Casidhe, reaching up with both her hands and cupping Casidhe's cheeks. "Yes?"

"This is all new to me; I have never been with anyone before. But I have never wanted anything so much in my life. I don't

know who you are, but you have driven me half-mad with desires I can barely imagine." Casidhe had slipped her arms
around Dana's waist and pulled her in tightly. "Dana..." she
said again before Dana covered her mouth, kissing her and
ceasing all further conversation. Casidhe finally let herself go,
no longer trying to contain the hunger. Her mind slid back
while her body and her instincts commanded her. Caged for
too long, wild tremors shot through her whole being. She
clung to Dana with everything in her.

The kiss quickly became a fight to taste, to explore, to release. Dana's desires matched her own. Casidhe's hands
found their way under Dana's top, craving the touch of her
hot skin. Their lips never losing contact, Dana's hands began
undoing Casidhe's teal top, opening the front to reveal her
black bra beneath. The kiss increased in intensity as breathing became far less critical. Dana pushed Casidhe back
against the wall, pressing their bodies together, her hands
seeking skin. Casidhe moaned into the kiss, tasting as much
of Dana as possible, unwilling to miss anything.

She moved to the side and swung Dana around simultane-
ously, now pressing Dana against the wall with her body.
Dana pushed back until Casidhe leaned back over the end of
the couch. She stopped at the edge and then fell over it, landing on her back. Her eyes closed as she felt Dana's weight on
top of her. But they flew open again, flashing brightly as Dana
buried her face in Casidhe's neck, biting down lightly. Dana
half groaned, half growled, her body moving against Casidhe's.
Reaching up with both hands, Casidhe gripped her lower back
pulling Dana into her, at the same time arching her hips up,
increasing contact. The temperature in the room reached
blast-furnace level, and Casidhe didn't know if the heat would
consume them.

Dana groaned again but fell sideways off the couch when
she tried to shift her weight. Casidhe followed her down to the
floor. Their lips barely separated before diving back into each
other again. Trying to catch her breath, Dana pushed back,

a provocative smile playing on her lips. "Let's go to the bed where it's more comfortable." She said between kisses.

"Good idea," Casidhe said but didn't move to get up. Instead, she continued to unbutton Dana's blouse, her lips following each button's release. Their clothing half undone, Dana finally pushed Casidhe up and over. She understood and rolled as Dana moved to sit up, straddling Casidhe, her own eyes bright gold.

"Too hot, must remove this clothing," was all Dana could get out between deep breaths while pulling her blouse completely off. Then she rose to her feet and ran to the bedroom, flinging her top as she went, knowing full-well Casidhe would be on her heels. As she reached the bed, Casidhe tackled her, and they both fell onto the blankets, laughing.

They lay side by side for a moment, golden eyes matching. Casidhe's heart pounded, her skin red-hot. She sat up and pulled off the rest of her clothing before turning her attention back to Dana, who had done the same. Casidhe leaned into Dana slowly, now nothing between them. Dizzy with desire, their bodies met fully, hands and mouths explored without restraint. Casidhe felt sure the bed was on fire. Growls and groans escaped them both, and soon they howled. Just when they thought they were satiated, the inferno leaped to life once more. Sometime after 3:00, they fell asleep, tangled in the sheets, and each other. That night, Casidhe shed her loner identity completely.

At one point, Dana noticed the symbol burned into her hip. "When did you get that?" She whispered.

"I'll tell you about it later," Casidhe dozed off contented.

Late the next morning, they were both starving but had to settle for the cold pizza Dana had bought for the night before. After they devoured it, they ate soup out of a can. Dana had on a bathrobe, Casidhe was wrapped only in a blanket. It didn't matter much because soon they were back in the bed and didn't leave it again until nightfall.

"Is there a place to hunt around here?" Casidhe later asked absently, running her fingers through Dana's hair.

"Not really. I usually go out to the Ranch. It's not safe in town."

"We're gonna have to get more food soon." Casidhe's legs were wrapped up in Dana's, and she nuzzled lightly into her shoulder as Dana's fingers danced along her arm.

"Let's order Chinese food." Dana rolled over slightly without uncoiling their legs, the blankets pulling away, revealing her beautiful torso. Casidhe was tired and hungry but enjoyed the view. Dana grabbed her phone from the bedside stand to call a local restaurant already in her speed dial.

"I see this is a favorite place?"

"It's delicious. What do you want?"

"Whatever you get, but order triple! And she bit into Dana's shoulder lightly.

"Hey! Wait for the food."

"If you insist." Casidhe rolled back, exhausted but happy. "I'm going to go get some water. I'll be right back."

As Dana ordered the food, she didn't miss the scene of Casidhe leaving the bed without a stitch of clothing on. Casidhe knew she was being watched and laughed as Dana fumbled her order on the phone, having to close her eyes to remember what she was doing.

When Casidhe returned, she handed Dana a full glass and went into the adjoining bathroom, stepping into the shower. The hot water freshened and relaxed her. She felt terrific but knew if she didn't eat soon, she'd have to go hunting. In a minute, Dana joined her, and the shower became something completely different. A knock at the door pulled them apart from an embrace that threatened to drown them both. Dana scrambled out, put on the robe, and ran to the door. Casidhe stumbled out, flushed, reaching for a towel. After drying off, she found one of Dana's t-shirts and some sweatpants on the back of the door and put them on, joining Dana at the bar. No one spoke while they consumed every morsel of food. Then they decided the couch was the safest place for a conversation. Cuddled up as close, Dana asked about the initiation and her time with the White Wolf.

Casidhe told Dana the details of her first couple of transformations and the difficulties she had. Dana was not surprised. "It's hard for everyone the first time or two. That is why we are called State Changers. We have to change our state of mind to shift physically. You must believe, to do it. The moonstone helps with the first shift or two, but after that, you have to remember and believe. Then the outside transforms." Casidhe nodded, giving an account of her time in the woods and the moment she saw Dana run through.

"Did you do that on purpose, to bring me out of the wolf mind?"

Dana smiled shyly. "Yeah. We were all watching you closely and knew you had not returned to the Initiate Shack. We were racking our brains on how to bring you back but didn't want to risk interaction. It was my idea to just run past you. I hoped I would catch your attention."

"Oh, you did, and you do." Casidhe kissed her tenderly on the cheek. "Then there was the test at the end. Others were attacking you in the pack with your mom. It was hard to watch. If you had waited one moment longer before you turned the tide, I would have jumped into the fray to defend you."

"I knew that. I was so nervous about doing it. I knew I wasn't in any danger, but you didn't know that. Which was, of course, the point of the test. I am so glad you waited."

"One more second . . ."

"I could tell. I seem to have a keen sense of your emotions most of the time."

"Hmmm. I asked the White Wolf about us."

"What did she say?"

"Well, I told her I had trouble controlling my desire for you and that I had never felt anything so strong before."

"You did not say that!"

"Yeah, I kinda did. It confuses me. I have always been a loner. I have never felt anything even close to what I feel with you."

Dana smiled and leaned in to kiss Casidhe lightly. Dana pulled back and asked, "What did she say?"

"She told me not to control it. She said I should let go and allow it."

"Oh, really? Remind me to thank her the next time I see her." Dana leaned in and kissed Casidhe again, and they stayed at it a little longer than intended. Before they got too heated, Casidhe pulled back this time. Dana breathed hard into Casidhe's neck. "Damn."

After Dana could speak again, she asked, "Are you going to tell me about the State Changers symbol on your hip?"

"There's not that much to tell. During the eclipse, when the moon was darkest, I felt a burn on my hip. It hurt like hell, and I could smell it burning my fur and flesh. I tried to make it stop but couldn't. It only stopped burning when the moon returned from behind the shadow. I couldn't see it that night and didn't know what happened until the next day when I noticed it in the mirror. I asked the White Wolf about it, but she told me not to worry about it but to keep it to myself. Which is strange if you ask me."

"Very strange. We should ask Mum and Da about it."

"I'd prefer if we didn't, for now. As much as Saoirse downplayed it, I feel it means something important. She's just not ready to tell me yet. We should keep it to ourselves for now. Okay?"

"Okay, but I want to know when she tells you what it means."

"Well, it would have been hard to keep it from you. I will tell you if she says anything."

"Anything else?"

Casidhe hedged a little, unsure if it was too soon to speak of mating, but she didn't want to keep it from Dana. "She said you were a good mate for me, that it gave me good positioning in the pack as Kelly and Lesslyn are your parents. It keeps me close." Casidhe relayed the information quickly, hoping to get it all out before Dana got the wrong impression. "I told her that wasn't why I was attracted to you and that I have no interest in leading the pack. She told me I needed to consider that I was a Keneally. More or less, she gives us her blessing, but not for the reasons I would have wanted."

"Cas, don't worry. I don't think you are trying to take over leadership of the pack or using me to gain power."

Casidhe visibly relaxed. "Oh, good. Because I am not; I have entirely other interests in you." She smiled wickedly.

"But others might think it, just so you know. Still, anyone who knows me will not believe that you are playing me."

"Why is that?"

"Because they will think I am playing you."

"Oh, is that right? And is that true?" Casidhe taunted, but Dana got serious for a moment.

"Casidhe Keneally, I am falling completely and passionately in love with you. I think that thwarts any abilities I might have to play you."

Casidhe was shocked by this revelation of love but pleased. She cupped Dana's face in her hands and gazed into those eyes. "Well, that is good because I feel the same way, and if you did not return these feelings, then this could be uncomfortable for you." She smiled broadly, and Dana slapped her shoulder off-handedly. But then they fell into a deep kiss and were about to head back into the bedroom when Casidhe's phone buzzed. She had forgotten it completely; no one had called her in so long. She went to her bag to see a text from Lesslyn.

"Casidhe and Dana, please come to the Ranch tomorrow for a lunch meeting regarding the party." Casidhe showed it to Dana. "I think you got the same text."

"What party is she talking about? Brody and Blaire's mating ceremony?"

"It might be my birthday party."

"What? Birthday party?" Casidhe realized she hadn't told Dana about this part of the visit with Saoirse and dove into the explanation.

"Makes sense. I guess you'll get to meet your brother."

"I know. Have you ever met him?"

"No, I don't think so. I don't remember anyone from his pack coming down our way. I mean, I could have when we were children, but I don't remember it. Do you ever think about when we were children? We probably knew each other then."

Casidhe thought about this. "I guess you're right. But I would have been less than a year old, and you would have been two, almost three? We wouldn't remember."

"Right, but I wonder if something happened that has caused this connection we have now."

"I can't imagine what it could have been. But we certainly have a strong connection." Casidhe kissed Dana on the top of her head and then got up from the couch, grabbing Dana's hand and leading her back to the bedroom. "Let's investigate this further, shall we?" Dana willingly followed in after her.

CHAPTER TWENTY-TWO

They did get a little more sleep that night after a long, slow passionate interlude. The next morning, they both showered, dressed, and left the apartment arm-in-arm. Dana had promised Casidhe a fantastic breakfast at the local diner. She couldn't wait; she was always so hungry around Dana. After they were full of bacon, sausage, eggs, toast, hash-browns, and coffee, they went to the Ranch. Dana would have to go to work tomorrow, but she promised not to leave Casidhe's side a moment before she had to. They left Casidhe's car at Dana's apartment, deciding to get it later, and drove together in Dana's car. On the way, the conversation turned to Dana's parents.

"Should we tell your parents about us? Is it too soon?"

"Not in my opinion." Dana smiled.

Casidhe knew it was soon in their relationship, but she didn't care. "Should I say something?"

"Let's do it together."

"Okay, so what do we say? You know this is all new to me, and I don't just mean the pack but having parents."

Dana squeezed her hand. "I think we simply tell them we are seriously dating. How's that? In pack matters, there are two types of mating. It is the act of being intimate together, which I would say we qualify." Dana's eyebrows popped up and down in a seductive smile. "And there is the lifetime commitment, which is also called mating, but means marriage in pack-speak."

"Yeah, I figured that out by how Brody and Blaire were talking. But where does that put us?"

"In the middle. We're mating but not mating." She laughed out loud.

"Well, at least that's clear." Casidhe rolled her eyes.

"Don't worry about it. We'll just say we're dating. Okay."

"Okay. I will follow your lead. They are my Alphas, but they are your parents."

"Right. I'm not worried, so don't you be. Besides, I'm pretty sure they already know."

"Yeah, I may have confided in Lesslyn," Casidhe cringed.

"Oh, really?"

"Well . . . I was confused, and she was willing to talk about it."

"See, it will be fine."

They reached the Ranch long before the party meeting and tried to sneak up the stairs without seeing anyone. They should have known Blaire would hear them coming a mile away. They weren't to the first landing when she said, "Oh good, you're back." She smiled at the guilty looks on their faces.

"I was hoping to change clothes before the meeting."

"Yes, that might be wise." Blaire walked away. If you didn't know her, you might not know that she was teasing. Casidhe and Dana ran up the stairs before encountering anyone else.

"You can never get away with anything when Blaire is around."

"Yeah, she has a way of knowing before anyone else. I'm gonna change. She obviously noticed these are the same clothes I had on when I left here two days ago."

"Do you need any help?" Dana asked with a suggestive look.

"Ah, no. Not if you want to make it to the meeting on time." Casidhe gave her a smirk and took off to the bedroom, leaving Dana to wait in the sitting room. It wasn't long before Casidhe returned wearing clean jeans, a North Carolina sweatshirt, and sneakers. It was casual, warm, and comfortable.

"Nice," Dana said when she entered. Casidhe went over and embraced her. It had probably been all of ten minutes apart. Casidhe felt a little pathetic but didn't care. "Can you stay over tonight?"

"Maybe, but I have to go to work tomorrow, so I will have to get some sleep."

"Of course." Casidhe tried to look innocent but couldn't pull it off. "We could also go out as wolves together later. I would love that."

"Me too. Okay, it's a plan, after this meeting and dinner."

They released each other and went down the stairs, holding hands. When they got to the great room, only Kelly and Lesslyn were there. It seemed like good timing, so they told them about the dating, and Lesslyn smiled. Kelly appeared a little more stoic, clearly thinking this through.

"Oh, Da. You know I'm gay, and that's not gonna change."

"It's not that, Dana. I love you the way you are. It's the pack. Some will struggle with you and Casidhe together. I am just thinking about the different reactions. It's more about heritage and that damn Twin Curse. Pack business, you know."

"I know, Da. We know it could be an issue for some, but we'll figure it out. Right."

"Of course, we will," Lesslyn said. "Besides, I think it is good. This allows us to keep Casidhe close without seeming like we are giving you preferential treatment. We can use it to our advantage."

"Yeah, that's what the White Wolf said. But you both know I am not interested in Dana for a position in the pack, right?"

"Yes, darlin', we know."

"Good! As long as you both know."

Brody and Blaire walked in together. Brody had the same happy look all over his face as the last time Casidhe had seen him. She thought her expression probably matched his. Blaire held his hand. "Know what?" she asked.

"That Casidhe and Dana are dating," Kelly informed them.

"Not news," Brody smirked at them.

Dana slapped him lightly on the shoulder.

"Okay, you all, we have some things to discuss." Kelly got down to business. "Saoirse has suggested that we have a birthday party for Casidhe and Cian and invite the Calgary pack to show solidarity and strength to any Fae that may want to cause them harm. Also, if State Changers see Cian and Casidhe together getting along and celebrating, fears about the curse may subside. We all know these fears can become a self-fulfilling prophecy. No one knows, not even the White Wolf, if there really is a curse or not. But what does it matter if everyone believes it's real? It causes harm, anyway. So, the party is to help alleviate fears on all sides.

"If it works, that is. It could also play right into the hands of whoever would want to do Casidhe or Cian harm. It would make it easy, wouldn't it? Put us all in one place, easy to do a lot of damage at once. So, we must prepare now to keep everyone safe. We'll have an all-pack meeting mid-week, but I wanted you, our family, to begin thinking about this now. This will be a very important event, and it's only a month away. We still have trouble with Fae getting on the Ranch and have not yet figured out how to prevent it.

"In the meantime, in a couple of weeks, Brody, you and Blaire will be mated. That will involve all our pack, and we don't want to overshadow your celebration. You must not think you are any less important to this pack."

"Kelly, we do not think that. We are excited about our mating, of course. But we will also help plan and prepare for the birthday party on March 1st."

"Good." Kelly pulled on his beard. Lesslyn reached over and took his other hand. He visibly relaxed, looking at her, and smiling. "Saoirse also wants Casidhe to train with her. Everything the White Wolf does is important, but I feel she is being particularly prudent in how she is positioning our pack. Casidhe, as you know, your parents were the Alphas before us, and you are a Keneally. You come from a long line of Alphas, and your blood is pure State Changer. This will cause questions within our pack and across all packs. Many will anticipate a shift in power and loyalties. Uncertainty will surface within our ranks. I think you will need to address our pack soon. Tell of your intentions. They may or may not believe you, but transparency will help."

Casidhe had always run away from crowds and public speaking, but as she felt Dana's hand in hers, she knew how much she had changed. The wolf in her was much more confident, far less afraid. She winked at Dana and said, "Of course. I can do that."

Kelly beamed immediately. Casidhe thought he half expected she would need convincing. She was very different than the timid girl who had shown up at the bar a few weeks ago. She was a State Changer now.

"Great. At the pack meeting on Wednesday, then. The sooner, the better. You and Dana can also announce you are dating. I suspect there are a couple of males that will be disappointed." His eyes twinkled, but Casidhe was surprised. She had not thought of that. Dana squeezed her hand again.

Lesslyn spoke. "Good, that's settled. We need to plan the mating ceremony for Valentine's day. We'll be in the pack room, and there will be a party afterward. You two will want to go to the cabin up at Whitefish lake for a few days. After the birthday party, if you want to take off to warmer places for a while, that's fine too."

"Brody and I would not leave the pack during such an important time. We'll be here."

"Good. The rest of the pack will help, and I know it will all come off fine." Lesslyn sounded like she was convincing herself more than the others.

"Lesslyn, it will be great, I'm sure. Our expectations are simple." Blaire said reassuringly.

"Blaire, you know how important mating is to the pack. And you are important to us. It will be grand!" Lesslyn promised.

"Okay, enough for now. Plans will continue with the rest of the pack on Wednesday; let's go eat."

The rest of the evening was comfortable. Brody remained very attentive to Blaire, who had to give him chores to keep him out from underfoot. But Casidhe could tell she wasn't really annoyed. Casidhe felt more comfortable showing her affection for Dana openly in front of the family and found opportunities to touch her often. Sometimes they brushed up against each other or whispered into each other's ears. Kelly and Lesslyn appeared to be okay with it and content to have their family around them.

After dinner and cleanup, Casidhe, Dana, Brody, and Blaire went out for a run as wolves and didn't come in until midnight. Casidhe and Dana escaped to the Keneally suite, not caring where Brody and Blaire ended up. Dana did get a little sleep that night, but not enough.

As the sun came up, Casidhe was buried in a dream. She was running down the halls of the Maze when one of the doors opened, and two beings walked out. They looked almost human. Someone had told her that many Fae can look any way they want. Casidhe didn't know what type of Fae they were, but as soon she walked with them, their faces changed into leathered root-like faces, with beady little black eyes and deep wrinkles. They were speaking to each other, but she didn't understand them. She wanted to ask them how far it was to the White Wolf's chambers, but when they turned around, they attacked her. The next thing she knew, she was on the ground, her lip bleeding and a bump on her forehead. She couldn't walk, so they were dragging her along the wooden floor to an open door. She still could not understand the high pitch squeaks of their language. Once they crossed the threshold, the hallway disappeared, and they were in a dark, damp dungeon. She tried to call for help, but no one came.

Dana shook her awake. "Cas, what is it? I'm here. Cas, wake up."

Casidhe woke up with a start and clung to Dana. The dream faded, and Dana's presence reassured her. Still, Casidhe worried. She knew her dreams, or parts of them can become real.

"What did you dream, Cas? Are you okay?"

"Yeah, I'm okay. Just a bad dream. Sorry."

"Don't be sorry. Do you want to tell me about it?"

"No. I don't want to make it any more real."

As they laid in each other's arms, Dana immediately fell back to sleep. When it was time to get up, she struggled. "Cas, I may need to stay at my place tonight. I am going to get fired for sleeping on the job. And classes start soon. I have to study," she yawned.

"I know. I understand. But you'll be here on Wednesday, right?"

"Yes. I'll stay on Wednesday. I'll catch up on sleep tonight." She slumped down in the covers nestling into Casidhe, wrapping her tight. Casidhe knew the struggle well but also knew it was time to get going.

"Nope. We are going to the shower. If we want to stay together, then we have to help each other get moving the next day. I'll get the hot water running." Casidhe extracted herself to Dana's dismay and went to the bathroom. Dana reluctantly followed.

Casidhe saw her off to work, kissing her passionately goodbye and holding on tight. "I don't want you to forget," Casidhe said breathlessly.

"Fat chance of that. I'll call you later."

"I'll get my car on Wednesday. I won't need it to get to the Maze."

"Right. Good luck with Saoirse today."

"Thanks."

They kissed one more time before Dana ran to her car, not feeling the cold at all.

CHAPTER TWENTY-THREE

C asidhe went in and got another cup of coffee. Brody was supposed to accompany her to the Maze as Kelly and Lesslyn had pub business to attend that morning. She thought of the dream.

"Ready, lassie?"

"Ready. Thanks for taking me into the Maze. I would get lost for sure."

"Of course, but the White Wolf will meet us in the first room and escort you in, so I don't have to go far today. She has another entrance, which is much closer to her quarters, but she is working on securing it better."

They drove in the direction of the back portal, soon walking through the opening at the back of the cave. "I don't like this portal as much as the other. Too far to get to the main rooms and too far from the house. It used to be our only portal, but Saoirse opened the one closer to the house a few years ago. I hope she reopens it soon."

"What is she doing to it?"

"Well, I suspect because it is the one the Fuath used to kidnap you on New Year's, she is having it redone with new protections."

"Oh, right." She didn't think about that night much, but since the morning's dream, she wondered if the Fuath were plotting against her again. That attempt on her life had been a terrifying experience, but it happened before she had become a wolf. The wolf's nature didn't allow for feelings of nervousness often, and she was glad for that. She knew she wasn't bullet-proof, but she felt confident.

As they walked down the first hallway, just ahead of the first fork, one of the doors on the left side opened. Two Fae came out like in her dream. Her eyes grew wide, anticipating the worst.

"We'll accompany Casidhe to the White Wolf," one said to Brody.

Brody was wary but not overly avoidant. "Are you sure? I thought the White Wolf would meet us."

"Saoirse will be detained for a few minutes and asked us to bring Casidhe to her chambers. We will call you when it is time for her to return." It seemed official and clear, so he turned to Casidhe, "This is Keera; she works for the White Wolf. I'll see you tonight."

Casidhe did not move to go with them but reached out for Brody's arm. "I am not sure about this, Brody." She looked him in the eye, concern on her face. "Maybe we should go back to the Ranch until Saoirse is available." She squeezed Brody's arm harder.

"Sure. Maybe you're right. Keera, we'll come back when the White Wolf is available." Casidhe began to relax as they turned to go.

But they never left the Maze. The two Fae, who pretended to work for Saoirse, changed before their eyes into the angry Fuath from Casidhe's dream. The one closest to Casidhe blinked her beady black eyes and crinkled her nose, causing the wrinkles on her face to deepen. She reminded Casidhe of an old, dirty turnip with a few, single long spouts of hair on top. She had no teeth Casidhe could see but didn't want to test that theory. Her body loomed large with multiple thick limbs that hardly resembled arms and legs.

They went for Casidhe first, their clear objective. Brody had shifted into a wolf quicker than she thought anyone could and attacked the one closest to him. Growls, yelps, yells, and high-pitched squeaking filled the hallway. Casidhe began the shift into her wolf form, but the one who had pretended to be Keera jumped high into the air and came down in a rolling side swipe onto both of Casidhe legs with so much force, Casidhe was sure both legs were broken. In the same moment, something like hands pummeled her face, causing her lip and nose to bleed and her eyes to swell. She didn't have a chance to change states, and she wasn't prepared for that kind of assault. She was down, lying and bleeding on the wooden floor within moments from when the attack began. The other Fuath who had been fighting with Brody came closer, and together, they picked her up and dragged her, one Fae under each of her arms. Her legs were no longer able to support her as they lugged her along the hallway's wooden floor and through a doorway. Casidhe squinted back through half-slit, swollen eyes to see Brody's wolf form lying unconscious and bloody down the hall. She prayed he wasn't dead. She tried to call his name, but her mouth would not work right. She croaked out a yell, but they yanked her over the threshold; the hall and Brody disappeared.

She knew this place from her dream. They dragged her into a dark and dirty dungeon Casidhe knew was far from any person she cared for. They heaved her body over to the filthy wall where shackles were hung, ready. She tried to fight with her arms and hands, not wanting to give in to them. She made contact with the mid-section of one of them as a deep growl escaped her throat. But this did not affect her assailants. Instead, it felt as if her wrist snapped. A scream followed her growl. She tried again to transform into her wolf body, but there was a darkness in the dungeon which would not allow it.

They shackled her arms and legs to the wall. Her broken legs were crumpled under her, angled in unnatural directions. The pain was excruciating. The root-faced people spoke to each other in their own squeaky language, then turned and left her there, alone.

She called out for Brody, for Dana, for Kelly and Lesslyn. She called out for Saoirse too. But no one came. She half sat, half hung, crumpled there against the wall. She lost consciousness for a long time but had no idea how long. When she came to, nothing had changed. She was still in the filthy dungeon with no one else around. *Didn't they say you could get lost in the Sidhe and lose your life forever?* That is what she knew those root-faced people hoped for. For a State Changer, forever could be a long time.

The wolf doesn't allow fear to take over; it merely transforms and attacks no matter the outcome. Casidhe tried again
to shift into her wolf, but some type of dark magic would not
permit it. Nothing happened. She remained a wounded human and alone. She tried to stand, but her legs collapsed
beneath her. In her human mind, she felt fear, but she was in
too much pain to stay conscious long.

Time wore on. The ever-present pain in her legs and wrist
began to numb her mind. Her body shook and began to sweat.
Shock ravaged her. Still, no one came. She was too deep in
the darkest part of Tír na nÓg. The root-faced Fuath did not
have to kill her. That would have been too nice an ending. No,
they intended to leave her here, unable to change state, unable to call for help, unable to run. Her body would slowly rot
and die, and in that order.

The next time consciousness left her, she had a vision of
Dana. She had been crying, but she was yelling at Kelly. She
insisted someone go in after her. Lesslyn and Kelly tried to
comfort her, but she would not allow it. She said she would
go after Casidhe herself if they did not. Kelly forbid it. "We are
doing everything we can, Dana. Saoirse is working inside Tír
na nÓg to get to Casidhe. The Fae council is searching. We
cannot go in and disrupt the Fae. We must wait."

"The Fae don't care about Casidhe or us! They won't bother
to look very hard for a State Changer!" She spat back at him.

"They don't all feel that way, Dana, and you know it. You
must stay put; you could risk your life and the entire pack if
you were to go in there."

When Casidhe regained consciousness for a few minutes,
she cried out for Dana. She tried to send her the message with
her mind to stay away. She did not want Dana to get killed or
the pack put in danger.

Casidhe's mouth was so dry; she had a hard time swallow-
ing. Her stomach grumbled with hunger causing more pain to
her already failing body. She had no idea how long it had been
since her abduction. In the dim light, she could see purple
bands around her wrists from the shackles. She didn't feel the
ones around her ankles, and that horrified her. What if she

would never regain the use of her legs. What if she were par-
alyzed? What did it matter? She would die here soon, alone in
this filthy place.

The stench of death and decay was crushing. She wretched,
but since she had not eaten, nothing came out. She hung
there, hoping for death to take away the pain. Ronan's voice
came into her head. "Whatever you focus on is your experience. Remember your training." Right. I must not allow these
thoughts. I must stay alive. Maybe they will find me. No. No
one will find me here. Ronan could not expect her to focus
here.

Time marched on. The shock wore off, but the hunger and
thirst grew far worse. Her lips cracked and peeled. She
couldn't reach the dried blood crusted on her face, which
itched as it flaked off. She knew she was frightful, her hair
matted and caked with blood and grime. But as bad as she
looked, she felt far worse. Thankfully, she lost consciousness
often.

In one vision, she watched Brody and Blaire stand together
at their mating ceremony. Brody had his arm in a sling and
crutches. It was a bittersweet ceremony. She searched around
the room; no one was very joyful. Kelly stood before them,
looking haggard. Lesslyn sat in the first row, deep circles under her eyes. She looked older than Casidhe could imagine.
She scanned for Dana, locating her in the back. She was not
watching the ceremony, not looking up at all, but sitting
slumped over, dazed and staring at the floor, tears flowing
down her face. Her hair was tangled and had lost its luster.
She fumbled with the napkin in her hands. This scene broke
Casidhe's heart. She could hear Kelly saying not to lose hope
and that the pack must continue. As Casidhe regained consciousness, tears flowed down her face. She sobbed to herself
as there was no one to hear her. Even to lose consciousness
was torture to her.

Did the fact that Brody and Blaire were mated mean two
weeks had passed? Surely not. She could not survive for two
weeks without water or food. She would be dead by now,

which is, of course, what her captors had in mind. There was no way for her to tell the passage of time. There was no way for her to escape. She had no strength left. The wolf seemed to have disappeared, gone. Dana, gone. Her pack, gone. She despaired and wished to die and end the suffering. She wished there was some way to facilitate the end, but she had no weapon; there was no magic at her disposal. The intrinsic magic of long life and health, which every State Changer possessed, was now her bane. She would suffer as long as it is possible for a State Changer to suffer before death made its claim.

When despair consumed her, Ronan's voice entered her head again, telling her the story of the Fae Princess he had told her before. Only slightly conscious, she listened attentively, allowing it to take her attention away from her pain and hopelessness. After it ended, she completely lost consciousness once more.

This time she dreamed of the door to the dungeon flying off its hinges. She heard the loud bang and voices all around. Casidhe heard Saoirse speaking, but she sounded furious at finding Casidhe dead. Saoirse was too late. At that moment, Casidhe knew for sure; it soon would be over. It might take a while for this body to give up, but in the end, it will die here in this horrible dungeon.

She should have stayed in North Carolina. At least she would be alive. *No!* She screamed in her mind. She would not trade becoming a State Changer, becoming a wolf, and feeling the freedom and power of running through the forest. *No!* She would not change meeting and loving Dana. *No!* She would not regret. If this were her fate, she would accept it. She had fully lived and loved, even if only for a short time. Far better than the lonely existence she had for almost 18 previous years of her life. She had obtained what she had always wanted. A place to belong. A family. Love and belonging had been hers for a brief moment in time. She would not trade it, no matter the outcome.

As she resigned herself to her fate, a new thought occurred to her. *If Saoirse finds me too late, how can I dream it? Am I dreaming of my own death? That seems odd.* She remembered what her mother had told her in another dream, which now seemed a long time ago. "You may also have your father's power to reshape events." But didn't her father tell her she needed a talisman? She didn't have a talisman "to control it." Maybe she didn't need to control it. Perhaps she needed to use it. *Am I dreaming of dreams? Is any of this real? Would any magic work here?* Her wolf form did not come forth, but would Fae magic? She didn't know. They had told her as a Keneally, she had great power, and she might be able to reshape events. *Well, I can't think of any other event I would like to reshape more than my death. Still, how do I access this power? The dreams had just happened.* She thought about it long and hard, but no new ideas came. The vision of her parents drifted away into memory, and she cried alone in the dungeon once more.

Her hunger and thirst became so acute she felt like a wild animal ready to chew her own skin if she could reach it. She knew she was losing her mind. She would have preferred to stay unconscious and die that way. Her filth assaulted her nose. She could smell her legs rotting from under her. She wretched again and again. Her head seared in pain. She knew the end would come soon, and she no longer cared. She wanted it to end. Like her dream, rescuers would come too late.

In her last effort, she used every ounce of strength she had left and thrashed about with arms and legs, and in that second, she almost dropped her mother's ring as it slipped off her thinning finger. She had forgotten about it. Managing to grab it before it fell, and she clutched it hard in her hand, allowing her nails to bite into her grimy palm. She tried to scream out, but only a scratchy, garbled croak made it to her ears. In her head, she yelled out, *Mother, Father, I have never known you, and I have never known what it is like to be a Keneally, but everyone says I have power, and yet I hang here rotting and dying, away from those I love. This cannot be my fate. I do not want this fate. If there is some power in me, some ability to alter this event, then show it to me now!* The words reverberating off the walls of her mind.

At that moment, in that desperate plea for her power to come to her, a bright light shot out of the ring through the gaps between her skinny fingers, filling the room, nearly blinding her. The shackles sprang open and flew away, unable to hold her any longer. Her legs straightened and righted themselves, snapping loudly back into place. She screamed out, and this time the sound echoed around the cavern. Her wrist realigned and became whole. Her wounds dried up and disappeared. Even the filth vanished, dissipating into thin air. She stood, tall and fully whole and radiant, as if no time had passed and she had never been attacked.

Before her, an immense cauldron appeared. She peered inside to find water. She dunked her head in and drank her fill. Then it overflowed with delicious food, which she ate until she was satisfied. After it had served her, the cauldron disappeared once more. She put the ring on her finger, and she strode toward the door. As she was about to turn the knob, someone else came through from the other side. It was Saoirse, her hair gleaming, her eyes bright. But she looked surprised by what she found, blinking with her mouth agape.

Casidhe filled the silence with a deep timbre to her voice. "I would like to have my father's staff, please."

Saoirse closed her mouth and smiled only slightly. "Of course, it is yours. Will you follow me?"

As they exited the filthy dungeon, Casidhe glanced back, and for a moment, she thought she saw herself hanging there dead and withered, a pile of stinking skin and bones. But the image dissipated, and she knew that path was gone; she had changed it somehow. She wasn't sure how, but she hoped the woman in front of her might know. For now, she needed to get back to her pack and Dana.

"How much time has passed?"

"25 Days."

"How is that possible?"

"It isn't."

No, it wasn't possible. There is no way a human could survive 25 days without food or water. But she wasn't exactly human, was she? She was more than human. She followed Saoirse to her chambers and over to a locked cabinet. Saoirse waved her hand in front of the lock, and it clicked open. Reaching inside, she pulled out a twisted root staff of light blonde and deep burgundy wood. It had nicks and dings around its center, but it was beautiful. "I believe this is yours."

"Thank you. I have much to ask you. Much to learn. But I must go to my pack now."

"Yes. I believe they have all but lost hope. I will take you another way out, and you can return when you are ready of your own accord. I do not believe there will be another attack so soon. Anyone with your power will be feared. I can help you learn to control your magic."

They had reached the other portal, which opened at the exact rock outcropping where she had slept as a wolf, away from the wind, during her initiation. Casidhe turned with a sharp expression to Saoirse.

"Yes, I have been watching you closely. Come back soon, my granddaughter."

"I will." Casidhe did not miss what Saoirse had called her.

♪

CHAPTER TWENTY-FOUR

Casidhe left the portal and immediately shifted into her wolf form, allowing the feeling of freedom to wash through her body. She breathed deep, grabbed her father's staff between her teeth, and ran as fast as her four legs would carry her to the house. She entered the back door and transformed back into human form quicker than she ever had before. She seized a robe from the changing room, throwing it on as she entered the kitchen. Only Blaire was there. Shocked, she dropped her mug and ran at her, hugging Casidhe tight. "I knew you were still alive. No one believed. They were afraid, but I knew."

"Thanks, Blaire. Will you tell the others? Where is Dana?"

"I'll get them. Dana hasn't left your room in over a week. She dropped out of school, lost her job. She eats little. Her parents are distraught."

"I'll meet everyone in the great room after I see Dana."

Casidhe yelled this as she ran up the stairs taking two at a time, not stopping when she heard the squeals of delight below. She opened the door to her suite, but Dana was not in the sitting room. She went into the bedroom and found her lying on the bed, curled up asleep. She looked frail and grey with dark circles under her eyes.

Casidhe went over and quietly sat on the edge of the bed, reaching up to stroke her hair. "Dana, love. It's me. Dana, wake up."

Dana stirred, opened her eyes a little. When finally recognizing Casidhe, her eyelids flew open wide. She cried out and threw her arms around Casidhe's neck, sobbing hard. They clung together for a long time until Dana's sobs died to a whimper, and she was able to pull back and look at Casidhe.

"I thought I had lost you. I thought you were dead. I couldn't . . . I lost myself. Oh, Cas." Tears streamed down her face.

"It's okay." Casidhe soothed her, kissing the tears away, stroking her hair. "I know. I'm here now. I'm so sorry. I did almost die, and I have lots to tell you, but it's going to be okay."

Dana nodded her head and buried her face in Casidhe's shoulder once more. Casidhe held her in her arms until the familiar heat rose between them. When Casidhe could see the color return to her face, she kissed her tenderly. Finally, Dana was able to get up and dressed. As they descended the stairs to the great room, Dana held on to Casidhe, both hands clinging to her arm. She would let go only long enough for Casidhe to embrace Kelly and Lesslyn, who were overjoyed and crying as they entered the great room.

Brody came storming in, having heard the news. Big tears were falling into his thick beard. "Casidhe, I'm so sorry."

Casidhe embraced the big guy. "It's okay, Brody. I know you tried to protect me. I'm just glad you're okay! I'm sorry I missed your mating ceremony."

"It's okay," he sniffled.

Casidhe and Dana cuddled up closely on the couch as Casidhe told the story of what happened. She didn't speak of the worst of it in order to spare them the pain of such torture. And she left out much of the enchantment at the end, glossing it over as some magic her mother left in the ring. She tried to act clueless as to what had happened, which wasn't too much of a stretch since she was still confused by what transpired in that dungeon. She knew they suspected more had happened, but no one pressed her for details. If they had asked, Casidhe would not know what to say. Her only clue was the ring.

Dana regained her spark, but she was weak. Later that night, she told Casidhe how ashamed she was for becoming so fragile.

"Shhh. Do not speak poorly of yourself to yourself. It will only weaken you further." Casidhe repeated Ronan's wisdom.

Tears fell down Dana's cheeks again, but she smiled knowingly. They held each other close that night, loving ever so tenderly. As Casidhe drifted off to sleep, Dana wrapped in her arms, she heard her whisper, "I love you, Casidhe Keneally."

"And I love you, Dana Moore. Always. Will you be my mate?"

"Yes." Dana kissed her deeply, her heart open. "But let's wait until after your birthday party."

"Deal."

Casidhe thought about how much she loved this woman and how wonderful it felt to belong here with her and the pack. She thought about Aunt Colleen. *She was wrong not to tell me about the State Changers. This is who I am and where I belong. I am a wolf.* Being a wolf gave her confidence; it gave her surety. She knew her place in the woods, with the pack, and with Dana.

Casidhe still did not understand her new Fae powers or what really happened in that dungeon. But she hoped with the White Wolf's help, she would learn. Soon, she would meet her brother, and they would break the curse together. She would find a way. She had to.

In a week was her 18th birthday, which was a milestone even if she felt far beyond that age. Still, she couldn't wait to see what the next year would teach her. She had learned and changed so much already. How much more could there be? It didn't matter, so long as Dana was by her side. Casidhe ran her fingers through Dana's hair and drew in her scent. This was her happiest moment so far. With this woman, she was no longer a loner or alone. *I am a State Changer.*

CONTINUED . . .

STATE CHANGERS

BOOK 2

COMING IN 2020!

Sign up for notification of the release date of FAE:

www.statechangers.com

If you loved WOLF, consider:

- Sharing it with your friends in person or on social media, see the share page on my website
- Writing a review on Amazon or Good Reads
- Checking out my blog for insights into my writing, characters, and other fun stuff

Acknowledgements

To my brother, Mark – in life, we struggled to find common ground; in death, our bond of love remains. Thank you for the inspiration.

I want to thank Lawrence Knorr at Sunbury Press; his continual support to authors inspires me. Special thanks to Shiobhain Doherty, my favorite Irishwoman and friend who helped me with a multitude of references, ideas, and license to tell some of the old stories in new ways. Thanks to my beta readers: Tami Shaw, Julia FitzGerald, Lauren Evans, and Trina Hoefling. You helped make this book better, and you gave me positive feedback when I needed it most. Thanks to my editor Erika Hodges. And special thanks to my family, without whose love and support, I could not begin to spin out these stories. Finally, I'd like to express my sincere gratitude to Esther Hicks – if you know of her, you know why I'm grateful to her.

ABOUT THE AUTHOR

Photo by Lynn Johnson

CHRIS FENWICK is a storyteller, writer, editor, marketer, and former eCommerce professional. Her first novel, *the 100th human*, published in 2006, remains one of Sunbury Press' all-time bestsellers. This is the first novel of her new four-book fantasy series: STATE CHANGERS. She lives on a farm in rural Pennsylvania with her family and a multitude of animals.

www.chris-fenwick.com
www.statechangers.com

www.ingramcontent.com/pod-product-compliance
Lightning Source LLC
Chambersburg PA
CBHW020637260626
47157CB00008B/2781